# About the author

Paul Kingsnorth is the author of two non-fiction books, *One No, Many Yeses* (2003), and *Real England* (2008), and a collection of poetry, *Kidland* (2011). A former journalist and deputy editor of *The Ecologist* magazine, he has won several awards for his poetry and essays. In 2009, he co-founded the Dark Mountain Project, an international network of writers, artists and thinkers in search of new stories for troubled times. Much of his writing can be found online at paulkingsnorth. net. *The Wake* is his first novel.

# The Wake

## Paul Kingsnorth

unbound

This edition first published in 2014 ❧ Reprinted in 2014 (twice) ❧ Unbound, 4–7 Manchester Street, Marylebone, London, WIU 2AE ❧ www.unbound.co.uk
❧ Typesetting by Bracketpress ❧ Cover design by Mecob ❧ A CIP record for this book is available from the British Library ❧ Printed in Engand by Clays Ltd, Bungay, Suffolk ❧ ISBN 978-1-908717-87-0 (limited edition) ❧ ISBN 978-1-908717-86-3 (trade edition) ❧ ISBN 978-1-908717-85-6 (ebook)

# Contents

*I have persecuted the natives of England beyond all reason.*
*Whether gentle or simple I have cruelly oppressed them.*
*Many I unjustly disinherited; innumerable multitudes*
*perished through me by famine or the sword.*

*Having gained the throne of that kingdom by so many crimes,*
*I dare not leave it to anyone but God.*

**Deathbed confession of Guillaume le Bâtard, 1087**

*England is become the residence of foreigners and the property of strangers ... they prey upon the riches and vitals of England; nor is there any hope of a termination of this misery.*

**William of Malmesbury, 1125**

the night was clere though i slept i seen it. though i slept i
seen the calm hierde naht only the still. when i gan down to
sleep all was clere in the land and my dreams was full of
stillness but my dreams did not cepe me still

when i woc in the mergen all was blaec though the night
had gan and all wolde be blaec after and for all time. a great
wind had cum in the night and all was blown then and broc.
none had thought a wind lic this colde cum for all was blithe
lifan as they always had and who will hiere the gleoman
when the tales he tells is blaec who locs at the heofon if it
brings him regn who locs in the mere when there seems no
end to its deopness

none will loc but the wind will cum. the wind cares not for
the hopes of men

the times after will be for them who seen the cuman

the times after will be for the waecend

who is thu
who is thu i can not cnaw
what is angland to thu what is left of angland
i specs i specs
but no man lystens

*songs*
*the songs from the holt*

songs yes here is songs from a land forheawan folded under by a great slege a folc harried beatan a world brocen apart. all is open lic a wound unhealan and grene the world open and grene all men apart from the heorte. deofuls in the heofon all men with sweord when they sceolde be with plough the ground full not of seed but of my folc

aefry ember of hope gan lic the embers of a fyr brocen in the daegs beginnan brocen by men other than us. hope falls harder when the end is cwic hope falls harder when in the daegs before the storm the stillness of the age was writen in the songs of men

so it is when a world ends

who is thu i can not cnaw but i will tell thu this thing be waery of the storm

be most waery when there is no storm in sight

*feoht*
*tell them*
*feoht*

loc it is well cnawan there is those wolde be tellan lies and those with only them selfs in mynd. there is those now who specs of us and what we done but who cnawan triewe no man cnawan triewe but i and what i tell i will tell as i sceolde and all that will be telt will be all the triewth. triewth there is lytel of now in this half broc land our folc wepan and greotan and biddan help from their crist who locs on in stillness saen naht. and no triewth will thu hiere from the hore who claims he is our cyng or from his biscops or those who wolde be his men by spillan anglisc guttas on anglisc ground and claiman anglisc land their own

   ah but we is broc now dreaned we is too small to feoht mor we has borne it too hard we secs now only to lif. and if there is any left who thincs to lif after his triewth or after the laws of the crist if there is any thincs him self abuf this through luf or through mildness of heorte then he will die with his wif and his cildren for all is broc now
*all is broc*

   still i will stand and i will tell the triewth the triewth of what i done and for what i was feohtan and how i was brocen by those ficol hores what i stood and cwelled for. i has not forgot i has cept it for there is micel must be telt

3

and words now is left my only waepens and none wolde
sae i has efer been afeart to wield what waepens i has

because of what is wispred it moste be telt what befell

i was a socman of the blaec fenns a free man of the
eald danelaugh where there was no ealdors too high for
the folc to cum to and if they wolde pull down. thu wolde
not cnaw it to see me now my nebb blaec all is broc a lif
in fenn and holt but i was a free man of angland a man of
parts in my land i was born this way i is still a free man i
is still a free man

to them i wants to cnaw it i is named buccmaster of
holland

*the songs will be sung for a thousand years*
our fathers was freer than us our fathers fathers stalc-
ced the wilde fenns now the fenns is bean tamed efry
thing gets smaller. for efry cilde born there is sum new
law a man sceolde be free and alone on his land the world
sceolde not cum in until he ascs it. freodom sceolde there
be in angland again lic there was in the eald daegs in the
first daegs of the anglisc

*freodom in angland*
now if this bastard is gifan to lif the fenns will be succd
of the sea and gifan to the land gifan ofer to man and the
gods of the secg and the water will die and the spirit of
our folc in these lands will die. the wilde will be tacan
from these fenns and the wilde will be tacan from in me
for in efry man there is the wind and the water and his

worc until he is tacan is to cepe the wilde lands from the tamers

cwell the bastard
cwell the bastard
cwell the bastard

in these places there is wihts uncnawan to man there moste be no law put on us by sweord or by word of ingenga cyng

bastard tamer with stan and style the wilde is all

wood not stan

it will tac thu baec

water not the lea

it can wait long

the hafoc not the ox

but we colde not wait long we colde wait no mor

an unfree land breeds an unfree folc

and i moste go baec now baec before the storm baec to when things was still lic the springmere

go baec yes
go baec

see i had cnawan yfel was cuman when i seen this fugol glidan ofer

a great blaec fugol it was not of these lands it flown slow ofer the ham one daeg at the time of first ploughan. its necc was long its eages afyr and on the end of its fethra was a mans fingors all this i seen clere this was a fugol of deofuls. in stillness it cum and slow so none may miss it or what it had for us. this was eosturmonth in the year when all was broc

what is this fugol i saes to my wifman

i cnaw naht of fugols she saes why does thu asc me of these things

wifman i saes lysten this is sum scucca glidan ofer us what does thu mac of this

naht she nefer saes naht

i tell thu sum thing is cuman

sum thing is cuman she saes lic specan my words will scut the mouth they cum from. sum times this wif she needed laws though there was many wimman things she was learned in. it is not a mans job to spec of the loom nor the water pael nor to asc of brewan nor of reapan all these things my wif done well and in stillness. many was called to beat their wifs mor than i many there was whose cildren ran wilder sum whose wifmen was drifan nacod from their hus for the fuccan of their neighbours behind the raecs at haerfest but this wif of mine most times she was a good wif only she did not lysten

it is no good to spec to thu i saes these is not wifman things i will spec to sum other

what thu wysc my husbond she saes

so what i done i gan to the ham. my land and my hus was apart from the ham as is right for a socman this land was good land good ground it was the land of my father i will not spec of my father to thu

i was no i is a socman of holland a part of the scir of lincylene where the ground was blaec and good and deop. our ham was an ealond in the fenns on all sides the wilde on all sides the dabcic the water wulf the lesch and the deorc waters. our folc cnawan this place lic we cnawan our wifmen and our cildren. we cnawan fiscan and fowlan the gathran of the lesch the ploughan and the pannan of the salt we cnawan the paths through the fenns the ways with the ael and the alor mastors we was of the blaec lands

so i will go to the ham i saes to my wifman and i will asc what the gerefa macs of this fugol. she was wefan on her great loom in my great hus as i left this hus was sum thing to see. raised of ac timber it was the roof laid with secg from the fenn all carfan on the door frames wyrms

and the runes of the eald times. treen we had and sum
seolfor things a great crocc greater than many in the ham
many men was lustan after my hus

three oxgangs of good land i had and two geburs to
worc for me on it and four oxen of my own for the plough
this was mor than any other man in this ham. baerlic i
had and rye sceap and hors also i had swine pasture holt
my own water aeppels on many good treows

a great man i was in my ham all cnawan me a seat i had
on the wapentac and free i was from the worc of other
men. this was my land it was my fathers land i will not
spec of my father. geld wolde i gif but only to the cyng
not to the thegn. sum lytel worc wolde i do for the thegn
for this was how things was but no man was ofer me no
man will be ofer me

socmen was free men socmen is free men still. in other
parts of angland men was thralls in thrall to the thegn
their land their lifs gifen to ealdors and higher men and
now to the frenc men but not in holland not in lincylene
not in the east. free men we was in the fenns free on our
land free men we is still naht will mof us not the frenc

i was specan of this fugol i will not spec yet of the frenc

i gan through my lands i gan along the path to the ham
where there was six hus six cynns most not free men with
land but with micel owed to the thegn. when i was seen
these men was always in awe

buccmaster they all saes gretans to thu buccmaster
sum times i wolde sae naht to this for i was a socman

with my own lands with three oxgangs and they was thralls but this daeg this fugol was in my thincan

what of this fugol i saes what of this fugol thu has seen this yes

fugol they saes fugol. dumb lic hunds was these men

this fugol i saes this great blaec fugol cuman ofer fugol

oft i lost my mynd with them

the heofon is full of eorcas this daeg has thu men seen naht

well saes one jalf was his name sum gebur he was sum esol not free. well saes this jalf there is many fugols here of course buccmaster it is odd thu sceolde spec of one when all is the same to mine eages

fewer of these fugols wolde be better saes sum other they eats my beans

there is noddan at this. fewer fugols saes all these esols

has thu no eages thu nithings blind thu moste all be blind

of course they saes naht to this only locs at their feet

thu wasts my time thu geburs where is ecceard find me ecceard

ecceard was the gerefa of this ham in sum ways a man to tac care around. he colde tac geld or spec of thu to the thegn micel colde he do to harry thu if he ceos. but ecceard was also a plough owner of sum greatness ecceard wolde cnaw about this fugol

ecceard was in his hus doan naht drincan ealu only

sittan. his hus was smaller than my hus though he was gerefa his floor all straw not clene his windows smaller his fyr smaller though his ealu was well brewed

it is a good lif as gerefa yes ecceard

buccmaster thu is well cum here it is always good to see an eornost man

has thu not worc ecceard sum geburs to harry sum hors to loc at sum geld to tac from sum eornost man

has thu cum here to tell me my worc buccmaster

i jocs i saes and i laughs. no i has cum here to spec with thu of this fugol

the great buccmaster cums to spec to me of fugols well this is an odd daeg

now lysten i saes i is sic of this ham. lysten i was standan in my feld and abuf me passed this great blaec fugol this was a scort time baec. this fugol its eages were afyr it had arms lic any man it spac to me lysten. this fugol i seen it it was glidan ofer the ham there is sum thing cuman

a fugol of the deoful then saes ecceard well these is sum tidans indeed

this is no cristian fugol

there is no cristian fugols ofer thy land buccmaster

do not joc with me ecceard this is a graef thing

none wolde dare joc with thu buccmaster of holland my wise freond. well sceal we send to the preost to ring the bell or sceal we call to the thegn to cum and hiere us spec of fugols or sceal we call a moot of the wapentac to

thinc on this. it may be we colde mac this fugol gif geld
for its misdeeds

    does thu mocc me ecceard

    buccmaster i moccs thu only with mildness

    this fugol was an yfel thing

    well i has seen no fugol none here has seen such a fugol
buccmaster or i wolde haf hierde of it. men in this ham
thu cnawan them sum hara passan through their baerlic
at night they tacs as a word from crist their cildren
coughs and it is the deoful specan. a specan bird with
eages of fyr if this had cum here i colde not cepe down
the madness across all this scir

    it was a word but not from the crist

    then what sceolde i do buccmaster about this thing
what wolde thu haf me do

    sum thing is cuman ecceard

    what wolde thu haf me do tell me what is cuman

    this is what i want to cnaw

    then go buccmaster and loc to the heofon again and it
may be thy fugol will tell thu

    well ecceard was no help these geburs they was no
help the smith the fuccan preost the cottars none seen
this fugol. this is why i is a man of greatness while others
still lifs off water snaecs from the fenn these men has no
eages in their fuccan heafods. o fugol they saes o buccmaster has thu hierde he talcs of sum fugol o

    next month it was

    next fuccan month they cums to me and now there is

no smerc on their nebbs

    not three wices after the fugol and now buccmaster is sum wis man

    next fuccan month we seen the star


*a grene treow will be heawan in two and one half of this treow will be tacan awaeg three furlongs and there planted deop in anglisc ground. and not until this treow is hol again and bers aeppels again with no help from man will angland be hol also for thy god has ceosan this folc to feel his wrath*

    *synn is upon this grene land biscops moccs the word of god earls fucc in the sight of the crist ceorls drincs ealu and is druncen. there is deop synn all through this land and thu will be strac down o angland for what thu has done*

    *i see in the heofon a haeric star this star will beorn for eight daegs and nine nights gods hand is upon thu the word of his wrath is upon thu. and in my bed my death bed now two capd men of the crist i sees and they specs to me*

    *o edweard cyng they saes o ealdor of angland thy folc is in thrall to the eald deorc deoful they has wandred from the path and now the lord will stric them down. soon thy sawol will be tacan o edweard cyng and thu will be gifted the cyngdom of heofon for thy worc but on thy folc there will cum a great fear. the sea will teorn to blud and braec upon thy southern strand and thy cyngdom will be gifan into the hands of the deoful for this be his will*

    *o what can be done i saes to them what can be done for my*

*poor folc and they saes there is naht to be done edweard cyng*
*that thu has not done by now through thy triewe cristian luf.*
*the treow will be heawan it is the will of the crist and time*
*alone and death will bring it together. lie in thy bed o cyng of*
*men and cum now to the end that will bring thu to the wide*
*felds of heofon and thy folc to the open gaets of hel*

when we was in the brunnesweald nebbs all blaec hydan
in the grene holt lic the afeart bucc oft i was thincan of
my grandfather. a great man he was strong in all he wolde
weep to see what angland has becum. efen he strong man
that he was wolde weep lic a cilde to see us hidan there
runnan from ingengas in our own land that is no longer
our own land

   tales he wolde tell me of many things. of the great
scips he seen cuman in from the sea with the wilde denes
all afyr callan for the blud of their gods. of eald aethelred
cyng he who broc us of the great death at maldon the sea
druncen with anglisc blud. of cnut who was denisc then
becum anglisc and other tales from farther baec of the
time of his grandfather of great aelfred and of aethelstan
of the eald wundors of angland

   of this haeric star i was specan but my grandfather a
great tall man he was hwit beard hwit haer his own
sweord all on the beam of his hus what becum my hus.
he wolde spec micel of the eald daegs of the anglisc of
our folcs cuman here to these grene lands from across

the wid sea. and those daegs he wolde always sae those daegs was best for our folc for we was as one agan the ingenga and we was free. no thegns there was then no preosts no crist no cyng of angland but free men alone in the wilde tacan the land men in freodom not in thrall. marc this he saes this is how angland moste always be gif no geld lysten to no law if thu can run from it for always they will cum to tac from thu what is thine always the gerefa the thegn the wapentac the eorl the cyng always this thought is in them what can i get from these free men how can i tac from them and cepe them down. mor years of this saes my grandfather mor years of this and we will be thralls lic the wealsc tac heed

thu will see why i tells thu these things but lysten now the haeric star

o but why sceolde i spec now of these things why sceolde i tell thu all is gan now all is too laet. what can cum now by specan of these things at efry teorn the gods was agan us

for so long i felt sum thing was cuman try to lif thy lif when sum thing is cuman when ahead of thu on the path is sum deorcness. try to lif lic this none can lif lic this the deorcness waitan for thu i will not tell thu mor i can not

no i will go on i will tell it i moste

it is early in the mergen it is gan eostur now when the land waecens from winter all the land is cuman open all is grene and waecnan. water crows is callan in the fenn the alor treow is grene haras is in the felds fugols in the water and the heofon there is micel goodness here beyond what man has macd. my folc was in the fenns before the crist cum to angland this ground is in our bodigs deop

two geburs i had to worc for me on my land these geburs was bound first to my father they did not loc up to him none did but they locd up to me for what i done. they was bound to me two daegs in efry wice and three daegs at haerfest

this mergen early with the sunne high in the heofon the wind clene a wundor it is to be in the fenns in these times a wundor it was before the beornan cum. this mergen i was on my land i was sean to my geburs they was sawan flax. one man he was called gamel i had put him to haro the blaec ground with blaec thorn twigges the other he was called asger he was sawan the seed after. this asger i moste tac care of always for he was an esol of a man. bound to me he was but it wolde be better sum times for my swine to do this worc so dumb was he

thu will haf my wifman to answer to if this does not cum up i saes to this gebur. my wifman she colde spin flax from all of angland so micel linen does she mac if there is no flax i will haf no scyrte and thu will haf no hands a blue feld i wants to see two month from now. asger he saes naht to this only locs at me. to be triewe to him i wolde haf to sae that asger is a good man though with no wifman and no cildren thus he must worc for me but his hus is not the wyrst still he is a gebur and dumb lic a hund

there was a barn by my hus and ofer the winter sum timber had gan rotin and i was needan to see to this. i was about to be leafan this asger to his luc when i hierde the sound of folc from the path what cum ofer the fenn from the ham

buccmaster cums this call buccmaster and ecceard is cuman up to me under the welig and alor treows from the west and not alone. ecceard has with him two men from the wapentac of course i is thincan they is cuman to put sum thing on me

this is my ground ecceard i saes and there is naht thu has on me. i can find twentig oath helpers in one daeg to spec agan what efer thu puts on me do not cum here with these men to afryht me on my own ground my grandfathers sweord is in my hus i is a free man

ecceard cums to me with these two ealdors eadbert it is from crugland where there is a great abbodrice and also lidmann of the holt by durwins water. these is high men of the wapentac nefer has i seen them near this ham befor

buccmaster of holland saes ecceard thu is thincan wrong now loc thu cnawan these men. he is right i cnawan these men lic them i has a seat on the wapentac as a great man i greets them well now as i seen they is cum in freondscipe buccmaster saes ecceard how is it thu is worcan on thy ground lic it is any daeg

thy ham is all afeart saes this lidmann all hams in these parts is

sum thing is cuman saes ecceard this is what thu saed buccmaster thu spac to me of sum fugol and i mocced thu well it colde be this was wrong of me

it cannot be seen from this ground saes eadbert he is locan to the heofon all these treows

lic him i locs to the heofon then and my geburs they locs too

the fugol is baec i saes does thu smerc now ecceard

no saes ecceard no there is no fugol cum with me we moste go a lytel way. he walcs then ofer to my hus and past my hus and my barn we gan beyond the ox hege and to the east of the strips to the ecg of the holt where i has my swine

now loc saes ecceard and i locs baec ofer to where these geburs sceolde be sawan my flax but they has cum with me and i cannot harm them now for the heofon has sum thing greater for all of us and it is scinan lic another sunne efen in the daegs bryhtness

what is this fuccan thing i saes

this is a haeric star saes lidmann buccmaster of holland it is cum to spec to us

we is telt thu seen sum other sign before saes eadbert a fugol

this is triewe i saes it was wid lic a hus it spac to me it

breathed fyr it saed buccmaster of holland sum thing is cuman

this fugol spac thy name saes eadbert in sum wundor. of course i colde haf saed mor but loc at this haeric star. the daeg was high and clere but this star it was bright lic the mona as if it was mid night and lic the mona it cum ofer the heofon and from it a tael lic fethras

we has spoc to the preost saes eadbert he has hierde from the biscop this haeric star it is bad for angland

the preost i saes thu might as well spec to my oxen

buccmaster thu will not spec these things to the men of the wapentac saes ecceard and he specs to me lic it is a warnan

it is the cyng saes lidmann then and he specs lic a man what is dragged from water

what saes ecceard

it is this cyng the crist is agan him

spec not this way of our cyng saes eadbert

well there is none to hiere in this fenn the biscop specs thus when there is none to hiere. this cyng he is not of cyngs blud he brings the frenc man and the dene on us for his corona now there is this haeric star the crist is tellan us our cyng has synned

harald godwineson is our cyng saes ecceard gifan the corona by a witan of triewe anglisc men. who wolde thu haf as thy cyng there is none other he is an anglisc man a man of wessex not to be tacan from his place by ingengas

the crist will tac him if he ceoses saes lidmann there

has not been a thing lic this in angland that any lifan has seen. fugols specan to thy socman here now this haeric star in the heofon

sum thing is cuman i saes i has telt thu

then it may be sige saes ecceard sige for angland

thu will lysten next time ecceard i saes

this is from the deoful saes lidmann it is from the deoful

so thu seen what men was lic in these lands thu seen they was not ready for what was cuman. i saes men but they was mor lic wifmen sum of them runnan lic cycens round their ground not ready for fuccan their wifmen not ready for what was cuman all afeart of sum star. but who wants to see what is cuman who wants to see if what is cuman is blaec lic the graef. none wants to see all wants to haro and plough and drinc and fucc lic the blaec will nefer cum

lif is a raedel for dumb folc but the things i has seen it is not lic they sae. the bocs and the preosts the bells the laws of the crist it is not lic they sae


*to the cros road i walc to the wilde cros road by the wilde grene holt where there is no hus of man and at the cros road a man hangs from a pal for crimes agan his folc by law of the wapentac after ordeal and beneath this pal is an other man and this man he lifs*

*this man capd he is in grene and he wers upon his heafod*

a wid hat and until i is near i cannot see his nebb. and then
he teorns to me he locs at me with his one eage one beornan
eage

   upon the pal then there is a raefen
   from the holt then a wulf calls to an other
   this man then he specs to me he saes only one word


it is lic my grandfather saed to me lic what i saed to
ecceard to these wapentac men this hwit crist he lies. it is
hard to sae these things they moste be saed in thy hus
only if thu is hierde the preost and the thegn and the
gerefa and the wapentac they will tac thu down. but it is
lic my grandfather saed before the crist cum our folcs
gods was of anglisc wind and water now this ingenga god
from ofer the sea this god he tacs from us what we is.
there is sum of us saes my grandfather still cepan alyf the
eald gods of angland efen in these times and he wolde
spec to me of these things when my father was not
lystnan a thrall was he to those who wolde tac from him
what macd him man

   this is not of what i was specan not of my father of
him i does not spec but it seems to me thu moste cnaw it
was the crist and the bastard what toc from me what i
was what i is for men of all places was afeart of both. all
is afeart in this world is not fear what cepes the gebur
from cwellan the thegn who cepes him down is not fear
what cepes us from slittan the throtas of the preosts

when they tells us we is born to die that we synns by
fuccan or drincan is not fear what macs us hyd lic hunds
liccan our beallucs when we is telt
   angland was not in synn angland was in fear
   now the bastard he grows fatt on it


sum daegs it was after this time sum daegs after the
haeric star. folcs in the ham was runnan around cloccan
lic cycens for all the time this star was in the heofon and
for ecceard at last there was sum thing to do in cepan
these men stille for there was lytel worc done while this
star was with us. my geburs they was moanan lic the ox
in the lihtnen storm they muttered and loced to the heofon all the daeg lic this star wolde fall on them lic the
crist wolde cum up abuf the alor treows to stric me down
and tac them from their worc to his fathers hus
   well the crist nefer cum for them as the crist nefer
cums for no man. the haeric star it beorned for one wice
but the cyng was still the cyng by the end and angland
was still angland and my gebur asger was still dumb lic
my swine and the sunne it cum up as it cum up for my
grandfather but still i cnawan this was not the end of this
thing for had there not been sum time betweon the
cuman of the fugol and the cuman of this star and had
not that time seemed lic ten years past or ten years to
cum. yes and all was well but all was soon not to be well

and i colde see this colde feel this colde feel this lic i colde feel the regn cuman. i colde feel things what other men was too dumb to see this is how i still lifs while others from that ham is rottan in the ground this is why i was cyng of the grene holt lic my sistor wolde sae my brothor thu is not lic other men

i is not specan neither of my sistor to thu these is not things to be specan to thu

but loc after one wice this star was gan. i cum out of my hus early in the daeg the grasses is wet with dew lic hwit silc ofer my land the sunne risan to the heofon the fugols callan the treows wacan all is fresh and grene and open no man is to be seen or hierde only the greatness of the fenn and all its lif

so i cum out one wice or mor after this star was in the heofon and i locs for this star as i had efry daeg since it cum and this star is gan and all is as it was in the heofon and on the land. and i has my swine to loc to and there is madder to be sawan but i is wantan to cnaw if there is any men in the ham has not hyd in their hus or run to the holt for fear of this star so leafan the hus to my wifman and my cildren i walcs the path to the ham

in the ham i was hopan to see all those cycan men runnan i wolde haf smerced at this i wolde haf thought ah buccmaster of holland safe thu is on thy land and strong while these lytel men is runnan from stars but this was not what i seen. there was a stillness in the ham on this mergen the mergen after the haeric star had gan from angland a stillness lic the fenn in winter lic a curse was gan from the land

our ham was lytel it was not sum great tun there was six hus on the straet and sum four mor hus set baec from it around fenn and feld but no mor than this a lytel place only and what was good it had no circe. a preost there was who cum oft to lie to us for there is no part of angland now can hyd from these things but there was no hus of the crist. efry sunnandaeg men of this ham must go ofer three miles of fenn to the circe at bacstune there to be sung to of hel and of all the things that they moste do efry daeg to cepe them selfs from it. many lic ecceard and others on the wapentac seen that i was not at the circe on many daegs and this did not mac them blithe and sum there was talcced of ordeal for me and saed this was not right and that sum thing moste be done for the crist was mocced. and i belyf sum thing might haf been done i belief sum thing was cuman for me that the men of the crist was cuman for me wolde do sum thing to cepe me down in the eages of the folc to cepe the eald gods down but then the beornan cum and all was broc

so in the ham on this daeg in the bright mergen there was sum stillness and i seen why as i cum to the gathran place where the straet from the west cum in. the folc of the ham had stopped worc though in this ham there was little worc done on any daeg this was why my geburs was so weac. there is sum thing in this fenn macs sum men weac. esols they is here cycan men it is best to cepe awaeg from them. but on this mergen they is gathered round sum other folc all is there efen ecceard as i cum up he locs up lic he does not want me there

buccmaster he saes buccmaster of holland it is early to see thu

what of it ecceard i saes

he saes naht gretans that is all my freond

the star is gan ecceard

the star is gan buccmaster and sum thing has cum saltmen

they has cum with tidans

the star did not beorn for saltmen this fugol did not call for saltmen

well loc buccmaster they is here

saltmen has cum on this mergen to the ham from the pans at offerthun on the saltpath from the east. they pans salt from the wid sea and they tacs it all across holland they cuts it efry man cnawan this they is not to be trusted but still it is bought to cepe the mete of the swine through the winter

there is two saltmen i cnawan i has seen them before but now there is sum other man i has not seen before and it is this one what is specan and all is gathred round him. he is a thynne fello eald in his loc a long cenep but no beard he is lic sum ghast. nebb long and hwit haer thynne he is not yonge and i sees cwic that he is no saltman neither though he has cum with them. this is a gleoman a teller of tales bringer of tidans from other places

if this gleoman does bring tidans he first has dumb folc to spec to so i moste stand and lysten to his rot and his raedels or they will be restless for they is dumb folc in this ham and to laugh is all they wants they wolde be blithe to haf naht but laughter and fuccan and ealu all their lytel lifs

ah i is a freond to all wifmen saes this gleoman he is holdan this lytel throng with his words

my stem is hard he saes in a bed it is standan proud

all these esols they laughs hard at this

i is haeric under neath

coughan and spittan

and now sum girl she tacs me in her hand she holds me hard she runs her hwit hand along my hard stem

they is almost ceocan now

and she peels me and she tacs my heafod in her mouth

the gleoman is blithe with himself here. it moste be the same in all hams all ofer angland when he specs this raedel. sum of these geburs they is almost rollan on the ground it is hard not to cicc them

and lo i will mac that girls eages water

a pintel cries sum dumb gebur thu is a pintel

thu is dumb saes his freond this is what thu is meant to thinc it is a raedel

a hund saes sum other is it a hund

a fuccan hund thu is a hund

i is saes the gleoman puttan an end to this with a roll

of his eald heafod a leac

a leac a leac saes all these fools as if they had always cnawan. well i will not listan to mor of this scit i is a socman with three oxgangs

gleoman i saes does thu bring tidans

this gleoman then he locs at me and his eages is strong this one he is not a dumb man

tidans i saes what of this haeric star what of angland

of angland he saes now what is angland

do not be dumb i saes i is a socman of these parts i is not sum gebur to be mocced with raedels tell us what tidans of angland now that we has seen such things in this land

of angland he saes i can tell thu naht. i colde tell thu of hams in wessex in the land of the golden wyrm and of the hwit clifs in the south where they locs ofer the sea in fear and i colde tell thu of the holtmen of the andredesweald who belyfs they is safe beneath the great ac treows. i colde tell thu of the great blaec duns what macs a line betweon mierce and the wealsc and i colde tell thu also of where the tees runs a deop deorc ea what foams ofer the fells of the north where the hams of the folc is cold beneath. i colde tell thu of west wealas where the folc specs a tunge spoc by no anglisc and where blaec folcs in scips from hot lands tacs their men efry daeg to be thralls far from this ground in their land of dust. but i colde not tell thu of angland for this word is too lytel for all the folc of this land to lif within

these gleomen they thincs they is great men

lysten gleoman i saes i is ascan thu of angland and its wyrd. tell us what others macs of this haeric star in other lands tell us if sum thing is cuman

what of the cyng saes ecceard and sum geburs they locs at him then lic this is not a thing to sae

tell us without thy raedels i saes

it is not wise to mocc raedels saes this gleoman locan at ecceard and i raedels is what thu is macd from. but if thu wolde haf sum tidans then tidans i sceal bring to thu for i see why thu is ascan

what of the cyng saes ecceard again

well saes this gleoman smercan sum well i has not spoc with the cyng this daeg but harald of wessex is still cyng as efer he was but his eages locs to all strands in north and south and his men locs for scips for lic eald aethelraed this cyng has those wolde haf his corona and this haeric star is their light

tell us saes sum gebur

what can i sae that men does not cnaw by now saes this gleoman. two men they thincs to be cyng of angland they thincs to tac harald cyng to hel and wear his corona. one is the duc of the frenc geeyome he is called a man of sum deorcness a bastard he is a strong man in his land but his land is lytel and his folc is thralls and weac from his strength. he may cum it is saed he may cum with sum scips from the south but he is too lytel to haf this cyng-dom he is a duc only who wants mor than he may haf. he wolde do well to thinc on what harald cyng done to the wealsc

and what of the other saes ecceard

ecceard saes this gleoman ecceard of holland thu is gerefa of this moste great ham now what can i tell thu that thu cnawan not. this other man he is the cyng to be afeart he is the man what harald cyng waits for. he builds his fyrd and he waits on his scips cuman from the cold blaec sea to the gold strands of angland he is the landwaster

the landwaster calls jalf the gebur who is this land-waster. this is all scit this is sum game efry man in angland cnawan of who the gleoman specs but when a gleoman cums there is things men will do for they thincs it is what is done and all of us moste stand and lysten

ah the landwaster saes the gleoman and now he is all lic it is sum raedel again or sum tale of the eald times not lic the tidans what i was ascan him for. loc now he is bendan his cneows and raisan his arms and locan from lyft to right around all the men of the ham lic he is around a fyr in sum dim holt talcan of wyrms and the gold of the geets.

harald landwaster he saes cyng of the denes he who dwells in high blaec fjords lord he is of those cold lands. he is ten foot high born sum saes of a wyrm and with the strength of one and with an ax what cuts through three men with one swing and cuman he is cuman from the north with a thousand long scips to tac the corona of our harald cyng and to rule us hard lic a cold beast from the ys lands

now i has things to do this mergen there is madder to be sawan and how is i to saw madder when my geburs is pissan them selfs in the ham due to sum gleoman specan of wyrms and ys and ten foot men i is not needan this

gleoman i saes when thu has ended with thy cildes tales colde thu tell us if there is any thing thu cnaws that is not a raedel or a game for dumb men. in these parts we has seen things we has seen many fugols of the deoful they has filled the heofon and has been specan to me for i is a socman and we has seen the haeric star cuman low ofer us. now sum thing is cuman all here cnawan this and i is locan for sum wise man who can tell me of what is to cum now is thu that man

now the gleoman locs at me again and now he does not smerc. well he saes well great socman of these parts here is the tidans from angland. this haeric star has been seen in efry part and all has been afeart of it. if it is tidans of war or of death what thu is ascan me for there is naht i can gif thu but this. harald cyng is raisan his flota in the south and soon he will raise the fyrd too and in this ham thu may be called. for tostig the brothor of the cyng who was sent out of angland for his synns he is cum baec with scips he harries the south strands and who cnawan if he is with the frenc duc or the landwaster or with others who cnawan but here is the the tidans for thu socman. sum thing is cuman yes it is cuman from the sea. saw thy flax plough thy ground fucc thy wifman drinc well for sum thing is cuman to thu from ofer the waters and this year will be lic no other in the lifs of all men in this land

it was odd in sum ways this gleoman he spac lic my grandfather in raedels of the eald times in tales of what is to cum and of how things sceolde be. my grandfather micel he had to sae about how things sceolde be for to him naht was right in angland. at times it seemed no man was right for him but me. i was his ceosan son for his lifan son my father was no son to him

still i will not spec of my father this is an oath his name is gan from my tunge he is naht to me i will not loc at his graef as i pass for what he done. but at the low grene graef of my grandfather i will sitt in stillness though he did not want no graef at all

i will tell thu of this time my grandfather toc me trap-pan the ael i was a cilde a lytel cilde but my grandfather he wolde sae that the ways of the fenns moste be taught yonge or will nefer be cnawan

there was so many aels in the fenn what cum near the ham the fenn betweon bacstune and our ham this was what has macd us who we is as folc this place for none cums here that does not cnaw it and none cnawan it lic us. writhan it was with aels long and blaec sum times thu colde almost walc on them across the water so many was they after bredan time in the sumor early. this was the time when the yonge aels was out and there was so many they wolde seem to cum from the water to thu to be eatan and this was when my grandfather toc me in his boat. a lytel boat it was macd from ac timber with two of us in it was hefig in the water and low and right for mofan through the deorc undeop waters of the fenn. with him my grandfather toc a rusc light for it was still early in the daeg and also he toc his glaif macd of ac. this glaif it had a long handle and on its end four spere points and with this the ael is tacan from the fenn only at that time yonge was i and i did not cnaw this

grandfather i saes what thing is this

it is a glaif he saes thu will see

is it for cwellan beras i saes or wulfs will a wulf cum in to our boat grandfather

no wulf will cum into our boat and there is no beras in angland not since our folc cum

is it for aelfs

there is no aelfs here neither aelfs lifs in the holt not in the water this is for the ael

and he locs at me smercan

and also he saes for any ingenga who cums here

what ingenga will cum here grandfather

none will cum if always thu has a glaif or a sweord or a scramasax he saes always thu moste be guardan we moste hold this land it is how we cum here

who cum here

anglisc folc cum here across the sea many years ago.

wilde was this land wilde with ingengas with wealsc folc with aelfs and the wulf. cum we did in our scips our great carfan scips with the wyrms heafod and we macd good this land what had been weac and uncept and was thus ours by right

was thu in these scips grandfather these great scips

this was many years before i was born

was there years before thu was born

yesterdaeg i was yonge lic thu marc them they will fly lic the crane all of thy years

but this is our ground now yes

it is our ground for we has macd it ours but there is those who wolde tac it from us he saes i will teacc thu what i has cum to teacc thu loc

while talcan grandfather has been rowan through undeop deorc waters. it is early in the mergen mist is risan from the waters and on the top of the waters is mos grene lic the grenest daeg and deop below deop in the blaec water can be seen great leafs what is suncan almost from sight. all is flat all this land is flat naht stands abuf the reods. low we is and we gan slow through the green and naht is to be seen but the water and any man passan by wolde not cnaw he was any thing but alone here. on efry side the lesch and the saw secg what has leafs what cutts any man felan them. naht but lytel fugols callan naht but water runnan slow

we cums to a pool to a place carfan it seems into the secg and this is where grandfather stops paddlan and ecges the boat up to the lesch and the rusc and tacs his glaif then and lifts it abuf him. cwic he is cwiccer than i can see and he has thrust it then in to the water and pulls it out again cwiccer than the hund tacs the hara and on the ends of his glaif is six writhan aels blaec and scinan in the sunne what is risan now ofer the yeolo secg

fast he saes tac them fast and thu will haf as many as can feed all of us in our hus and all in the ham

slow he saes and thu will hungor till thu is wasted

i locs at these aels still on my grandfathers glaif he holds it now up to the heofon that i may see in the sunne what is cum how he has gifan me sum thing i has not had. the aels is writhan but slower now slower they is dyan and i is yonge and dumb and this seems a sad thing

grandfather i saes can thu not cwell them cwiccer they is dyan slow

they is aels he saes only aels

but still i saes it seems hard

i will tac thu he saes sum daeg i will tac thu to a holt where a blaec ea runs. many craws there is in this holt and efry efen thu may hiere them screaman lic hel itself is cum for them. by this holt there is a hafoc a great fugol with a carfan bec what can tear and efry night it cums to the holt and it cums for these craws. thu may sitt thu may sitt by the path and watch this great feoht sum times the craws they drifs off the hafoc but sum times the hafoc it tacs down sum craw and this then is the greatest thing to see. to see this hafoc and this craw to see them rise and fall to the ground to see this hafoc tear at this craw this is to see the lif of all of us and it is to asc thy self if thu is hafoc or thu is craw. or if thu is ael for sum men writhes without efen feohtan

thu moste see the hafoc tac down the craw he saes and thu will see that all of the world is blud and thy worc is not to lose thine before thy time. be the hafoc not the craw nor the ael for this is how we cum to this land and it is what we is

well i has been specan micel of my grandfather but this was not my tale it is not of what i meant to be specan. it will cum though i thincs efry daeg of what things wolde be now if it had nefer cum for i wolde still be with my glaif by the secg in the sunne. aels is the best thing to be eatan i was in the holt for so long berries i was eatan nuts leafs sum times fugols the hara it is naht to me i is naht. the ael thu tacs its heafod off and its guttas out thu cocs it in butere and petersilie it is the best thing in angland my wifman she wolde coc this so well

it is hard to thinc here sum times it is hard to spec but i will spec of these times they moste be thought of still though we is gan now. lysten i has telt thu of the spring of that year now i will tell thu of the sumor for it was in the sumor that efry thing begun to cum wrong for our folc for efer

*the clouds is blaec torrs and around these torrs the lihtnan*
*of thunor is writhan lic an otr tacan from the fenn. i hieres*
*specan among the torrs and betweon and under the sound of*
*the folc of angland the fear they specs*

*there is wundor in this fear wundor in the wepan of the*
*folc*

*the blaec stoccs of cloud lic stoccs of the ac in the storm*
*they writhes faster thunors light sends sparcs betweon them*
*so that the heofon is light so that the wepan seems louder*

*now from betweon the torrs lit up hwit cums a capd man*
*and as he cums to me he casts off his cape and his nebb is lic*
*sum eorca sum deoful. from his mouth there cums fronds lic*
*the sceots of blosms they wafs as he specs there is no haer*
*upon his heafod but the hide is thicce and craccd cuman*
*away in places and his eages is blaec lic night on the water*

*he specs*

*he saes thu cnawan me*

*thu cnawan me*

*he saes name me*


i was thincan of things in these times sean things at night
and sum times in the daeg and not cnawan what i was
sean til later. did he cum at this time or was it after i thinc
he cum to me after the beornan i thinc. it is hard i wolde
asc my wifman i wolde asc odelyn but odelyn is gan

odelyn was my wifman i has talcced of her she was a

good wifman to me gifan me luf and cildren and duty lic a wif sceolde. all men lusted for my odelyn thynne she was of wifly scape i will sae only that all things a wif moste do she wolde do and if she did not she wolde cnaw cwic about it. we was wed after my fathers hus becum my hus when i becum man. her father he was a socman also though of two oxgangs only he was from bacstune where we was wed in the grene felds by the ea. then i toc odelyn to my hus what had been my fathers and my grandfathers and in that hus in the mergen the sunne cum up ofer the fenn it was sumor o the sounds of the land was a wundor in the sumor. when we woc that mergen i gif her the mergen gift what was bidan by our folc i gif her three aecers of land and a part of my holt and i gif her a gebur name of annis for her needs in the hus and she was smercan wid i lics to see her this way. thu is a good husbond she saed to me we will haf many cildren buccmaster of holland my husbond. and i was thincan then that to haf a wifman lic this was good for many other men wants her and yet she is mine

with odelyn i had three cildren fyrst oswiu my cilde fyrst son to his father and his folc oswiu who did not lif a year. the fenn fefor toc him lic it tacs many but he was not weac only yonge yonge cilde my cilde in the duns will we meet after this lif is gan. then dunstan cum then eadberht true sons of the fenn they growan to be men growan to cnaw this world but not to lif through what the bastard brought. these was my cynn i will haf blud for their blud i is not done i will haf my wergild in frenc blud

but lysten i was talcan of that sumor when efry thing gan wrong let me spec of it to thu now let me tell thu of weodmonth. in weodmonth there is worc to be done all ofer and for my two geburs then there was no time to be slac on my land there is no slac. heges there was to be macan my barn to mac new timber to heaw in the holt other things also but abuf all things weods to be tacan from the ground. not for naht was this cnawan as weodmonth to the eald folc of angland. i had my gebur asger tacan weods from my ground all daeg in this time from the flax feld from the bean rows from the lines of waet all daeg wolde he be walcan my land with his hoe and this for asger was a good thing for he was dumb lic a hund and liccd small things he wolde sing as he teorned the turf

this daeg i will tell thu of asger was in my waet felds with his hoe singan and gamel he was with me in the grene holt we was cuttan timber for the year to cum. we wolde cut this and taec it to my barn for one year so that it wolde burn triewe. of course we did not cnaw then that in one year there wolde be no barn here for this timber no hus neither to warm with it no fyr but the fyrs of ingengas all on angland all on what we was. no and we did not cnaw neither that in one year the holt not the hus wolde be our dwellan lic we was swine only fuccan swine in our own land

but this daeg we was in the holt a lytel holt this was only for in the fenns the ground is ealonds in the water and the treows there has not micel ground to grow deorc and wide. the wilde holt is where our folc cum from the wilde grounds is what our folc is and in the grene holt walcs grim when the daeg is short and there rides weland and ing of the waegn and erce is all around the eald gods of our folc is deop in the ground and the treows. but it is also triewe to sae that sum lytel holt lic this is good for our swine and is good to cut timber in without fearan the aelf what walcs in the great holts and will sinc his shot in thu for thy cuman. for the aelf needs micel ground to lif so the lytel holt is safe from him and is safe also from nightgengas what stalccs the deorcness when the sunne is gan and from all scuccas what has a mynd to cwell any anglisc who is dumb in not fearan the wilde lic he sceolde

so we was in the holt and asger in the waet feld and odelyn and her gebur annis was in the hus doan sum wif things lic weafan or macan loafs or brewan ealu a good brewer was odelyn our ealu was better than that of most in the ham and all cnawan this. also on that daeg my two sons was worcan on my barn. these boys well though i was still callan them boys due to my bean their father they was men now. eadberht had seen feowertiene sumors and dunstan eahtiene or seofontiene they was men and fit for worcan on my ground and so i had them worcan. dunstan sceolde be gifan to sum wif by this time i had saed this to odelyn many times but dunstan was wilde and wolde not settle he wolde spec of lands other than angland wolde spec of goan to the land of the frenc goan to scaldemariland and of feohtan in fyrds for gold. he wolde spec of feohtan wyrms and denes and sum times i wolde beat him for this rott and tell him he was a socman of holland an anglisc man the man for who i tilled my ground and cept the sweord of my grandfather but though i wolde beat him efen with staefs he wolde not spec lic a man

eadberht though he was not wilde eadberht he was lytel where dunstan was a long man and where dunstan wolde feoht with me until i beat him eadberht wolde sae naht only sitt loccan. dunstan i belyf he thought eadberht weac but still he wolde stand with him agan any man and when eadberht spac he wolde lysten

so we was in the holt and asger in the feld the wifs in the hus the yonge men at the barn and all of us then we hierde the sound what cum up the path from the ham the path what went then by us and into the fenn ofer to bacstune and then to the wilde lands. this was the sound of many men and so we cum cwic from our worc to the hus for we cnawan this sound may be sum ingenga cum to cwell us or sum scucca from the fenn or sum out laws from the holt cum for they had hierde of the wundor of my wif or the wundor of my land but it was not this the sound was many men from the ham and sum from other parts and they was cuman to my land and they was waepened these men but not waepened lic a triewe feohtan man. sum they had scra-masaxes rusted from their fathers sum had eald speres nefer used others they bore sithes or efen hoes and those without hoes or who colde not gif them up from their land had only staefs and on to this staef was tied with line a stan. and with these men was an other who i had nefer seen and this man he was not sum esol gebur he was a feohtan man and upon his heafod he was wearan a seolfor helm that was bright lic the daegs light and at his side a triewe sweord

my sons and my geburs we was standan by my hus my wifman and annis was standan in the door loccan and i was thincan to get my grandfathers sweord but sum of these men i cnawan. jalf the gebur was there and others from the ham and then also i seen ecceard for he was with this feohtan man who was saen naht but who was langer than all in his stillness

buccmaster saes ecceard this man is sent from the cyng to holland. harald cyng is callan out the fyrd from the folc of this scir as thu cnawan is his right by anglisc law. harald cyng he calls all anglisc men fit and of feohtan age to cum to him for angland is threatened from ofer the sea and its men must feoht for angland

this is no good ecceard i saes it is weodmonth

buccmaster saes ecceard all moste send men it is the

word of the cyng all moste send their strength in this time thu will see many hus in this ham is now with no men at all

we has timber to heaw i saes a barn to mac good i is a socman of these parts i has three oxgangs who will worc my ground the fuccan swine

then this feohtan man he steps toward me in his helm of light sum dumb swine he may be under this helm but wearan it he locs of sum greatness

he locs at dunstan and eadberht and he saes thu will cum go bring what thu has. he locs at my geburs and to gamel he saes thy cyng is in need of thu bring what thu has. he locs then at me and at asger and he saes naht then he teorns baec and he macs his lytel band to teorn baec with him along the path in to the fenn

ecceard locs at me lic he is with me but he is not with me he is doan what he is bid by other men again for this is his worc in his lytel lif

it may be there will be no feohtan buccmaster he saes they will be baec for the haerfest for this is the duty upon the cyng

i saes fucc the cyng but so ecceard only colde hiere and he locs at me then in sum ire and saes naht and teorns and walcs with the fyrd down the path and naht mor he specs. ecceard has always been a hund he will tac scraps from any man who has them and no care will he gif to who is fedan his fatt mouth

well then all is madness on my land. gamel has gan

from me he is walcan the path baec to his hus to tac what lytel things he has and go after the fyrd. in my hus my sons dunstan and eadberht is macan around with their things also and odelyn is frettan lic a moth who can not reach the bright mona through wattle. ah my boys she is saen my sons thu is yonge to be feohtan ah my husbond she saes to me do not let these boys cum to harm

of what is thu specan i saes does thu thinc i can cepe these boys they is men why does thu not asc the cyng to cepe them it is no tasc of mine. i was in a great ire i was thincan that no man in angland is left alone no mor that my grandfather was right that all was cuman apart around us that sons and geburs can be toc away by sum hore in a helm without efen gold bean gifen. if ingengas is cuman we sceolde feoht them on our ground in our way not in sum other land for the will of harald of wessex

then dunstan is stood by me he has a sacc with his things in and in his eages there is blud. eadberht he is mofan slow lic there is sum curse upon him lic sum deorc wyrd gathers him in but dunstan he is lic a fyr risan to the heofon

father he saes i sceolde tac the sweord

of course i cnawan of what he is specan for he is locan at my grandfathers sweord all on the beam of my hus lic in his own time

i is a feohtan man now he saes i is feohtan for angland i sceolde haf a sweord thu is goan to a fyrd with sum herd of geburs i saes thu is not aelfred. this sweord is not sum cildes thing thu has not nefer swung it efen it is as long as thu

it is a sweord for cwellan ingengas saes dunstan this is what thy grandfather telt thu

do not fuccan spec to me of him i saes to dunstan and i macs my words hierde then in my hus loud. thu did not cnaw him all thu has seen is his graef this is not a sweord for the fyrd where will thu be cilde in sum fuccan feld in wessex loccan at the sea all daeg. this sweord is for when this hus moste be feoht for it is not to be tacan from my land

dunstan then he locs at me and in his eages there is ire agan me i has seen this many times but also it seems there is sum other thing what is not ire but is sum thing smaller. odelyn is locan at me lic i is doan sum misdaed but it is her misdaed locan at me this way before my cildren

to dunstan and eadberht then i specs lic a father sceol-de. go i saes and do what is ascd and do naht mor and cum baec. tac what thu needs from the barn there is sithes there and axes. cum baec cwic for there is worc to be doan and thy mothor will pine as mothors do. dunstan then he locs at me both these things still in his eages and i wundors what this feoht will mac him and i saes go then or they will cum baec for thu and both my sons after grippan their mothor lic cildren again both my

sons is tacan from my hus and one of them only saes
faren wel

i stood loccan at them go and sean also my dumb
gebur asger goan baec to the waet feld locan for weods
and singan as if naht had cum and when all had gan from
my sight i teorned baec in to my hus. here was odelyn
only standan and at her side her gebur annis who was
not lic my wif in no way. odelyn was thynne but annis
scort and fatt and while odelyns haer was gold annis
had blaec haer with all graeg in a widewe was she her
husbond had been sum gebur and when the fenn fefor
toc him she had naht and cum to worc for me for what i
colde gif her

thu sceolde haf gifen him the sweord saes my wifman
she cnawan this was a misdaed as soon as it was
specan

sceolde i saes
it is only my thought she saes it is naht my husbond
again i saes sceolde. now she macs with annis to go
baec to her loom lic she had saed naht lic there was naht
in the air but she cnawan there was

thu fuccan tells me what i sceolde sae to my son i saes
what i sceolde do in my hus

she saes my husbond it was only my dumb thought
thy dumb thought and thy dumb locan i saes thy locan
at me before my sons lic thu is tacan waepens agan me
i wolde nefer tac waepens agan thu she saes but this is

not enough if she belyfs words will right her lies she does not cnaw who is mastor of this hus. i saes to her that she is settan me up for a liar and a dumb esol in front of my cildren and what does she thinc she is doan and she saes naht only locs down at her feet lic a hund lic always and stands still to mac her self lytel. she has no pryde and pryde is neded in a wifman i saes and i strics her about the nebb that will teacc thu to haf sum pryde in thyself i saes. sum times this is enough with her and no mor is needed but this time she saes naht does not efen loc at me it is lic i had done naht. well this is not right and it is triewe i was in a great ire now lic any man wolde be my sons was gan my gebur gan also and i was thincan of how this man in the helm loccd at me

loc at me when i is specan to thu wifman i saes i is the man in this hus i has lost two sons and a gebur to sum cunt in a helm this ground will fall asunder and thu is with those who wolde mocc me. i will not be mocced by no fuccan wifman who sceolde stand with me and i strics her again and she falls then and she strics her heafod on the stans what is weightan down the warp threads of her loom and she is on the flor hwinan lic a cat in a water pael all blud and spit and annis runnan round her lic an ael on a glaif and she is weac weac it is a sad sight to see

what wolde thu do without me i saes who wolde teacc thu these things who wolde teacc thu to be a wifman. but as she has no pryde she does not answer

*i is the eald one*
*dweller in the beorgs*
*i walcs the high lands*
*i macs the hwit hors and the hwit man*
*i is forger of wyrd and waepen*
*cweller of cyngs*
*i walcs through deop water to cum to thu*

*name me*


at this time with my sons and my best gebur gan it seemed to me that all was lost but in triewth naht had begun efen and if i was triewe to my self efen then i wolde haf saed so. sum thing was cuman still the fenn was tellan me this and the fugols and the treows and though sum lytel thing had cum it was only the first sparc of the great fyr

well this fyr has cum now it has cum and it has beorned high and strong and for many years and it has eten all angland in it and now angland is but a tale from a time what is gan. if thu can thinc on what it is lose efry thing thu is thinc on this and if thu belyfs thu wolde do sum thing other than what i done if thu thincs thu wolde be milde or glad to those who wolde heaw away thy lif from thu then thu is sum dumb esol who lifs may be in sum great hus with all warm fyrs and rugs and sum cymly wif and has nefer suffered naht but as there is a time after angland so there was a time before and i thincs of this sum daegs when i is moste weary and i thincs of when my grandfather toc me to see where the eald gods lifd before the crist cum. this place was sum way from our hus it toc us one half of a daeg to reach this place i was still a yonge cilde and until we had cum to it i did not cnaw what we was doan for my grand-father he wolde not sae he was a man who wolde not sae. he had toc me from my fathers hus early in the daeg it was in the month of litha when all is bright when blosms is open and buterefleoges is floteran on them. we was in his boat again and on to the water of the fenn and in litha with all bright and hued wyrmfleoges and all the heofon writhan with lif and with the risan sunne on the nebb of the water the fenn what can be so blaec and deop and cold on this mergen was a thing of great wundor

micel rowan did my grandfather do through the secg and the lesch below the reed and down streams deorc and windan and nefer did i thinc we wolde find our way baec efer to our hus so far was we in to the fenn. the secg had been cuman in ofer us for a long time and it was locan lic we was in a deop place in the ground but after many hours we cum to a place where it fell baec and there opened before us a great mere hecged around with yeolo secg and singan with the call of coot and hraga

my grandfather then he rowed us slow to the middel of this mere and he stopped rowan and he toc the ars wet and dryppan into the boat and we roccd then with the

wind and the water. and my grandfather he saes to me
loc into the water cilde loc down

and i loccd then into the deorc water and at first i colde
see naht but the blaec and the ael and the writhan caddis
and the grene ropes of mos on the water still but my
grandfather was specan lic he meant to hiere a good
answer from me so i cept locan and then lic sum masc
had cum off my nebb sudden i seen the treows

under the boat under the water and not so deop was
the stocc of a great blaec treow torn to its root lic a tooth
in the mouth of an eald wif. a great treow it was wid and
blaec as the fyrs aesc blaec as the deorcness beyond the
hall on a night when the mona sleeps and as i was locan i
seen another and another and i colde see that under this
mere was a great holt a great eald holt of treows bigger
than any i had seen efer in holland and ealdor i was sure
ealdor efen than my grandfather. and through the waters
these treows they seemed to stir though in triewth they
was still as the graef and blaeccer

then i specs to my grandfather lic he is sum wicce what
is this grandfather i saes what is this holt under the water
what world is this. i was thincan many things that afeart
me then i was thincan this was the land where aelfs cums
from or that ents or dweorgs was here or efen that it was
the hall under the mere in what grendel was lifan and
that his mothor was cuman for me under my lytel boat.
until my grandfather spac i efen thought he was him self
an aelf or an eorca in a mans masc cum to tac me to his

world of blaec and yfel and me no place to run

my grandfather then he left the ars still in the boat and we was driftan slow on a wind that was so lytel we colde not feel it and naht near but the yeolo secg and naht hierde but fugols and wyrmfleoges and driftan then ofer the great blaec treows he telt me of the holt of the lost gods of angland

he telt me that in the time before the crist angland was ham to a hus of gods what was born of this ground and what lifd in it among the folc. and these gods he saed was not lic the crist they was not ingenga gods bound about in lies and words not gods of fear unseen in the heofon what priccd man sore and bound him with laws and afeart him with fyr but these was gods of the treows and the water lic we is folc of them

the ealdor of these he saes was woden also called grim who walcced the duns and the high hylls woden cyng of the gods of angland from who all triewe anglisc cyngs is cum in blud. and before the crist saes my grandfather and i hierde from others after that this is triewe though then i wolde not belyf him before the crist he telt me it was woden what was hung fyrst on a treow and woden holed with a spere until waters cum from him and woden who fell lic he was cwelled then cum up again and in risan was gifen the wisdom of the world in the runes. and woden then was called upon by anglisc folc in holt and feld and now the preosts they tells us he is the deoful himself though they has tacan his lif for the tale of their own god the hwit crist who nefer cums

woden has a wifman my grandfather saes also and her name is frig and for all wifmen frig is a freond in the birth of cildren and in luf and in all wifly things. and the first son of woden and frig was thunor freond of all wilde places god with a hamor what waepen brought on the lightnan itself. and his brothor was balder whose beuty was greater efen than the beuty of the fenn in winter efen than of my wifman edith. and his brothor also was ing ealdor of the holt who steered the waegn of lif through the grene months who colde becum a boar for feohtan and for specan to the land and all wihts

and these gods saes my grandfather these gods was lic our folc lic my edith to me and thy good mothor to thu before she was tacan. these gods was lifan here in this holt in the daegs before the waters cum and drencced it. this was the holt of the eald gods for they had no hus lic us now they was not weac lic us they was of treow and ground

and ofer all these gods he saes ofer efen great woden was their mothor who is mothor of all who is called erce. erce was this ground itself was angland was the hafoc and the wyrmfleoge and the fenn and the wid sea and the fells of the north and efen the ys lands. and great erce it was who brought the waters to cum ofer the holt of the eald gods and to drenc the treows so they is now lytel stoccs for she seen that the folc of angland had teorned from them to this crist the lyan god who specs of heofon but cnawan not our own ground. for erce she is the ground herself and until anglisc folcs sees what they has done the holt of the gods will be for efer under the deorc waters of this fenn and the gods will be lost to us.

and the gods he saes the gods them selfs waits still beneath these waters for us to cum baec and when angland is in need if we call them they will cum all of them from the eald holt below this fenn mere and feoht again with anglisc men agan any and heaw them down

the treows in the mere was beorned in to me that daeg and until i is in my deop graef always i will see them. ah my grandfather the crist he saed wolde nefer cum all the strength of preost and biscop he wolde sae all their hold ofer men is in this one lie that the crist will cum to recen with them all but he nefer cums. and my grandfather he had seen this for when he was a yonge man micel of the world was in high thryll for it had been a thousand years since the crist cum saed all the preosts and biscops and for many years it had been saed this was the year he wolde cum again

and for one full year folcs was wepan and biddan and sean signs in the heofon and all preosts and biscops was saen it will be tomergen and then again tomergen. and then when the year was gan at last with a thousand fyrs on a thousand hylls ofer angland and folcs callan up to heofon on them and when it was done and the crist was still not cum then the preosts and the biscops they saed naht mor and it was nefer spoc of again. and then saed

my grandfather then their lies was claere and yet dumb
men still belyfs them and triewely he saed most men is
hunds or esols and not to be loccd up to

well my grandfather was a wise man in many things
and of the hunds and esols he spac triewe and of the crist
also. but of the lost gods under the mere the eald gods
who wolde cum again when angland called well i was
callan them i was callan them from fenn and holt and
they did not feoht for angland. woden thunor ing they
did not cum for harald cyng for dunstan or eadberht or
odelyn lic they had not cum for all the men of sanlac. lic
they had not cum to stand agan the bastard and send
him baec to the sea with the frenc hunds he bring to eat
our land lic goats

but i sceolde spec with care for i did call and sum thing
sum thing cum
sum one cum
sum one cum and is still here


but i will spec now while he is still i will spec to thu of
the fyrs beginnan as was seen in fugol and in star and in
many other signs what the fenn gaf to me.

my sons and my best gebur was tacan from me in high
sumor and i did belyf this wolde cwell us. i had to go
with asger to the meado and sithe and succ was the grass
and succ the month that odelyn also and efen annis
moste sithe though this is not wifmans worc their worc

bean to reap only. but naht mor colde we do and so annis moste sithe and lay the grass in windrows and then we moste all mac riccs for the hig and dry it and tac it to the barn what was still in need of worc. and later also annis moste help in cuttan and feccan in the waet and the baerlic at haerfest then gleanan and grindan the flour for the loaf for though ecceard had saed my men wolde be baec they was not and on our land the crops grow cwic and the weods long. and the swine too was needan worc also the sceap and oxen and our one hors and the treows and when the aeppels was growan annis moste mac of it what she colde for the winter and also do all other wifly things and i moste be worcan on barn and heges and heawan in the holt and tendan to the haerfest and locan at asger that he not cut off his hand with an ax or sum other dumb thing

well ecceard had not gan with the fyrd he bean gerefa and he bean also a man who is gan when hard things cum and many a time i was wantan to go to the ham and tell him how i felt about this but i cnawan in triewth it was not ecceard who was wrong. oft i thought i wolde lic to see harald cyng cum and worc on my barn as he had toc my men but other times i thought that if it was triewe about the landwaster and the frenc duc and the brothor of the cyng and all then harald cyng wolde be needan mor than my gebur and dunstan with his ire and his cildes dreams and then it was seofon wices after the helmed man cum and from the treows on the path i seen sum one cuman. locan from the waet feld what asger and i was ploughan for the autumn sawan i seen by how he was mofan that i cnawan this man and from the barn odelyn cnawan the same and she was runnan to him cwic for it was eadberht cum baec

eadberht my son she saes my cilde thu is baec and she locs at him all ofer and i gan to him also and seen that he was micel the same

mothor father saes eadberht

where is dunstan saes my wifman then and in her eages there is fear

i does not cnaw saes eadberht for he was sent to other places and i has not seen my brothor in many wices

then did thu feoht the dene i saes or the frenc or the aelfs of the holt for thu is not micel bruised for a feohtan man

there was no feohtan saes eadberht and as efer his nebb is straight he smerccd lytel this one he was a stille man. there was no feohtan naht cum harald cyng he feared the cuman of the frenc duc from the sea to the south for he hierde the duc had many scips on the frenc strands with hors in and many waepend men ready to sail. the duc was cuman it was saed and this harald cyng feared and still fears and so the fyrd he placed along the strands and clifs of the south and the flota all in the ports and there we satt for six wices and from the sea we seen naht but fugols and the wood and weod that cum in on the waefs

it is as i telt thu i saed sittan in felds in wessex locan at the sea when there is haerfest to be gathered in holland

well sum men saes it is not so saes eadberht and i seen that bean in other parts had macd him mor braesen in his own hus. triewe feohtan men he saes and those who has been to other parts saes harald cyng is right to be wary of this for the duc of the frenc belyfs he is triewe cyng of the anglisc. it is saed around fyrs when it is wise to spec that eald edweard who was cyng before harald bean frenc in half his blud gifen the corona of angland to the duc and that harald saed also to this geeyome as he is called that angland was his by right and now the duc geeyome is in a great ire and will cum to tac the corona from harald and his heafod with it

then why is thu baec saes my wifman

he is baec i saes for the cyng may asc six wices fyrd duty from a man and no mor in any year and good it is that he is cum baec though it is six wices too long for the barn is still broc and micel of the waet is forspilled

and the strands of angland is now open to all saes eadberht and if the duc cums now he will tac mor from us than our waet

for three daegs then odelyn fretted and clucced lic a cycen for she was afeart that her dunstan was gan may be tacan by the sea or by out laws or may be the duc had cum in the end and there had been a great feoht and him with no sweord though she was wise not to sae this. me i was wantan dunstan baec and my gebur gamel also for it was sawan time and we was micel behind in worc but gamel he nefer cum baec and where he gan or what wyrd he found i nefer cnawan. gamel had sum lytel land in this ham and a hus both gifen by me and for this he moste worc for me a lytel and gif me sum lytel geld it was a good lif i gif him so why he wolde go i do not cnaw. but sum men secs in other lands what they belyfs they is due though in triewth what they has is better than they thinc

in these three daegs also i saw sum new things in eadberht for though he was still gifan due in his talcan to me he was also waxan mor lic a man and it seemed that in his goan to other lands he had left sum part of him out there still. not efen feohtan but only walcan in other lands can do this to men as i cnawan well. also i seen it triewe when after three daegs dunstan cum baec ofer the felds

it was the efen when he cum deorcness was gathered in and we was in the hus around the fyr with was a crocc of broth of lamb and baerlic and we was all eten this with the good baerlic loaf what odelyn macd well and we was eten with micel lust for the daeg had been long. then it was that sounds was hierde from without and before efen we colde stand dunstan cum through the door with his lytel sacc and a new seax at his belt that had not been his before odelyn runs to him as wifmen does and eadberht also stands and he grips his brothors sculdor and saes brothor in such a way as i had not seen

dunstan my cilde i saes not standan up sitt with us and eat thy mothors broth for i hiere it has been hard for thu feohtan with sea weods and with the water. this was a joc but dunstan he did not understand jocs and as he had done no feohtan it seemed he wolde do it here. he locs at me then with that fyr in him that i was hopan wolde be cwelled by his goan

father he saes i see things here is as efer they was

yes i saes this is triewe the barn is still broc and the weods is still in the felds

and thu is as efer thu was also he saes. eadberht and odelyn they both locs at him lic he sceolde stop and in triewth he sceolde haf

i is still thy father yes i saes and i is tellan thu now to eat for in the mergen there is worc to be done i has lost one gebur and will not lose mor worc than i moste

thu thincs this is sum joc he saes and he is loccan at me right at me and now i sees it is time to end this he is still a cilde though he may thinc not. i stands

tell me what is a joc cilde i saes

thu thincs he saes and now that i is standan there is sum flicor in his fyr but still it beorns thu thincs our fyrd worc was sum joc is this what thu thincs

i thincs i saes that i was right it wolde cum to naht and thu sceolde haf been here i thincs saes dunstan that triewe men gan to feoht for their cyng and land agan the ingenga

ah i saes the ingenga what cums in the scape of the sea weod

then dunstan he starts to yell lic he has wanted to from when he first cum in. what is thu he yells talcan all my lif of thy grandfather and anglisc gods and thy great sweord what thu has nefer efen swung and talcan of our folc and ingengas and feohtan agan all from outside and now they is cuman thu is sittan here on thy arse talccan scit about barns

thu will scut thy fuccan mouth now i saes but as he is across the fyr from me i cannot beat him without goan to him and he is cwic i will sae this for him

i will not he saes for i is man also on this land and i has been with the fyrd with triewe men with feohtan men who cnawan what angland is and has feoht for it and all saes there is sum great thing cuman from the sea and i will be with them these men feohtan agan all who cum and if my father will stay here with his fuccan waet and his sweord what rusts and all his fuccan words then that is his lif

dunstan saes eadberht thu sceolde not spec this way to our father. he is right in this but then he locs at me father he saes to me has thu not saed sum thing is cuman since the daeg thu seen this fugol and we all seen the haeric star. well he saes is this not what is cuman and moste we not stand if it cum well i had saed this and right i was to sae it though none wolde lysten to me i cnawan sum thing great was cuman to angland and not a good thing. but i wolde not haf this not from no cilde lic this if there was feohtan to cum it wolde be me who saed when and where we was feohtan not dunstan nor ecceard nor efen the cyng but me

i will not hiere this from cildren i saes

i is no fuccan cilde scouts dunstan i is a man and mor fuccan man than thu

thu is no man i saes

thu is no man he saes before i has done thu is no fuccan father who will not feoht nor let his sons feoht. and he is gan then baec through the door to the deorcness and sore cene i was to go after him then but i seen odelyn and eadberht locan and i thought stillness was best that it wolde mac dunstan loc lic the lytel esol he was bean

so i sits baec down still and i saes we will cepe eatan and after a lytel time of them locan at me eadberht and odelyn they sits down also lic they wolde rather not but they cnawan their place and still and saen naht i cept eatan lic naht had been done. in me though was a great ire and i was thincan of what dunstan wolde get from me cum the mergen and i was thincan also of why i was cursd to be all the time with esols and those who was agan me

i cnawan odelyn was agan me and eadberht too now

for the way he had spoc and dunstan had been agan me
for all time. annis was agan me gamel had not cum baec
to me and ecceard and many in the ham was agan me
also for i was wiser than them and wolde let them cnaw
it. all was agan me lic all had been for so long since i was
myself a cilde my own father had been agan me my dumb
yfel father who sent me away for he was agan my triewth
and only my sistor only aelfgifu to stand with me only
aelfgifu who efer cnawan me triewe. and otherwise all
folc in the world forsacan my word and who i was who i
is who i fuccan is these folcs does not cnaw they thincs
they cnaws but they is hunds all to the last fuccan one

*where now is the bans*
*of weland the wise*

well dunstan the daeg after this he cept claere of me. that
night he slept in the barn and the mergen after i hierde
him worcan on it and later eadberht went to him and
they worcced together and so micel did we haf to do that
i colde not spare the time to beat him but i waited to see
what he wolde cum at me with. but he cum with naht
and for nearly a wice he spac naht to me only worcced on
the barn and in the holt and feccan and heawan

well this colde not go on and had we not so micel worc
i wolde not haf let him do this for once this cums in to a
mans hus it is lic a rat or the wyrm in the wud if thu does
not cwell it it will bring the hus down on thu. but there

was not time for me to do naht for after a wice or it colde haf been less efen after this time our freond with the seolfor helm cum baec and this time he spac mor and he spac cwiccer

this time he cum to our land with not so many folc as before and those he did haf from the ham was not lic before when they was talcan and singan and in high sawol. ecceard again was with him but this time the helmed man he cum to me first and spac for he colde see i was in no mood to see him again

buccmaster of holland he saes and he cnawan my name this was good it gaf me my due buccmaster of holland he saes thy sons has done angland triewe in these last wices and for this i thancs thu

my sons is good i saes strong and they does what they moste and now they has done their six wices as thu cnawan in thy fyrd

the fyrd of angland saes the helmed man is not mine nor is it that of harald cyng it is for all and though six wices as thu saes has been done i is cum to call the fyrd again for angland is under a great slege now lic it has not been since the time of great aelfred

the duc is cum then saes dunstan it is the first time i has hierde him spec in many daegs and on his tunge there is a great thryll

the duc is not cum saes the man it is worse in the north the landwaster has cum with a thousand long scips and he secs the corona of angland. harald cyng is ridan to

lincylene and then to eorfic and we moste bring feohtan
men as we go and we must go cwic for as we go north the
south strands is left open to the frenc

i will cum saes dunstan and he walcs to this man
before any word is saed from me and he locs at me standan by this man who has cum again to tac from me

father he saes i will not feoht thu again i will feoht the
ingenga. i is goan father do not stop me

then eadberht he gan to this man before he efen ascs
me and he saes i will cum also and to me then he saes
father thu will see that this is a time when all men is
needed efen if they wolde stay on their ground. thu has
spoc to us many times of how we must feoht for what we
is so now we gan to feoht and thu will be proud

so now he is tellan me i will be proud and me standan
there lic a cunt while they is toc. what wolde thu do i ascs
thu what wolde thu do thy sons tacan from thu again lic
this. i locs at this man at ecceard behind him who is locan
at the ground i locs at my boys and at the geburs and cottars gathered also and then i sees asger is there betweon
them asger with his hoe and his dumb smerc and i sees i
has lost it all now so i teorns and i walcs baec to my hus
and naht i saes to any of them

fare well father calls eadberht but i saes naht there is
worc to be done

well there was worc to be done but i did not want to
do no worc then and what worc colde i do with no geburs
and no sons it was a fuccan joc they was cwellan me. well

i sceolde haf cnawan the fugol had saed this and the haeric star i sceolde haf cnawan but still i had not thought so micel colde be agan me

so i sat in my hus by the aesc of the fyr and i dranc ealu and i waited for odelyn to cum for she was frettan around my sons as they was leafan. she cum in soon enough and loccd at me lic to see how she sceolde be around me

wifman i saes and she saes yes my husbond in a tunge that saes she still felt what i had taught her before

thu cnawan i is a good man i saes

thu is a good man she saes

there is those saes not i saes to her but they is only men. one man may thinc what he ceoses of another but it is only the thoughts of one man

she locs at me lic she does not cnaw what to sae she nefer cnawan this one she needs me to steer her i lufs her when she lystens when she locs up at me she is proud

if i cnawan i is good who is to sae i does yfel

none can sae this

sum may i saes but the word of one man is as good as another in the world is it not

it is

thu cnawan i is a good man

i cnawan this

none can sae i does yfel if i does not belyf it

who saes this my husbond

folcs thincs this i saes folcs is agan me in all lands my

sons is agan me ecceard my geburs the cyng himself is agan me

my husbond she saes this is not so

it is so and i is thy husbond and i saes it is so

she saes naht to this as she cnawan it is triewe

this is the way it is in the world now i saes the way of things is all gan it is the crist who done this they cums with his boc loc they saes this deed is yfel this deed is good heed the crist

yes she saes

it is bocs that does yfel i saes all bocs the boc of the crist the boc of the cyng all laws from abuf mor efry year. i moste gif geld to the cyng i moste cepe the bricg i moste gif a hus to my gebur i moste gif land to my wif i moste gif my sons to the fyrd i moste sitt on the wapentac i moste gif haerfest worc to the thegn i moste gif a tithe of waet to the circe on sanct martin and sceap at pentecost i moste go to the circe efry wice and lysten to scit from the mouths of preosts i moste efen gif geld for my own graef

thu is a man of parts she saes thu has three oxgangs this is good

it is good i saes yes it is good is this why they cums for me with laws and bocs they is agan me for what i has. loc now they cums to me and they saes ingengas is cuman we need thy sons and thy geburs for we moste feoht agan the cwellers but efry daeg they is cwellan us the cyng and the crist. this ingenga god that they lufs he has nefer seen

an anglisc treow this god from a land of dust where there
is no night
    is there no night
    lysten to me i is specan lysten we feoht agan one yeoc
only to cepe our selfs under another this god does not
cnaw me how can he sae i is yfel can he see my heorte
    she saes none can see thy heorte
    then how can he sae i is yfel
    he can not sae this
    what man can stand ofer me what man
    no man
    is i yfel wif
    thu is not yfel my husbond
    this is what i belyf i scit on all bocs those who trust in
them they is in a gaol of dust and light light from sum
other scor
    dust and light she saes
    the crist can not harm me
    no
    the cyng can not harm me
    no
    none can harm me
    none
    i is not yfel
    no
    thu is a good wif to me

*where now is the bans*
*where now*

it was that night i had the first sight of him yes i see it now that night when all was first tacan from me though i did not cnaw then how micel mor wolde be lost. ah for micel time it had been cuman sum thing had been locan for me sum thing had been growan had been callan from the deorcness and when i locs baec now all is clere. that night i seen all things end in a great storm and from this storm cum a man and the man saes thu cnawan me buccmaster thu cnawan me and this man he was foul to see. from his mouth there cum fronds lic the sceots of blosms they wafs as he specs there is no haer upon his heafod but the hide is thicce and craccd cuman away in places and his eages is blaec lic night on the water

in his left hand there is a hamor the hamor of a smith the hamor of the great smith what lifs in the eald beorgs and in his right hand there is a heafodpanne the heafod-panne of a wifman and it is all ofer with gold and stans and cut in two lic it is a cyngs cuppe for wine or mead and the smith through his rottin mouth he specs to me again and he saes thu cnawan me

and i do cnaw him and he specs again name me but i thincs that if i name him sum thing will cum then that will nefer go and so i specs not and he saes again bucc-master of holland name me. but that night i does not

69

name him not that night and from this dream i waeccen and it is before the daegs beginnan and i stands and i walcs to my feld of flax what is now a feld of weods and abuf the treows the haerfest mona is great and yeolo and the ule is callan and all else is still. but in me is his tunge what is hierde abuf the ule and the sound of my breathan and it nefer stops all that night and it saes name me name me name me

there is no one lifan in angland now has not seen all they cnawan tacan from them. there is no man in angland in any part from mierce to northanhymbre to efen us the free socmen of holland has not seen efry thing they cnawan tacan and none of this in their grip. lic the wind what brings down the waet before haerfest there was naht we colde do to stand in the way of such a slege naht but to go out after with sicols and loc at our broc felds and tac what straw and seed we colde from the whole wide strip of broc lengths cut at the ground by what was called down from the heofon and us not gifen to cnaw why in this lif and it colde be not efer


this i cnawan now and so does efry other man in angland. that night when i seen him for the first time that daeg when i lost all my men to the folc of the boc that daeg i felt what i was losan strong i felt what fugol and star had brought to me. there was mor to lose yes i is cuman to this i wolde lose efry thing soon angland wolde

70

lose efry thing and though we feoht to cepe it we did not cepe it though if men had lystened to me done what i had spacan done lic i saed then we colde haf cept it but men is esols and dumb and does not lysten to the wise

my grandfather wolde sae men does not lysten to the wise for what the wise has to sae is not what they wants to hiere for what they wants to hiere is that their lifs is right as they is and that they is good folc and does not need to do naht. and most times saes my grandfather this is not the triewth most men is dumb and they lifs lic hunds and they does not see beyond their hus into the night or efen the daeg they does not hiere the fenn specan to them they does not see the eald gods under the mere they is blithe in their hus fuccan and drinccan while all in the wilde world falls away. those who is wise he saed those who is wise moste lead men moste show them what they can not see lic the swine moste lead us to the trufa or the hund to the hara

well there was no men for me to lead then and for many daegs i done naht though it now brings sceomu to thinc of this but i done naht for i colde not see why. i had no men to saw the winter waet and no men to spread the scit on the felds for winter and no men to cum with me to the fenn for secg for thaeccan the hus for when the cold months cum. it seemed to me then that there was naht to do but drinc ealu and eat what odelyn was macan eat hunig cicels and pies and loafs and sitt in the hus stay warm stay in with my wif and my grandfathers sweord what sum times i wolde tac from the beam and scine and hold while i was sitttan for out in the world there was naht for me all was agan me. and for many daegs this was my world and odelyn and annis they both cared for me but naht was saed for this was my hus and they both cnawan what the world had done to me and fed me while i was in my seat at the fyr

then after sum daegs the preost cum. i cnawan it from ecceard for he cum to my hus to tell me for he felt sceomu for what he had done and all he had tacan from me. the daeg was high with the sunne but i was in the hus in deorc and smoc with odelyn and ecceard he cum in then and seen me in my seat by the fyr with my ealu and he locs at me lic this is his worc

buccmaster of holland he saes odelyn wif i greets thu well in thy great hus i has cum to sae that eadweard preost of bacstune circe is cum to the ham and that thu sceolde cum hiere him spec

well i laughs at this i laughs with ealu still in my mouth and half of it gan on to the fyr

buccmaster saes ecceard before thu specs i cnawan thy thoughts on preosts of course and synnful thoughts they is and thu will be sorry for them after thy daegs here is done but this preost he brings word not from the crist but from the fyrd

of course odelyn hearan this had to go she wolde not stay in the hus if there was word of her sons so she wolde go to the ham with ecceard and i moste go also for i wolde not haf ecceard alone with my wifman on the grene paths around these parts things was saed about him and all cnawan what they was

down in the ham we seen the preost at the gathran place at the cros roads with folc all around him. most was wifmen with so many men gan to the fyrd but hwit haerd ealdors was there also and yonge cildren and those lic ecceard and me who was great men in the ham men of parts. the preost is in all his fuccan gold and he has out his altar of wud what he tacs to all the lytel hams where he lies to the folcs and he has his great boc on it what is all gold and in sum ingenga tunge the better to awe the dumb folc. he sees us cum then and he locs at me lic i sceolde not be there for this eadweard he is an eald man and cnawan my grandfather at the end of his daegs and cnawan as all did his thoughts on the crist

eadweard preost saes ecceard eadweard preost thu is well cum here in the name of the crist and his holy sancts and we bids their gladness on the poor folcs of our ham. eadweard of bacstune tell us what word is thu bringan from angland

well saes eadweard in his deop tunge i has telt these folc as thu can see there is gladness now in their heortes by the crists mildheortness but i will tell it again for none is too late to cum in to the word of god. he is locan at me then i sceolde beat him but i is not an esol he is the preost

i brings tidans from eorfic saes eadweard preost i

brings word of a great sige what has been gifen to harald cyng of angland through the hand of thy great triewe god these three daegs past. harald of the denes who is called landwaster who cum here with a thousand long scips to cwell angland has himself been cwelled through the will of the crist by the fyrd of our harald cyng. it is saed that our cyng gan north cwiccor than any man efer has done and he cum upon hardrada who is called landwaster near eorfic. this great dene had cwelled the fyrd of the eorls of the north sum daegs before and was thincan to tac eorfic and then tac angland but our harald cyng cum upon him when the denes was eatan and fuccan and drincan lic heathens will do who has not the triewe light of the crist upon them or within them. he was loccan at me then again i wolde beat him if there was any triewth but always there is mens laws stoppan triewth

and harald cyng gan on this preost in stillness for all folc locs up at him open muthd though they has hierde this already harald cyng he cum down on the landwaster at a place that is called stam ford by eorfic and on him he dealt a great death and under his sign of the blaec raefn the great landwaster was cwelled the crist guidan an anglisc strael in to his throta and the denes was drifan baec to the sea what ran red with the blud of denes to where sea becums heofon. and of the thousand scips what brought them to angland ten only was needed to tac them baec to the ys lands

there is a great roar then from the dumb folcs and efen

from odelyn and ecceard and in triewth these tidans was good that ingengas had been sent baec in blud though to me it seemed that a preost who tells us that the crist saed thu sceolde not cwell lufs too micel this tale of blud and straels and the cwellan of ingengas but this is preosts

what of the fyrd now calls odelyn what tidans of the men of this ham

i can not in triewth tell thu saes the preost and all wifmen locs sad but the crist he gan with all men who is of his flocc. sum will cum baec and sum not but all who feoht for the crist will be tacan in to his heofon and all who gifs their lifs for crist and cyng will see their god

when is my son cuman baec cries sum wifman

wifman saes eadweard and he locs ired lic he has had enough dumb folc and as a preost he has seen many wifmen and also fuccd them for this is preosts. their words is of the boc and the crist but their thoughts is of wifmen and ealu lic any man

i can not cnaw these things he saes we moste all trust in god and bid efry daeg that those who is cuman will cum soon baec to thu

well this is no good for odelyn this has only macd her fret mor for now she cnawan there has been a great feoht and her sons colde haf been in it. i tries to tell her this is good that dunstan wolde feoht and now he has done and that ingengas has been cwelled all ofer and will not cum again and that now we will haf our men baec and lif will go on. but she wolde not haf this naht wolde be right for her till her sons cum baec and in triewth though the folc of the ham was glad for the tidans and though ecceard saes this is what the haeric star cum to tell us of the great wyrd of harald cyng in triewth i did not belyf all was done. i still felt sum thing was cuman and i was right and in my heafod as the preost begun to spec of josef and his fuccan brothors again lic efry wice for he cnawan or can not read no other tale in my heafod was still the tunge of my dream saen name me buccmaster name me and i cnawan all was not still


*i stands on a long seolfor strand it is night all is deorcness but the mona thynne lic a sithe blaed the sea is cuman in and risan and fallan on the strand lic the beatan of a heorte but the heorte of a man who is roaran lic a wiht in blud. efry waef roars the strand roars behind is clifs high and hwit and there is no light on the strand no light on the clifs all is deorcness all around but for the mona*

*but for the mona and for one light out on the sea now so far out that it is only seen when locan away. out where no light sceolde be far off on the waefs one fyr beorns small and it mofs with the water and it nefer gan out and slow slow slow it can be seen cuman nearer to me nearer to the clifs nearer to the strand while the waefs beat blaec on the land lic no man was efer born*

76

moste i tell of what cum then moste i sae it i does not want to sae it all cnawan it now all in all lands cnawan it. in the frenc lands they talcs of what they thincs is their great sige but in the other lands also in the ys lands of the denes in the land of the biscop of the crist who gaf his flag to the bastard who set his god agan us in friesland in bohemia perhaps in hel itself they cnawan what angland has becum and their preosts uses it to tell dumb folc what befalls a great land what teorns away from their word

but he cnawan before what was cuman and in sleep i was sean succ things as has nefer been seen and it was only later that i cnawan what i was sean and why i was ceosan to see it. but i always cnawan i was not lic other men my grandfather wolde sae that lic he i was abuf the esols in the ham and this i colde see and not only my grandfather seen it. so when i was ascan why he cum to me efen that first night in the felds name me name me he was saen efen then sum part of me cnawan that if there was to be a man in holland ceosan for greatness then of course it wolde haf been buccmaster

ofer the next daegs it was lic waitan for the regn it was lic we was wifmen with the first cilde all will be new thu cnawan this but until it cums it does not seem lic naht will efer be other than it is and has been. i had saed it to all sum thing is cuman i had saed but efen i did not not cnaw then what this meant in triewth not until it cum not until it was here. it may be that he cum to tac away

77

the mist from off the water for me to see the deop triewe how deorc it was

so odelyn loccd out for her sons and efry daeg they did not cum was a daeg when sum of her heorte was gan. after sum time i left the hus and the fyr and the deorc and done sum small things i tried to worc on my land but it was gan now and late and so i teorned from it. i wolde haf sat again in the hus but we colde not lif on naht so i toc to fedan us by goan in my boat for aels. i gan to the parts my grandfather toc me to and tacan his eald glaif i brought baec aels though there was not so many as when i was a cilde. when i was not in my boat i was in other places for i colde not loc at my land now so broc was it

all them brocn daegs seemed a year or mor but in triewth it was only wices and then we was with cilde no mor the leafs cum from the treows and snow cum from the heofon and the waters cum up and we was drencced. it was in the mergen on a daeg of cold winter sunne when the gleoman cum again to us and this time he was not sum raedeler with the folc in his hand but he was lic sum cilde what has seen many folc drencced and is runnan to tell his mothor and his father runnan for where it is warm

the cyng is dead he saes the cyng is dead

all is broc he saes all is gan

we was down in the ham me and odelyn she was specan to other wifmen of sons gan to the fyrd of why they had not cum bacc after the denes was cwelled.

78

odelyn had cum to buy sum things and i had cum to cepe her safe from others and also to see the lie of things to see that others also was also small and broc as i. we did not see the gleoman cum he cum from the fenn but we hierde the wifmen gan fast to him and when we teorned from the gaet where we stood we seen him

when we had seen this man before he had been proud he had been strong in his raedels and tales. an old man yes but he had the strength what all men moste haf if they is to hold others to them. but this strength now it was gan and this man he seemed lic sum thing had scufd him away easy and with out efen locan. he cum then to the cros straet and he spac but it toc him sum time it seemed lic he did not want to sae what he had cum to sae for saen it wolde mac it triewe

geeyome has cum he saes straight there is no jocs with him now. geeyome duc of the frenc who is called by his own folc the bastard for his mothor was sum hund and his father a thegn of great yfel whose own folc was in thrall to him. geeyome has cum in scips from the frenc lands and all is gan

who is gan cries the wifmen what is gan

harald cyng saes the gleoman thu has hierde of his great sige ofer the denes well he and his fyrd and his huscarls they had not time to breathe when they hierde that the scips of the bastard had cum to the scors of the south near haestingas and landed and none there to meet them with what they sceolde haf been met with. well harald cyng he toc to the road again and gan south as fast as he had gan north but with half the fyrd dead from the denes and the other half broc and with the bastard fresc and with the flag of the biscop of rome

what fuccan flag i saes

the papa of rome he blest the bastards war on angland saes the gleoman he gaf him the flag of the crist to feoht under and when anglisc men seen this they was afeart and harald cyng though he was a great anglisc man though he was our greatest cyng since efer i was born and triewe well

he stops here and all is still in the ham lic i has nefer seen it

in a place called sanlac on the hyll of the graeg aeppel treow harald cyng drew up his men few and weary and this bastard with his flag and with the relicts of sancts around his foul throta and with men from all lands and none feohtan not for luf but all for gold he cum down on harald cyng and he cum down on him and he did not stop. and all daeg saes this gleoman all daeg our cyng held his line and wolde haf held it until deorcness and then sent the bastard to his scips again sent him baec with blud into the water but then sum thing cum

what thing i saes what thing

none cnawan he saes none seen it who still lifs but the bastards men cnihts as they is cnawan feohtan on hors they broc through the huscarls and toc the cyngs flag and they cut the cyng down cut him down on anglisc ground after efry thing he done for us and his blud is still there at sanlac and will not dry and the bodigs of his huscarls and of his brothors eorl leofwine and eorl gyrth all is gan all anglisc men is cut down and angland now with no sweords naht to stop the bastard from tacan all things in this land

then what will cum saes sum wifman

they gelded him saes the gleoman who is still at sanlac they gelded our harald cyng they cut off his beallucs these frenc men cut off his beallucs for the gold of the bastard and gold is not all he will tac now for he is cuman and he has not begun efen

there is a great moan at this a great fear mofan round all in the ham and i felt it also

i has cum to tell thu this saes the gleoman i is tellan all hams i cnawan and it it is all i can tell thu. harald cyng is dead the eorls is dead the fyrd is broc and the bastard is cuman down on lundun with sweord and fyr. he means to be cyng of angland and who will stop him now none i saes none will stop him. the roman biscop and his sancts has tacan down a great anglisc man and a bastard will be our cyng and angland will weep for a thousand years


*the feld is grene it is high sumor the long grass runs ofer to a bright ea and from across the water rises roccs great and deorc and high they rises high and on them is a great stan torr and in this torr a wifman yonge and with cilde. deop in the frenc lands in this torr this wifman she is to bring forth a grendel a cweller of cyngs a fyr deoful but now she cnawan naht but that she has been had by the greatest man in the land though she is not his wif and now is bound to him*

*and in this torr this blaec torr risan abuf the grene felds now this wifman dreams. from her guttas where this deoful is brewan she sees growan a great treow and this treow it cums up high abuf the felds abuf efen this great torr abuf all the lands of the frenc and it does not stop there it grows higher. and the sceado of this treow she sees spreadan and mofan out and out until all of this ducdom is deorc and then across the sea the sceado mofs and the treow still growan and the sceado cums upon an other strand and still it spreads until all this other land is in sceado also and when she wacans this yonge afeart girl all is deorc as the deorc stan what cepes her in*

hard it was to get odelyn to go efen baec to our hus that daeg after the gleoman cum hard to stop her wepan and cryan and wantan to go to the south to sanlac to dig on the hyll of blud for the bodigs of her sons what was cwelled there she saes cwelled for the cyng lic what dunstan had always wanted. i telt her none cnawan if this was triewe none cnawan naht her boys colde still cum baec they colde be hurt only or they colde be in lundun or sum other far place but no she cnawan she saed she cnawan they was gan she was their mothor she cnawan

82

and her heorte now was broc she saed and naht to lif for

well i was right when i saed none cnawan for none did but still i thought she was right that our sons was gan under the hors of ingengas or cut down by sweords or shot with straels on sum cold dun and for what for men feohtan ofer the right to tac our land and our rights and mac us gif geld to them and fall on our cneows if efer they cum by for fear of the line and the treow o our mastorful ealdors how we gifs thancs for our cyngs

well i got her to the hus and sleep she did in the end though it was late before she wolde and when she did it was a broc sleep. i cnawan i wolde not sleep not for the tidans alone but for what i was again hearan for what was bean spoc to me seemed louder now efen than that first night sum wices ago and now i cnawan why he had cum. sum thing is cuman i had saed and sum thing now had cum. i seen the fugol i cnawan what the haeric star cum to sae now i was hearan sum great thing from lands other men can not see and i colde see now why i was ceosan

that night i did not sleep for i did not try to. i did not go to our bed i went down the path across the fenn and i went as night was on all the land and deop in the eald holt of what my grandfather spac them years bacc the holt of hafoc and craw. this holt it was the same as efer it was efen though all other things was cuman down on us and the craws then was still for night was long begun. i has gan to this holt many times since i was a cilde and

satt always on one eald ac treow what cum down and is
now foda for all in the holt. when i was a cilde when i satt
in this holt as night cum i was afeart of eorcas and aelfs
and scuccas but not now for now i was grown now there
was naht to fear but him

for among the sounds of the night wud there was sum
thing cuman cuman for me alone sum thing what had
been locan for me ofer all this world

*name me*

and i cnawan who

*name me*

and i cnawan i is ceosan

*buccmaster of holland*

for he is tellan me now and he is not near lic he was

*thu is ceosan*

he is here right here right here in the holt with the craws

*name me*

and with me and with the fox in the blaec by the cwelled
ac

*buccmaster*

where there is no light and no men and naht but what
the land macs

*name me*

and i saes i name thu
weland smith i name thu
why has thu cum

84

why does they not lysten why does they not see

it is all that i is this why can they not see

i wolde teorn to the crist if they wolde see efen to the crist any thing i wolde do

all the lytel things cwelled the treows they tacs our names our names they tacs our tales our songs. i was grown from this ground the ground they has tacan my ground from me all that i is they tacs all

if my grandfather was here now he wolde cnaw me for what i is for i is weac in all things a small man i is all is dyan here all is gan and tacan through my weacness i is small and weac and naht i has nefer been naht

well they is naht also the fuccan frenc the fuccan ingengas may be i is weac and lic a wifman but all that i done i done for my land and my folc and all that they done they done for gold for seolfor. deofuls they is scuc-cas fuccan cunts all angland is gan in their fyr all that anglisc folc macd in a thousand years all gan in frenc fyr and all men in thrall and deop in sceomu

after harald cyng was cwelled the bastard he called for angland to mac him its cyng but angland wolde not. a witan of high anglisc men was called of all who had lyfed through the wars of the year of fugol and star and not many men there was but they cum together in lundun and they saed they wolde feoht the bastard though there was few men with efen axes left in all the cyngdom. this witan they called as cyng edgar aetheling whose grandfather was eald cyng eadmund when my father was a cilde. edgar was an anglisc cyng of anglisc blud but he was no mor than cilde and the witan what called him was macd of eald men too eald to feoht and the bastard he wolde not stop

the bastard he cum north from the place where he had cwelled harald cyng and all the way he cum in blud his men they fucced all anglisc wifmen they cum to and cwelled them when done and all hams and tuns they beorned in ingenga fyr. the bastard cum up to lundun fuccan and cwellan and beornan and the witan it seen what was cuman and it stepped baec and the last of angland that daeg was gan and we had a new cyng who spac not efen our tunge and ate not our foda and cursed us as hunds and curses us still

in the abbodrice of eald eadweard who was cyng before harald the great abbodrice in lundun what they sae is all macd lic sum ingenga hus for lundun is no longer an anglisc tun in this abbodrice on the daeg of the mass of the crist in the year of fugol and star this bastard was gifen the corona of angland. i has met men who was there that daeg or men who saes they was for all lics to sae succ things and they saes what befell then was to mac the bastard sore lic a hors with a thorn in its foot what is ciccan all things it sees.

the bastard duc geeyome was gifan the anglisc corona by the biscop of the crist who tacs his orders from his cyng not from his heofon and all men there then gaf up a great roar of wilcum hunds that they was and their brothors still rottan on sanlac hyll. but around the abbodrice the bastard had put his cnihts with sweord and hors to cepe him safe from anglisc ire and when the cnihts hierde this cry they belyfd it was a risan agan the bastard for they did not spec our tunge and did not cnaw our ways. and so they put fyr to all the hus around the abbodrice and they cwelled anglisc men who was locan on and all in the abbodrice fled but for the bastard who was alone with his corona and his ire and his fear. they saes the bastard has no fear but no man has no fear and on this daeg he cnawan what he had done to cum to angland lic he did and if he thought he wolde haf us easy lic he had our wifmen then he cnawan now he was wrong

well these deorc dreams was still cuman to me then dreams of blud of my wifman spered through the guttas by deorc ingengas of my sons torn by hunds of my hus beornan my lif beornan. efry night slepan the dreams cum as the fyr cum nearer to us i colde feel them cuman it was lic splotts on the nebb of a yonge man cwelled by sum deorcness in his high time of lif. and all the time he was cuman for now i had named him he was always with me not specan all of the time at least in the beginnan but always with me now i had been ceosan

my grandfather first telt me of the great smith weland what wolde he haf saed to see me ceosan for greatness by this deorc ealdor of all anglisc folc

but lysten to what the bastard done lysten now for though i will sae it still it is hard to belyf. since our thegn was dead in sum dicc his eages tacan by raefns his sawol by ingengas we was to haf new men ofer us and blaec they was to be. as the year begun ecceard he was called away sum place we was not telt of to hiere the new laws from them who had not the guttas to cum them selfs and tell anglisc folc what was to becum of them. he was gan sum three daegs then he cum baec to us hangan his heafod for what he moste sae but still he saed it. we was all bid to cum to the ham to hiere this snyflan scucca bendan to the will of others lic the dog hidan under the stool when the staef is raised

so in ire was i from what i hierde that my heafod was full of things i wolde do and sae it is hard for me efen now to tell what this weosul was saen that daeg

our new cyng he begins and he saes this lic it is triewe lic there was no fugol no star lic half our men was not gan and nefer cum baec. only our new cyng lic it is another daeg lic all daegs. our new cyng he saes he has telt me that as wulmaer thegn was cwelled feohtan under the flag of harald godwineson who was thief of the corona of angland his lands will be gifen to geeyome cyng and with them all lands in his thegnage and this means also the lands of all in this ham

then he stops and there is no sound at all only the breath of the mist all ofer the fenn. for it was a winter daeg in hrethmonth and on many daegs in this month the colde breath of erce wolde cum up out of the fenn and swallo us and it wolde be hard to see efen from hus to barn so thicc was it. well this was one of these daegs and though we was cum round near in the cold and though there was sum twentig or thirtig of us lystnan to this scucca specan these ingenga words hardly colde we all see our own selfs

still there was no sound none saed naht lic after efry thing that had already cum there was naht mor colde bring us pain and this seemed to fryht ecceard mor than if we had gan at him for he mofs about and swallos and his eages mofs lic he is sum cildes poppet

geeyome cyng of angland he gan on and his words now is hard to hiere as he finds them hard to sae geeyome cyng has gifen word that all men what can gif sceal haf the right to buy from him what lands they once held from wulmaer thegn who was with harald the thief at sanlac and whose land is thus gifen to thy rightful cyng

ecceard i calls here through the cold breath of the land what fuccan scit is this

ecceard he does not loc up he is specan low and slow

and he saes geeyome cyng will be raisan the geld for all men to two scillings for eacc carucate so as to mac good the worc what harald thief of coronas had not done to cepe this land safe from ingengas

now i was not the only one roaran out for loc what this cunt has saed. he tells us that we moste gif mor geld to an ingenga cyng to cepe ourselfs safe from ingengas. ecceard he still locs down he does not mete our eages he does not dare

thu is cwellan us all calls sum gebur for a few men is cum baec from the fyrd those men who colde cum baec and maybe those who colde not done better for to cum baec to broc land and now this it is lic bean cwelled many times in one lif

geld will be tacan in the eald ways saes ecceard through me as thy gerefa and for land in the same way and there will be hearm to thu if geld is not gifen and this is what thy cyng has to sae to his new folc

and this is all the cyng needed to sae for war had cum to angland with him and it did not end at sanlac or in lundun and it wolde not end now

*then what sceal be done*

sum thing sceal be done

*and what sceal it be*

it sceal be a war

*and who sceal lead this war*

sum great man

*what man is this*

the man will cum

*and what sceal his name be*

92

i does not cnaw

                              *does thu cnaw any thing*

i cnawan we moste feoht

                                      *then feoht*


let me tell thu of him now for when the bastard cum
upon us so did he. it was my grandfather telt me first
about eald weland the smith and the same tale i hierde
later many times by fyrs and from gleomen and scopmen
all ofer angland and efen in other places for weland he is
in our blud and our land. eald he is ealdor efen than the
lost gods under the mere eald he is lic the fenn and the
seas. for he cum ofer the seas in a time before time and
with him he brought what macd this land ours

                                   *gold seolfor blud*

in weland smith is what angland is what our folc is

                          *gold seolfor fyr on the water*

all the wundor in this land macd by him from the ore of
erce

                      *they broc my scancs they broc the land*

broc he was but he cum up again and lic the fugol was
abuf all men

                  *and a cyng i cwelled and all of his cynn folc*

cyngs who does yfel gifs away their coronas

                      *it is the small folc moste tac them*

for the great men is weac with gold and fafor

lysten i is tellan thu now the tale of weland the smith and i will tell it as my grandfather telt it to me by the fyr in the great hus to me and to my sistor aelfgifu yonge we was our hands held together as they wolde again many times o my sistor

luf is pure luf is triewe luf is all that is triewe and when thu has one thu lufs thu is a man gifen sige by the gods. weland was cnawan all through his lands as the greatest smith what has efer been and men cum from far parts to beg with him to mac them sweords for feohtan or rings for luf. weland lifd with his two brothors by a great mere in a place cnawan as wulfdale by a great holt called myrcwud. one daeg these three men they seen three fugols passan ofer from the holt three fugols of great wundor swans they was and they cum down by the three men and they becum wifmen for these was swan maedens of the eald times and in them was a great wicce craft

well these three maedens they was wed to these men and weland toc as his the wifman called allwise and for seofon years they lifd in wulfdale in bliss but in the eighth year these maedens they was gripped with a lust to go baec to their hams and while the brothors was slepan baec they gan on their fethras still lic the mona. when weland and his brothors woc in the daeg and seen their lufs had gan they was broc and bitter lic all light had gan from the world for efer. welands brothors they gan out for myrcwud to find their lufs but weland he stopped in wulfdale and he stood ofer the gold ring he had macd for allwise what she had left him and he called for her to cum baec

well she nefer cum but others cum to this eornost smith who worcced his strength and his craft on his fyrs in the wud and one of them was a cyng of great yfel who lusted after gold lic a cilde after hunig. nithad cyng he had hierde of the craft of weland and he sent men with speres to bring him from wulfdale with all he had macd and these deorc men they toc weland while he slept and all his gold. they toc him to nithad cyng and when nithad seen all weland colde mac he was full of graed. weland smith he saes to this poor man now thu will be smith only for nithad thy cyng and thu will mac what i tells thu and for me alone. and nithad cyng he toc welands sweord for his own and he toc the gold ring what weland still cept for his luf allwise and he gaf it to his dohtor bod-wild. and then this yfel cyng he bid that weland be toc to an eolond and the strengs in his scancs be cut so that he colde not go no other place but moste worc only for the cyng for lic all cyngs he was a thief who worcced not but toc from eornost men

weland he worcced for sum time on this eolond with his broc scancs and his broc heorte but all this time he was thincan of his wyrd and of the fyr he wolde put under this cyng for he wolde haf again his sweord and he wolde haf again the ring that sceolde be worn only by his luf. to this ealond only the cyng colde cum and all others was cept away but so great was weland that many wanted to go to him to see his worc. two who did was the cyngs sons who was in graed and gold lust lic their father and cene to see the hoard what wolde be theirs one daeg. they cum to weland as he worcced and ascd to see the gold and the things he had macd of the gold and here weland cnawan the gods had gifen him a gift. with his great hamor he stracc them down and then with his fyr he begun to worc and through the night the fyrs colde be seen from all strands of the blaec mere

when daeg cum weland called the men of the cyng to him and he gaf them gifts what he had macd for nithad and his cwen and his dohtor bodwild. to the cyng he sent two great cuppes set in seolfor and gold and to the cwen he gaf gems and to bodwild he sent two breost plates of sum wundor. sean them bodwild was tacan with their beuty and was mofd to see the man who colde mac succ things so lic her brothors she gan to the eolond when none was locan and lic her brothors then she was toc for the yfel her father had done. for weland then he toc her maeden head as he had toc her brothors lifs and he cnawan then he was done with this place for his wergild was gifen him

the great smith then he rose into the heofon lic his swan wif had done so long baec he rose on fethras he had macd of gold in the scap of a swans fethras and to the cyng he spac from the heofon one last time

o great cyng nithad saes weland thu has tacn my scancs from under me but not the heofon from abuf me. thu has tacn the ring i macd for my luf and the sweord i macd for my belt and for all these things i has tacn thy cynn and thy world. these cuppes thu drincs from they is the heafodpannes of thy sons and these gems of the cwens is the eages of thy sons and thy dohtor lies in my bed all bledan and on her throta the bans of her brothors teorned to gold by my fyr. thy eages will not see me again o cyng but thy yfel and thy synn will lif with thu until thu is in the ground

and gan he was then gan ofer the heofon to myrcwud to loc again for his luf and locan he is still it is saed and sum nights thu may see him on his great gold swan wings grippan his hamor still and callan her name under the mona


well i wolde not gif them geld no i wolde not gif naht to this ingenga bastard for what he done. i had naht to gif after all the wars and the fyr what had cum from him and these cyngs all feohtan ofer the right to play with small folc lic sum fuccan game and this is what i telt the fuccan weosul when he cum to me for geld

ecceard cum to my hus and i sceolde haf toc down my grandfathers sweord and gelded him and macd him eat his fuccan beallucs with hunig

thu cums here i saes to him when he cums on to my land this cold daeg and the mist here again and him cuman from it lic sum ghast. thu dares cum to me thu who has tacan my sons and my land and now wolde tac all that i still has. cuman from the mist macs all men loc lic they is from the other world but ecceard as he cum nearer he was loccan lic this for real thynne he was and with his weosul words gan it seemed

buccmaster he saes my freond do not sae these things i is gerefa i moste do what i is biddan by thegn and cyng

i moste do what i is biddan i saes macan my words lic his o yes ecceard thu moste do that for when did thu efer do any other thing. if they bid thu to get on thy cneows and bare thy arse to their frenc pintels thu wolde do this with a great anglisc smile wolde thu not

buccmaster he saes do not sae these things i moste tac the geld i moste

i moste i moste i will tell thu ecceard of holland thu moste get away from my fuccan land or find thyself in the fenn with no fuccan heafod on thy scealdors

now he cums near up to me and here is another man broc by the cuman of the frenc loc at him it is lic his flesc hangs from him

buccmaster he saes i moste haf the geld i moste haf it i moste tac it to the thegn if i does not do this there will be blud

there will be fuccan blud i saes o yes let them cum then these fuccan frenc what we has nefer efen seen let them cum to our ham and spec to us in our fuccan tunge let them cum and tac this geld let them see us let them tell us why we sceolde licc their fuccan arses but no they sends their lytel anglisc hund to do their biddan

98

buccmaster

i will not gif geld

thu moste

i will nefer do this ecceard and there is others in this ham will not neither

has thu been specan

many has been specan ecceard in this ham many folc has spoc who did not spec before and we will not do it ecceard of holland we will not lie in the straet and be walcd on so thu can cepe thy beallucs if thu efer has had any

then what will i do he saes and he is lic a cilde who has lost his poppet in the fenn and thincs his world is gan

go fucc thyself i saes and let thy frenc freonds do the same

he cums to me then and he tacs me by the sceaoldor and this is not sum thing he has efer done he is a man who cepes away. then he specs in a whisper lic he does not cnaw who stands beyond the mist

they is eorcas he saes they is eorcas thu does not cnaw thu has not seen them. they is eorcas cum from the sea to cwell us for what we has done thu moste see them buccmaster thu wolde not spec this way they is not men lic us their neccs is bare their heads is shafd

shafd

shafd lic moncs they has no ceneps no haer on them

all men does

not these frenc no haer and all their nebbs is set lic style all they lufs is gold and the beornan all they lufs is deorcness. worse they is than the denes for the denes has sum triewth but these frenc has only lust

then anglisc folc moste feoht

they has been feohtan buccmaster anglisc folc has been feohtan while thu was here worcan to cepe thy sons from the fyrd. they has feoht and has been cut down and who is left to feoht now. at sanlac harald cyng was cwelled also his brothors his thegns so many of the fyrd. the north still beorns from the cwellans of the landwaster what anglisc is left to do mor than bow the heafod as these scuccas cums from the sea to eat in fyr all that we has

we will stop them

thu buccmaster thu will stop them. will thu and sum eald geburs from the ham and their wifmen all ride out agan the bastard and his great fyrd

i will not gif all to them why sceolde i do this why sceolde any man

it is too late buccmaster thu has seen this cuman thu seen the fugol and the haeric star thu lost thy sons thu moste see that the crist is not with us buccmaster. it is lic the preosts saes we has synned lic in the boc now we is brought to the ire of god

where is this synn

all around our cyng was an oath brecer the biscop of rome gifs his flag to the shafn men the crist is agan us he sends the ire of his father with the duc of the frenc

this is all scit and beallucs ecceard crist and synn and

preosts we is men that is all. men with other men agan us if they stands ofer us we moste feoht them or we will die there is naht else in this world

buccmaster a fyrd was called if thu was wantan feohtan thu colde haf gan thu cannot feoht them now thu cnawan naht

and thu is a fuccan hund

how will thu feoht them will thu wait in thy hus with thy eald sweord till they cums with hors is thu sum great god agan a fyrd. it is too late for this now thu moste gif them geld or die there is naht else

thu is a fuccan nithing to sae this what is thu sum wifman in thy hus scittan in thy scirts does thu belyf we has no strength in this thing

the crist has the strength

the crist has cut thy fuccan beallucs off and the bas-tard will haf them ofer the fyr thu cunt scut thy mouth and get out thy fuccan sweord

i has no sweord i

then tac thy sithe or thy hoe or tac thy lytel fuccan pintel from thy breces and be a fuccan man


ecceard was a hund and a cunt but in triewth there was sum strength in what he saed to me for we was one small ham in the blaec fenns and now the frenc was here how was we to stand agan them. ecceard was a man made of fear always he wolde bow it was his first thought but the

first thought of a man sceolde be to stand agan other
men to cepe them out to cepe their hands from his land
and his sawol men moste be free or all is lost

but we was not free now and i wolde not gif geld and
others also talcan to me had saed they wolde not also
though in their eages sum thing saed to me that if the
frenc cum to them with their shafd heafods and their
nebbs lic style these men cwic enough wolde find what
was needed in their barn and their hus to cepe the eorcas
from their wifmen and the fyr from their thaecc. this is
men now this is men of angland weac weac weac and
unfree thralls for efer in their own fryht

*odelyn*

i does not want to

*all this beuty gan in fyr*

frenc fyr ecceards fyr

*the last thing a free man has*

gan

*tacan*

from me what was mine

but all moste cnaw these things as in the star it had
been spoc now in the aesc it was cum to be. lysten it was
sum wices on and i was out in my boat gan to tac aels gan
to the place my grandfather toc me to what was sum way
from my hus. i was gan early as the sunne cum up cold it
was and all the secg hwit lic cristal and odelyn when i gan
she was lightan the fyr and as i gan she smerced at me
ofer her sculdor and it was the last i efer seen of her

the aels was smaller than when i was a cilde harder to find there was mor folcs now and mor feohtan ofer what the land had for them and all belyfan it was their right to haf what they colde and so it toc sum time to get what i was needan and to mac my way baec to my hus. from far out on the fenn i colde see it as i cum baec fillan the heofon it had been a bright daeg but now the heofon was blaec lic the graef

*the graef of the frenc*

fucc the frenc loc at this loc at this loc what they done all of this all these things my grandfathers hus the land of my folc efry thing worcced for all of what i was all of me

all beorned it was. i cum out of my boat out of the fenn i cum through the secg and through the treows and my land is gan it is gan lic all had only efer been naht. all heges down all barns beorned my swine cwelled bledan in the holt my oxen slit open my sceop all blaec and cwelled their heafods off my aeppel treows cut all to the ground and then the hus

the hus my great hus all of its greatness gan up to the heofon callan for blud now callan where was thu cepan this land where was thu buccmaster tacan aels while thy lif gan into the ground. all gan it was i cum up to it and all was a great graef of smocan blaec aesc the blaecness risan lic treow stoccs lic the arms of thunor up to the heofon. i cum up near and it beorned me still the fyr was beornan hot in the aesc

103

in there was all the things of my lif all cum down in to
this hot and deorc place. i colde see the great beams half
gan colde see scaps in the fyr what i cnawan and beornan
i was in my heorte also beornan and wepan. and i gan
then i gan to the path through the treows and down to
the ham for smoc there was too cuman from that place
and risan up gifan all the blaec fens a blaec heofon

blaec heortes

and what they done well thu cnawan for they done it
all ofer angland they done this and now we is lytel hores
in their beds lytel cildren used they fuccs us smercan
they saes we is thy gods we has the flag thu will lie down
it is his will loc at this anglisc gold it is a wundor bend
before me cilde i is thy fuccan cyng

well all the ham was beorned efry hus was gan in fyr
and many still beornan and in sum hus colde be seen folc
blaec also twisted and becum mete beorned on the fyr
for the hunger of the bastard. in the gathran place on the
straet was two wifmen on the ground cut and fuccd all
blud and rags sum geburs wimman one dead the other
mofan in sum small way and wepan and bledan and it
wolde not be long befor she was tacan by craws and
hafocs and this a good thing for her eages was gan it was
lic sum great hund had cwelled his hunger in her

there was naht here no mor naht to see no hus and no
folc naht but this great blaecness this great stincan in the
heofon and this on a daeg what had been colde and clene
and full of micel beuty in the beginnan. the fugol cum i

saed the fugol cum to mac us see but we did not see so
the star cum and still we did not see and now it is done
and all is gan but buccmaster of holland for he is ceosan
yes ceosan for angland ceosan for what is yet to be gifen
to him


so sum was cwelled and beorned and sum was gan i
cnawan not where into the holts and fenns i was thincan
to cepe clere of these frenc scuccas to cepe their lifs and
in the ham there was no sound but the beornan. i gan
ofer to ecceards hus to see if the frenc had been good to
their little hund but i saw cwic he was fuccd as bad as all
for his hus too was blaec aesc and stincan smoc. i was
standan locan into the aesc locan for ecceard to see how
beorned he was when i seen a man cuman from the holt
what led out on to the fenn. this man he called to me and
on my belt was a scramasax and i tacs this in my hand
     do not cum here i saes
     buccmaster thu moste cum
     so he is not frenc i thincs and as he cums to me i seen
he is sum cottar from the ham. i has seen him but not
spoc to him for i is a socman with three oxgangs
     i is called grimcell he saes i is with ecceard thu moste
cum
     ecceard lifs
     ecceard wolde spec with thu he is in the holt we moste
cepe from the ham now cum

sum cottar tells me cum and most times i wolde beat him but these is hard times and i gan with this grimcell who is a strong man man i gan with him into the holt and sum way baec to where the ham can be seen but none from there can see into the treows. sittan on the ground leanan on a stocc of berc is ecceard and if before he was locan lic a ghast now he is locan lic he has cum from the graef still with blud and eorth on his cold bodig to call out the synns of his lif

he locs up at me and he saes buccmaster and i only locs at him he is a hund and a weosul this is triewe but he has been gifen blud for these things now. he has cloth ofer his heafod and there is all blud on the cloth it is on his nebb and his scyrte and efen on the treow and still cuman and from his eages water is cuman also

they has tacan my eares buccmaster he saes they cut them and threw them on the fyr that was my hus

my wifman is gan he saes and he can not spec well now my wifman is gan my godgifu she was dear to me and my hus gan all is gan now

and my hus gan i saes and my wifman my odelyn i has not seen her is she beorned is she fuccd has she gan to the holt i does not cnaw ecceard it is not only thu

they is eorcas he saes i telt thu buccmaster eorcas thu cannot feoht them they cums on the wind lic the fenn feofor

they may cum again saes this grimcell we sceolde go from the ham why wolde they cum again i saes they has fuccd and beorned all in this world there is naht left for them to tac

they has their own ways

i will not go from my land i saes where is odelyn where is my sweord there is worc to do

there is naht to do saes ecceard thu is gan from thy land now thu moste find other places other folcs where the beornan has not cum they will let none lif here. he stands then slow and he grips the treow

grimcell and me we is goan in to the holt he saes we is goan from here we is not esols. grimcell helps him stand and he locs at me then

thu sceolde cum he saes there is few anglisc and many frenc now to lif thu moste stay in the holt

well i was not goan with them for where was all of my world where was my wif i had things i moste find. baec to my hus i gan and to all the land around it and i was callan odelyn odelyn where is thu. she may haf gan to the holt or be hidan but there was no sound no sign from her nor from annis her gebur whose hus was also gan. in the aesc i was locan but the aesc was hot and smocan and i colde not go there and so there i was standan locan at all my cwelled lif all things gan in fyr and none to hold down for this none to answer to me only these frenc ghasts who has cum and is gan

well i cnawan then what i moste do so i gan to my boat and to the fenn i gan and i was rowan rowan hard pullan

baec my arms beornan with it i was mofan lic the swealwe through the heofon through the saw secg and the
grene water i gan

the holt of the eald gods was still as it was always still
and there lic when i was a cilde was the treows under the
water under the meos and the grene deop but there was
the stoccs and the stillness and lic my grandfather i put
the wet ars in the boat and i sat for a time locan only
bean with the stillness of the mere and of all that is eald
and triewe and then i spac

i is buccmaster of holland i saes a socman of this land

i is buccmaster son of ascetil son of leofric a man of
thy ways a man of the eald times a man of thy hus

i is cum to call thu to the feoht for angland is beornan
in ingenga fyr thy folcs is bledan their crist has left them
lic we saed lic we always saed he wolde

i satt then lystnan and the fugols spac baec at me but
from the water there was naht. i loccd down ofer the side
of the boat the stoccs was the same as efer blaec and deop
and still lic the graef

in the boat then i stands it is hard it mofs cwic and is
undeop but i stands and to the heofon i raises my arms

woden of the duns i saes one eaged gifer of lif lord of
raefn and wulf dweller in deorc beorgs ealdor of runes
hung up and cut down god of war and god of the graef
cum to us

thunor of the holt hamor of men ealdor of the leas and
the lihtnan born in ac and fyr cum to us

frigg of the hus of the grene lif of small things and

triewe of the heorte under the ban of wicce craft and all
that is growan cum to us

great erce mothor of all who is grene and blaec who is
wind and snow who is water and stan who is hafoc and
craw and blud who is lif of the bodig and death of the
bodig who is efry lifan thing in the wid fenn and the wid
world cum to us

i stands i brings my arms down slow

there is naht

naht cum but the wind and the wind then it tacs me
and it scufs me it scufs me lic a man or a god has scufd
me ofer the boat and in to the mere

well this holds no fear for me i can mof through water
as through holt or feld this was gifen when a yonge cilde.
the water is colde it is eosturmonth it is hard to breathe i
is ceocan breathan cwic but it seems to me i has been cast
in to the mere to be sum thing after the brocn land and
after the fyr

i tacs in a great breath then and i gan down

down i gan down in to the blaec but my eages is open i
gan down i pulls hard down to the treows i sees them
cuman up to me i sees them blaec and mofan with the
water i puts out my hand and i feels them cold and hard
and slimd and then the water tacs me baec up up to the
boat to the heofon to the world and i cums up ceocan to
breathe and now with sum thing i has nefer had that no
man has efer been gifan

*now thu has been there*

it is lic ys

109

*thu has been to the holt*

they did not cum

*they is here*

i called they did not cum

*does thu thinc they cums in fyr in the heofon*

what then

*they cums in thu*

when

*thine is the bodig thu ceoses the time*

it is lic ys

*be triewe*

that night i gan to the holt where my swine was before they was cwelled by the scuccas and i made a fyr to dry myself and i satt and locd at the fyr and all was still for a long night. when the sunne cum i rose from the aesc of my small fyr and i gan ofer to the aesc of the great fyr what had been my hus and was now cold and still

into this aesc i gan and for sum time i was in it delfan and secan and i was aesc then on my nebb and in my haer and beard and on all my clothes all was aesc and i was secan

first i found my sweord my grandfathers sweord still on the beam what had cum down all blaec and i lifted the sweord and clened it and carried it from the hus and laid it down on the ground. then i gan baec and for sum time i loccd and i toc sum other things what i was needan sum things what does not beorn what is made of style and gold and i clened these things and laid them on the ground with my sweord to tac to where i moste go. then i gan baec and this last time i found odelyn

all mete she was all of her lif gan in fyr blaec and beorned lic sum hara or cicen coccd on a fyr too hot and long. her scap was not wifman was sum thing not of this world for she had gan to the other. i seen not what had been done to her and was not there for her when i was needed and this is my weacness what now i sceal lif with for it is my curse and this wifman who none sceolde efer harm who was triewe and who was lufd by me and cept lic a cwen in all things now was gan in frenc fyr and this macd me a small man small and weac and with my sweord still on the beam and my self gan for aels while my wifman was fuccd and cwelled by ingengas. and why wolde these gods spec with me why wolde they not smerc at me scun me lic a sic hund a sic man a sic weosul

all gan all was gan and so i gan i toc what i had and i gan away from my hus and land. before i gan i dug a graef for my odelyn and i laid her down with luf and with curses for those who tocc her from me and with her i left sum ac wud sum treen from the fyr a scramasax sum leafs from the holt and sum secg from the fenn and i laid down also my wyrd and i saed i will tac them for thu i will haf my wergild in frenc blud and ofer her then i swept the eorth and all was done on my lands and nefer did i thinc to see them again in this world i spac to him then but he nefer spac baec

this weland this great smith who had ceosan me he had cum when all was teornan about in blud and fyr this great ealdor of all anglisc folc lic i saes i seen why he ceosan me for i was a socman of three oxgangs i had been gifen the sight of the fugol who cum to warn us and i was of the eald hus. now angland was in need and now i had been to the hus of the lost gods so it seemed to me i would be gifen a path to tac

but no path was seen then this smith weland he spac to me when he ceose and other times he gan and was not hierde for days and nights. sum times i was thincan he saes he is weland he saes he is the great smith of wulfdale but all i has is words i does not cnaw i has not seen him it may be he is sum deoful or sum nightgenga of the holt specan to me plegan with me succ things has been hierde of. when i was a yonge cilde many tales was telt to me by other boys in the ham of eald ghasts from fenn and holt what cum to men whispran to them of gold and luf. oft when men cums to land what has been ham to aelfs they will hiere micel whispran and be telt to cum to the fenn at night for sum maeden is waitan but naht is waitan but death

so at this time i still did not cnaw what to do and sum daegs was spent wandran in the holts around the eald ham for though naht was there but aesc now i did not cnawan where to go or what to do. i locs now and i sees that i cnawan in triewth what i moste do but then i was

afeart and so i cept to places i cnawan for to leaf wolde be
to cum to my wyrd in full and this thing was so great it
left me dreaned and small in its sceado

for in triewth i cnawan another reason weland cum to
me for this was what my grandfather telt me and aelfgifu
when we was yonge cildren when he was tellan us in his
great hus the tale of the smith and his allwise and
wulfdale and the yfels of cyngs. my yonge sistor she was
in awe of my grandfather as was i but i was the first son
of my father and so for my grandfather i was to be cyng
of his cynn to cum and he loccd at me this way. after he
telt me this tale of weland he stood and he tocc from the
beam his sweord what is now my sweord and slow he toc
it from its sceath and he mofd it about in the light from
fyr and door and from it cum lihts of its own that swam
about the hus lic fisc in the water

cilde he saes this sweord thu sees but sceal not grip till
thu is man this is welands sweord. this sweord was gifen
to me by my father who was called guthrum a great
man and he was gifen it by his father and this sweord it
was macd by weland him self in the myrcwud fyrs this
sweord was born in the year angland was born and the
year my grandfather was born for these was all the same.
weland he cum to my grandfather at night for he was a
great man my grandfather and he telt me this when i too
was a cilde lic thu he telt me of when weland cum to him
and of the fear he was in for this great smith he cum one
night when my grandfather was cuman baec from the

fenn. and locan up he seen cuman out from the holt a
great gold man scinan with fyr in the cuman night

this man he cum to him and he was tall lic the treows
and on him he wore clothes of gold scinan with stans and
on his heafod was a great helm lic that of the eald cyngs
all carfan with boars and wyrms and raefns and scinan
too and all that colde be seen of his nebb was his eages
what was strong lic the sunne itself

and there by the fenn in the dyan light of the daeg and
in the cuman night this great man he saes i is weland
smith ealdor of this land gifer of tools and waepans and
to thu i has cum and why thu will nefer cnaw but thu
moste tac what i gifs to thu and not asc and this will be a
good wyrd for thu and thy cynn

and my grandfather he colde sae naht for he was afeart
and this great ent of gold then he specs mor he saes these
is new times now for all folcs in these lands is one folc
and to cepe thy hus free of denes and other ingengas thu
sceal be gifen this great sweord what is macd in fyr and
with the blud of many in its macan. and from his baec he
tacs this sweord what thu now sees and he gifs it ofer to
my grandfather who was still afeart and small

and there is one other thing also saes my grandfather
locan at me and also at my sistor there is one other thing
weland saes to my grandfather he saes that this sweord
thu moste cepe on thy land always for it is thine alone
and this sweord it is for thy cynn to cepe their selfs free.
and this may be free from ingenga folc from denes or it

may be free from others in angland from anglisc folc who wolde mac thu small it may be from those who wolde put them selfs ofer thu who wolde call them selfs thy

well my grandfather he saes no mor for it was then that my father cum into the hus he cum through the door and i colde see he had been hearan sum of what my grandfather had saed for he cums to him and to us and he is in sum ire

thu cildren go from the hus he saes go now and we can see he is not to be pleged with here and so my sistor and i we gets to our feet and not locan at our grandfather we runs from the hus and at the door i teorns when i is goan and i sees my father tac this sweord rough lic from my grandfather who stands and locs at him also in ire but my father is a strong man and he saes to my grandfather do not i has saed to thu do not i will not haf this efer in this hus. and then my father he teorns to me with ire and i runs out into the sunne with my sistor and a hwit place it is on the land all light and free after where we has been


well what i done after sum time i gan ofer to bacstune for this ham was one i cnawan and i wolde see if what had cum to us had cum also to others in holland. bacstune was sum hours walc ofer fenn paths and through the holt and on these paths i was safe for none colde walc these places but those who was folc of them so windan was they and so hard was the fenn on those who cum from

other lands. with me i toc welands sweord and the other
things i had toc from the fyr and sum aels and sum mete
from my dead swine what i had toc and smocd for i did
not cnaw how long i wolde be mofan or where i wolde go

   bacstune was not a long walc but i moste tac care for
who was in the holts now i did not cnaw who was in
angland i did not cnaw. in triewth though i toc care i seen
naht and no man in fenn or holt until i cum near to
bacstune on the path what went in to that ham and then
when i cum near a man cum from the treows and it was
this grimcell what had been with ecceard and he cum to
me

   do not go to bacstune he saes there is frenc there
   now
   they has been there i does not cnaw if they is gan
   where is ecceard
   ecceard is not long

   grimcell then he is gan baec in to the treows and he is
a strong man and anglisc and there is frenc in bacstune
so i gan with him he tacs me sum way in to the holt and
to a place where there is a fyr and a small hus macd of
treows and stoccs and leafs it seems they has been here
for sum daegs. i sees ecceard is lyan in this small hus and
not mofan

   dead i saes

   he will be far faran soon saes grimcell the sicness has
tacan him his ears blede grene and blaec he is cold i has
put sum hunig and salt on him but i has not any wicce

craft we needs sum wif to be with him with eced and senep and wyrts naht is growan it is still winter

i gan in to the lytel hus then and i locs down at ecceard who does not open his eages

i has gifen him water saes this grimcell he nedes mete has thu mete

no i saes i has no mete

ecceard then he opens his eages and locs up but what colde he see

it is thu he saes thu thu sceolde not haf cum all is blud now blud thu brings

see he is sicc saes grimcell

blud thu brings saes ecceard

well i will not lysten to this rot i will not waste mete on him he is dyan so i leafs this hus of bare treows and i gan out again and after sum time grimcell he cums out also

we sceolde mac a graef he saes he will be gan before night and wihts will cum

i has macd enough graefs i saes i has buried my wif-man these last daegs

i also

ecceard hored for the frenc i will not dig his graef

he done what he moste

and i do what i moste and thu also cottar and if thu moste dig then dig i is a socman i does not dig graefs

well for sum time then we sits or stands or walcs about in this small camp in the holt i gan to find wud to put on the fyr i cepes it goan and this gifs me sum thing to be thincan of but in triewth i had no reason to be in this place i was here only because there was no other place for me in this world. and where was he now when i was needan words where was his words now here i was as small as the fyr dyan lic ecceard naht i was naht when i sceolde be great

well i was sittan by this fyr thincan and this man grimcell he was gan again to loc at ecceard in triewth he was only waitan for him to go he had begun macan a graef. at this time we both of us hierde a sound cuman from the treows it cum from the path in to bacstune so i stands and i tacs my scramasax and this grimcell he has an ax and a good ax and he tacs this and we locs to this sound we gets behind the stoccs of treows for it seems the frenc has seen us and cum to clene us from our own land and agan these hunds i will feoht efen with a cottar

but what cum to us then was not the hors of the frenc but sum swine. six swine cum in to the holt and is locan about for food and snufflan and doan what swine does and grimcell and me we locs at them then and locs about and after the swine cums a cilde

this cilde is not a frenc cilde he has long light haer and his nebb is thynne he seems of denisc folc he is yonge as yonge as my dunstan i wolde haf saed and he grips a stic for the swine but he is locan not at them but at the hus where ecceard is dyan

i cums out from the treows then with my scramasax and i saes tac thy swine cilde and go from this place this cilde he leaps when he sees me but he stands locan and grimcell then he cums from the treows also and this cilde he locs at us

thu is men of the holt he saes

it wolde seem all anglisc is men of the holt now i saes for where is our fuccan hus and land

who is thu saes grimcell

tofe saes this cilde tofe of bacstune a son of gerd these is my swine they cums here micel where is thu cum from

do not sae grimcell saes i

grimcell saes naht

tac me with thu saes this cilde then

what and thy fuccan swine i saes i laughs at this the cilde he locs small

i has strength

go to thy hus cilde

my hus is gan and my mothor also did thu not hiere frenc has come to bacstune

thu has thy swine

they will mac me gif geld for them i has naht

go saes grimcell we is only men we is lost

all is lost without thu saes this cilde and he stands locan at us. but he sees we is saen naht mor and he teorns and he calls to his swine and slow he mofs away


that night i slept in the holt lic a swine myself and when i woc i seen grimcell tacan ecceard to his graef. the bodig of our gerefa was lic the stocc of a treow and grimcell was lyftan him as he colde but it was hard and he cept fallan. i was loccan for sum time and smercan when he fell lic an eald poppet but then grimcell he seen me locan and he ascd me to help him and help him i did for the sunne was cum up and fugols was specan and it seemed it colde be a good daeg for there was no frenc here and still we lifd

grimcell and i we dropped our gerefa into his graef in the holt and ofer him then we thrown the soft blaec eorth and grimcell he wanted to sae sum words about the crist and the lif after this but he did not cnaw none and i was blithe to see that he did not asc me for he cnawan i was of the eald hus though i had not telt him so

so what was we to do now where was we to go. all was blaec in these times and all we colde do was to walc to walc to other hams to walc in the holt lic the fox lic the swine. it seemed now i was to be with this cottar grimcell for in triewth there was no other place to be and he was not a bad man and colde be of sum use

so on this mergen this cottar and i we put ecceard in the eorth and we scoc the eorth from our selfs and we was goan to walc from bacstune through the holt and we was thincan to go north but before we gan we hierde again a sound from the treows and again we seen this cilde cum from the ham only this time with no swine only him and a lytel sacc. this cilde he cums to us and he is yonge only a cilde but he specs with set mouth

i moste cum with thu he saes my mothor is dead my father is dead all i has is swine and swine is naht without folc where is thy swine saes grimcell

at my hus saes this cilde

what can thu do for us saes grimcell

i can feoht if i moste saes this cilde feoht the frenc lic
thu does

feoht with what i saes

heorte saes this yonge cilde locan at me

get thy swine saes grimcell get three of them and bring
them and thu may cum with us

this cilde then he laughs lic the cilde he is and he is
runnan off again to bacstune i will be triewe to thu he
saes i will be triewe to the holt and gan he is in the treows

grimcell i saes to this cottar in sum ire what is this
what is thu saen to cildren. grimcell then he specs but he
does not spec to me lic he locs up to me he specs lic he
too is a socman

this cilde saes grimcell thincs us mor than we is and he
will follow us due to it and this cilde he has mete. we has
no mete buccmaster

no mete i saes this is triewe

buccmaster saes grimcell does thu cnaw of these grene
men

grene men

folcs saes things saes grimcell they specs in raedels thu
cnawan what folcs is. i has hierde tales and this cilde has
hierde them also. this bastard he cum from the frenc
lands and he cwelled all great anglisc men he broc us and
he toc our land for his own and when he had ate all he
colde he gan baec to his frenc lands and he is there now

and we is loccd ofer now not by a cyng but a biscop

a fuccan biscop

sum frenc preost named odo or sum thing he is brothor of the bastard he is eorl of cent now by the bastards
will. it is saed he is a man of blud macan his brothor loc
lic the crist and what his brothor toc now he tacs again.
there is frenc all ofer now cwellan who they will tacan
what they can beornan if they will fuccan all our wifmen
and efen the bastard wolde not let his new cyngdom be
beorned in succ a way as this

ingengas i saes ingengas

anglisc men is feohtan buccmaster though many is gan
in blud sum has gan lic us to holt and fenn and they is
not dyan as they is telt. folcs is gathran buccmaster they
is gathran in the holts and on the duns and in the fenns
and they is gathran waepans

i sees none

they is there

if this is triewe it is good

thu hierde this cilde folcs is waitan for them they is
callan them grene men. they is grene lic the treows and
the treows is all they has now and this cilde he tacs us for
them

and he has swine

and maybe we is them buccmaster for we is in the
treows and the treows is all we has

well grimcell spac of treows and treows there was in
this place mor than there was in my ham for the land
mofd as i walced it. those who does not cnaw the fenns

hears of them only in tales and oft these tales is lies or is telt to cildren to fryht them. it is saed the fenns is all deorc waters and deop mud and that walcan in them thu will be drencced and it is saed also that the folcs of the fenns is scuccas or esols or is yfel wihts of the mere

these is the things folcs saes who does not cnawan naht of what they is specan for the fenns is a place of wundor to those who cnawan them. yes there is deop meres and waters so blaec that oxen is lost in them and nefer seen and there is muds what strecces for miles ringed by secg and lesch and if thu does not cnawan the paths through these places and thu gan in thu will not be cuman out again as man. these is the blaec fenns where the eorth and the waters is all blaec lic the graef. there is also fenns of sand what is brun not blaec and where things is not the same and the treows and plants is not the same and efen the heofon has another loc

but while the low places is wet the high places is dry and there is many ealonds in the fenns what gifs us foda and good lifs. welig and alor treows is growan here and sum times ac and aesc and there is micel ground on what can be growan waet and baerlic and holts where swine can be lifan and micel good ground on hwicc to lif as folc. and as these ealonds is in meres on all sides with paths what only fenn folcs cnawan it is hard for those from other parts to cum in though as i had seen it can be done when those ingengas has fenn folcs at their call to lead them to the hunt

all around the fenn lands there is treows. ofer to the

south and west ofer to where the frenc cum from is a great holt that is called the brunnesweald and this holt has been in this place since our folc cum to this land. ham it is to wulfs it is saed and boars and aelfs and other folcs it is an eald place eald it colde be as the hus of the eald gods under the mere. this brunnesweald i had nefer seen before i left my ham but i was to see it later for it was there the enemis of the bastard cum to gather to feoht those who broc them

now in this small holt by bacstune locan at the treows i was thincan that these frenc they wolde gif all these things other names. i was locan at an ac treow and i put my hand on its great stocc and i was thincan the ingengas will haf another name for this treow. it had seemed to me that this treow was anglisc as the ground it is grown from anglisc as we who is grown also from that ground. but if the frenc cums and tacs this land and gifs these treows sum frenc name they will not be the same treows no mor. it colde be that to erce this treow will be the same that it will haf the same leafs the same rind but to me it will be sum other thing that is not mine sum thing ingenga of what i can no longer spec

will they gif angland another name also i saes to this treow what will we call our cildren

what is it thu saes buccmaster saes grimcell to me hearan this

i specs to the treow i saes to him it colde be we is grene men now without ceosan it

124

where will we go saes grimcell

other hams i saes let us go to other hams let us stay in the holt cepe walcan with this cilde and his swine let us see what the frenc has done in the fenns and let us see who else is in these wuds now

*now does thu see*

where has thu been i has been callan

*it is not for thu to call*

who is thu

*thu named me*

but i cannot see

*i has been waitan for thu to see*

still i is blind

*cepe walcan buccmaster of holland*

show me the path

*find it*

grimcell and i then we gan ofer to langetof to see what the folc there was bearan. as we gan through the holt we was specan and i cum to see that grimcell was cwic of mynd for a cottar and no esol lic sum was. he telt me he had not gan with the fyrd due to bean sic with the feofor when the call cum but his brothor had gan and his son and neither cum baec and lic me now his wifman was cwelled by the frenc when they cum through lic the wind and now we was left with the holt as all we had. we talcced then of the frenc and of what moste be done

when my father was a cilde saes grimcell our anglisc cyng aethelraed he was weac and men cum in scips then from the north lands to angland and aethelraed was cast out and cnut cum to us as cyng and he lic this geeyome was an ingenga a denisc man. and his men they set many fyrs and hams and tuns was beorned lic now and yet cnut when he cum he cum as an anglisc cyng and locd ofer us as one and he done well by us

well this may be so i saes but frenc men they is not the same mor lic hunds they is than men all their ways is ingenga to us. they has no haer on their heafods i saes does thu cnawan this no haer they is all shafn they locs lic frogs

frogs saes this cilde tofe then and he is laughan frogs he saes locan up at me. he is walcan along with us as we is goan through the holt we is talccan he is lystnan and callan and ciccan his swine to mof them before him

has thu seen them then saes grimcell

all cnaws this i saes thu does not haf to see it but lysten now does though cnawan of the daeg of sanct bricius and of what aethelraed done to the ingengas on this daeg

tell us saes tofe who is yonge this cilde but lystens to me well

this was in the time of my grandfather i tells this cilde who was a great man and at this time aethelraed he had many denisc folcs in this land but many was agan him and he was afeart at the cuman of the denisc cyng to tac his corona. and so aethelraed he telt his folc that on the daeg of this sanct all denisc folcs in the cyngdom was to be cwelled

cwelled saes tofe all of them

cwelled i saes and as the daeg cum up cwelled they was. anglisc folcs toc them from their hus and ham and cut them down and efen the circes of the crist was not good hidan places for them these circes was beorned for anglisc men colde not trust ingengas lifan amongst them

grimcell and tofe they saes naht to this for sum time only cepes walcan

it colde be done again i saes if we had a great man to lead us we colde tac efry frenc man in this land from his hus on one daeg if we had the will and angland wolde be ours again

tofe saes grimcell at last to the cilde this is a denisc name is it not

tofe he locs afeart then but he saes in a small way yes it is denisc

thy folcs then was denisc saes grimcell to him but he saes it lic a freond

my grandfather saes tofe again for we is in the dane-laugh is we not before the anglisc cyngs toc baec this place it was under rule of north cyngs there is many here of denisc stocc but they is anglisc now we is all anglisc now is this not so. he is locan at us in teorn lic he needs us to say yes cilde. grimcell he locs at me then but he saes naht to me

frenc is worse than denisc i saes loc and thu will see frenc is worse than denisc

when this geeyome our cyng cums baec from his frenc

lands saes tofe then it colde be he will rule us lic cnut lic a good man now the feohtan is done it colde be the beornan will stop

he is not our cyng and he will not i saes and i saes it in a way that stops them saen any things lic this again. there is not time for this there is no time. tofe ciccs his three swine what has stopped to root and we walcs on we is goan south

*thu will feoht then*

feoht who

*feoht them*

first we moste find them

*the gods locs on*

a time will cum

*they did not cwell thy odelyn with words*

do not spec of her

*she is here with me she locs on*

no

*she is here thy grandfather is here*

thu is lyan

*thy boys*

nefer this is scit

*in this place is all thy cynn folc they locs on*

i does not belyf thu

*who will feoht now they saes for our land*

they cnawan i is strong

*this sweord i gaf thu and nefer is it swung*

well we spent a night in the holt around a fyr with

these swine gruntan around us all the fuccan night and all night it regned on us and cold the regn was. we was wearan capes but we was wet through by the time light cum and in this way we gan south to langetof and i was felan lic a hund in triewth lic a man with naht

if i had again my hus and my fyr i saes and my wifman what i cept lic a cwen always and whose luf for me was triewe then all other men colde leaf me for efer and this i wolde not efen see

if i had been there i saes with my sweord then there wolde be no frenc in all these fenns

grimcell he walcs with me wet also and he saes naht to the things i is saen but this cilde tofe i has seen that he lystens always to me

buccmaster he saes this sweord what thu carries it is a great thing. a wise cilde he is this one and i saes to him yes this sweord is no sweord what small men has

small men has no sweords saes this tofe in my ham none had a sweord they is great things

this sweord is greater than any thu will see i saes for it is macd by weland the great smith of the eald times

weland saes the cilde weland i has been telt of in tales by gleomen but tales i thought they was only

gleomen is esols i saes they thincs they is only raedlan for poor geburs but in sum of their tales they tells great triewths though they is too dumb to cnaw it

in triewth saes this cilde was this sweord macd by great weland buccmaster triewth is all i tells i saes

but here i colde not tell as i had wanted the tale of my grandfather and of his metan with great weland in the fenn for grimcell saes we moste stop this specan now for we is cuman to langetof. i was in sum ire at him saen this but i saw he was right we was near for through treows we colde see smoc from fyrs. langetof was a small ham lic mine ten hus maybe and locd ofer by our thegn wulmaer who now was gan and his place toc by frenc hunds who still we had not seen

we cum near to langetof cepan always behind treows and we colde see that this ham was still lifan and that the fyrs we seen was not ingenga fyrs but only the fyrs of smiths or of folc in their hus and on their land. folcs was mofan around and talcan and worcan in the felds and hunds was lyan about and things was as things was in hams around these parts

there is no frenc here saes grimcell this is good

will we go to them saes tofe and tell them we is grene men and will feoht for their lifs

thu do this then cilde i saes and we will sitt here and smerc

tofe he locs small at this why does thu sae this buccmaster he saes does thu mocc me

tofe cilde saes grimcell we can not feoht for none with two men and one cilde and an eald sweord what was nefer swung. at this of course i tacs ire loc at thy fuccan mouth cottar i saes for these things is not to be spocn of in this way this sweord it is cum to me for greatness and for wars in times of great need

well so thu saes buccmaster saes grimcell and this seems to me a time of great need and this sweord not swung to cwell no man yet well perhaps thu is waitan to be telt by weland when to swing it

well i colde not haf this from no cottar and this cilde locan on and so i teorns to him and my sweord i tacs from my belt and at his heafod i swings it. grimcell he steps baec and he steps on the root of a treow and down he gan to the ground and on his breost i puts the tip of my sweord

thu sees cilde i saes to tofe lic naht had cum thu sees the runes on this blaed and the wihts thu sees the craft of weland thu sees what this sweord is

tofe he locs and saes naht but his eages is wid and grimcell he locs up at me in sum ire and my sweord ofer his heorte

who leads this werod cottar i saes and he locs up at me

werod he saes

who leads this werod

he locs up at me

thu it seems he saes slow and in his words there is naht to sae what he thincs of this

i is thy ring gifer i saes and thine too cilde. i is a socman of three oxgangs a man of the wapentac i has been spoc to by fugol and star i is buccmaster of holland i saes i has been ceosan

ring gifer saes tofe and he locs lic i is sum great man then

ceosan saes grimcell and he locs at me straight but saes naht mor. my sweord i tacs off from him now and puts it in its sceath

get up i saes get up off this ground man

grimcell he gets up then he clenes him self and does not loc at me

cum i saes cum grimcell thu is a good man only it moste be cnawan who is the strong one here yes. well he walcs away and tofe then who is locan on he cums up to us and specs before i has time to say any other thing

buccmaster he saes here is frenc to use thy sweord on

we locs at him and then both locs through treows at this ham of langetof and sum way from us on the straet through the ham we seen on a hwit hors a man

this hors it is a cnawan breed in these parts it is a hors lic any hors it is not an ingenga. scod and sadld the fenn way it is walcan through this ham lic any hors in any ham in any place in this land

but on this hors there is a man and of this man there is naht anglisc and naht triewe and he is not scod lic us. we is sum way from him so all of us all three men we mofs then as far in the treows as we colde be without bean seen from the ham and all three of us now not specan and mofan as a werod sceolde as one lic the fugols in the haerfest when they is leafan to tac to the heofon for the winter he is a frenc man saes tofe he is a frenc man i has seen him

grimcell and i who has seen no frenc before this we locs and now we sees what curse is on our land and the folcs who is bringan it. this man he is scort and he wers clothes in sum ways lic what anglisc folcs he wers scohs and scyrte breces and hose tunece and belt and cape but of all these things there is sum thing ingenga. i colde not see what thing it was that made them so but no man wolde tac these clothes for anglisc clothes for no men of these parts wolde wer them they was not right

but loc at his heafod now loc at his heafod for this is the thing what macs him what he is. his nose is lic sum bec lic the carfan bec of the hafoc and in his eages there is blud we colde not see his eages well but blud there was in them for sure. what did he do here by what right did he cum here this deoful. on his heafod where there sceolde haf been haer long and triewe lic anglisc haer there was lic a helm lic a scort blaec helm but it colde be seen that this was not helm but haer. this was frenc haer scapd lic sum lytel helm or corona sittan on top of the heafod of this thing and all shafd the necc the heafod the nebb

this is no thing of the grene world i saes

it is a hard sight saes grimcell

denisc men saes tofe denisc men when they cums they locs lic men lic feohtan men lic triewe men. and he locs at us again lic he wolde haf us sae yes cilde yes cilde

we locs on as this frenc man gan on out of the ham on his hors and to the west away from the fenn and towards the brunnesweald. we locs on and the sound of the hors then is gan and we is left with the sound of our breathan and of the treows mofan a lytel in the wind and of the folcs in the ham

now saes tofe and he saes it lic he is an ent now what is the grene men to do about this

what saes grimcell

well saes tofe loc here in our land is a frenc deoful and we is the free men of angland we is the sawol of the holt so what is to be done what is to be done buccmaster with thy great and triewe sweord

this cilde he was in sum great thryll now lic it was sum game with stics and stans lic he was feohtan with broth-or or girl behind the hay ricc in litha

well i saes. i did not cnaw what other thing to sae to him

loc i saes the deoful is now gan

*who will feoht now they saes for our land*

he will cum baec saes tofe he is of these lands now

he is not of these lands i saes

he will be of these lands if sum does not tac him from them saes tofe

*this sweord i gaf thu and nefer is it swung*

grimcell i saes i locs at him i does not cnaw what he sceolde sae. locan at me sum small time he saes naht

he will cum baec saes tofe again

then we will be ready i saes

ready for what saes grimcell with what. he is still smartan from what i has taught him

134

we will be ready saes tofe

*who will feoht now*

*i wacans in this wud in this deorc holt and though it is the deop of the night all is light all is light lic the sunne is cuman down on efry leaf in efry fox hole and efry piece of ground. i stands for i cnawan i moste stand and i walcs to the ham but where there was a ham there is now a strand and down from this strand a great sea a wid sea deop and deorc and yet light lic all the light that is now ofer efry thing*

*on this sea i seen a boat a great boat afyr in light and cuman near to me and once this boat was a small light in a deorc night but now it is here and lightan up all things and this light on my hands on my nebb and hot lic a fyr for a fyr it is*

*for this boat is no boat but a great scip with carfan heafod and with scields on its sides a boat of the eald times it is the scip of those who first came. and this scip it is afyr in great wafs of red afyr and yet mofan all afyr and in this fyr i sees scaps mofan scaps and these scaps now i sees triewe and i seen*

we lifd in this holt near to langetof for sum daegs we macd a small hus of timber and leafs we cnawan how to lif. we was eatan roots and leafs for the winter was gan and the spring was cuman and things was lifan again. we hunted the hara and i was eatan my mete from my swine though i was doan this when grimcell and tofe was not near for this was my mete and not for them. soon we wolde cwell one of the swine what tofe had brought but it was not yet time for we wolde haf to smoc or salt the mete to cepe it long and we colde not do that in this place so for now we ate the hara and the fugol

in this time we was locan at the straet locan for this frenc man. one of us was always locan and we seen him efry daeg cum down the straet from the west on his hwit hors and then he gan baec again sum time later. sum times he did this one time and sum times he cum and gan two or efen three times in one daeg. this cilde tofe this yonge cilde of mine he had saed he cnawan this man so i was macan him tell me all he cnawan. he telt me that this man had been seen also in his ham

what was he doan there i ascs

he is our new thegn saes tofe

thegn i saes

thegn saes grimcell

he is a fuccan ingenga i saes he has a shafd heafod he specs sum ingenga tunge this man can be no thegn of angland

he telt us he was the thegn now saed tofe he telt us that wulmaers land was now his land that we was now his men and that he was mofan around the hams to see the lie of the land to cnawan the fenns what now he was a man of. he spac anglisc to us but a lytel only and in an ingenga way

136

thy mothor saes grimcell thy father thu saed they was cwelled by the frenc was it him

no it was not him saes tofe it was sum others and it was not my mothor in triewth i nefer has had one. my mothor died in bringan me to this world my father has cept me since that daeg

did he cepe thu well

well enough saes the cilde all was well until the frenc cum and then one daeg three frenc men on hors cum into our ham. they locd lic this man and they telt us we moste gif mor geld for our land and all was ired but when they cum for the geld in the end folcs gaf it for there had been so micel blud and it was clere who was cyngs now. but my father he wolde not gif it and sum others wolde not gif it also and so one daeg these three frenc men they cum to the ham with sweords and they tacs those who wolde not gif geld from us and they saes we moste haf laws in this land and they tacs these men away into the holt and my father with them and they nefer cums out

what becum of them saes grimcell specan soft

after sum hours when the frenc had gan saes tofe sum of us from the ham went into the holt to find them to see if they was still there. we did not go far into the treows and we found them hangan from lines all cwelled. i seen my father hangan he was mofan as the treow was mofan his face it was red lic the sunne at dusc his tunge

the cilde then he locs down at the ground and naht mor he saes and grimcell he tacs him by the sceoldor and saes i is sorry cilde they is scuccas all of them

scuccas yes i saes for i does not cnaw what mor to sae

our folc saes tofe our folc we moste haf done sum great yfel for this. we moste haf done sum great yfel agan the word of god for this to cum to us so many good men tacan away by this ire and blud what is the yfel that we has done

there is no yfel i saes these is the lies of preosts there is no yfel

tofe then he is locan down for sum time and grimcell locan at me and not saen naht and then tofe he specs

i wolde lic to cwell this frenc man he saes

cwell him i saes. i did not thinc he wolde sae a thing lic this

we is grene men saes tofe we is free men we is men of the holt now. a wergild is owed on my fathers lif and who will gif it me

many anglisc folcs is owed wergilds saes grimcell who of us is not

what wolde thu do ring gifer saes tofe to me

oh yes ring gifer saes grimcell tell us what wolde thu do

cwell him i saes cwell him yes we colde we colde

and then how many frenc will cum here saes grimcell ten twentig one hundred and all will be locan for us with line

how many frenc is here now saes tofe and how micel line

the cilde is right i saes frenc men is in all parts beornan and cwellan what wolde thu do man sitt on thy arse and loc at them

well of course i will follow thu great buccmaster saes grimcell so now tell us what sceolde we do

well i saes we will tac this ingenga and we will cut him up send him baec to the frenc lands as a warnan to those who cum to angland in fyr and blud

yes saes tofe yes and he is smercan. grimcell only locs at me lic i is mad

how he saes

why does thu not fuccan thinc about this also i saes. do not sitt there saen how and why and what but help us man help rid thy land of these things

grimcell shrugs and saes i wolde lic to see no mor death now i wolde lic only to lif

thu will see see death in all parts i saes to him efen if thy eages is scut. does thu thinc thu can go baec to thy hus what is aesc there is naht now but death

death is in all parts saes tofe. he is a good cilde i is sean a good cilde and wise

grimcell locs at us both for sum small time then he mofs his head lic a hors mofs his to cnoc away a fleoge

well he saes what wolde thu do

the thought about the line was not tofes it was mine. i sent the cilde in to the ham of langetof and i telt him to get a length of line for if line was what cwelled anglisc men then line it was what wolde cwell frenc. he cum baec sum time later with a length of strong line though he saed it had not been easy to get with folcs ascan from where he was cum and what we wolde gif for it

well i had this thought and i telt it to grimcell and tofe and both saed it was good and we slept that night in our hus in the holt and the daeg that was to cum we saed wolde be the last daeg on eorth of this man what called himself our thegn. when the light cum up we cum up from our beds on the ground and we toc the line and i toc my sweord and my scramasax and we went down the straet to the west for one or it may be two miles. we went to where the holt cums up to the straet where no men is. we went away from the ham and grimcell and i we done our worc with line and treows and then we satt in the holt and we waited

it was sum time we waited in triewth. men cum up that path with small hors and with sacs and foda and wud and cycens and in the holt we satt grimcell and tofe and me we satt locan at them and they not sean us for we was in the treows and of them. then after sum time we seen him cum

from the west he cum on his hwit hors sittan straight cuman down this straet and he was alone as we had hoped and none others on the straet at this time. here the straet was straight for a way and this frenc man he colde see maybe half a mile before the straet teorned and was lost in the wud

now at the place where the straet teorned in to the

wud again a cilde stept on to the straet sum way ahead of this frenc man but where he colde be seen by him and this cilde he spoc

frenc cunt he saes frenc fuccer

this man then he locs at this cilde

frenc fuccer calls the cilde thu cwelled my father and i will cwell thu and all the hores thu calls thy folc and the bastard thu calls thy cyng. go home frenc cunt or thu will die. at this the cilde then tacs down his breces and teorns his bare arse at the thegn

this is what thu lics he calls thu and thy frenc men. cum and see if thu can get it cunt thu is no thegn but only a deoful

tofe has done well here and i was smercan as i stood by the straet in the treows. now he runs down the straet what gan to the ham and is lost behind treows him self. here we had hoped that this scucca wolde go after him and on this all things satt. the frenc thegn he sits it seems for a long time but in triewth it was i thinc a scort time and then he ciccs his hors and he calls to him to mof and he gan fast now down the straet to where he has seen this cilde gan

now me and grimcell we locs to our selfs. the line we had put ofer the straet was lyan down and us behind two treows on eacc side of it and when this hors cum up to us mofan fast too fast to stop i calls to grimcell and we both pulls baec around the treow and the line cums up ofer the path of the hors and the man and he sees it cuman at him and he roars out but he is mofan at succ speed that naht can be done for him and the line tacs him across the throta and baec ofer his hors and on to the ground

well this is what we had wanted and we is blithe to see how this has gan. all three of us we runs then in thryll to the straet where this man lays cluccan at his throta what is torn and gaspan and locan up at us and his eages locan through us to the heofon. here now is his great bec of a nose and his scafd heafod and his haer lic a helm and his ingenga clothes and he is writhan but we will not allow him to rise

so ingenga i saes thu saes thu is our thegn thu saes our land is thy land well loc now scucca at what thu is cum to

scucca saes tofe locan down at him. the frenc man tries to sae sum words but he can not mac his words cum

well cilde i saes well then. i locs at tofe and he locs at me also

well he saes

well i saes i is thincan on what thu saed. i wolde lic to cwell this man thu saed i wolde lic to cwell this frenc man well now then he is at thy feet.

o saes tofe and he locs lic a cilde again now. from my belt i tacs my scramasax and i gifs it to him

cwell him i saes

o saes tofe again and he locs down at the ingenga who now breathes hefig through his broc throat and locs up at us hefig too. his hors stands sum way from us locan about

folcs will cum down this straet i saes at any time they

moste not find us we moste be cwic. cwell him cilde haf thy wergild for thy hanged father

at this tofe locs at me and then grimcell who is standan locan on saen naht and then down at this man on the ground with blud on his hands and his nebb

i has nefer cwelled no man he saes i does not cnawan how

does not cnawan how i saes thu has a scramasax there is his bodig thu has cwelled swine has thu not

it is not the same

it is not the same because swine has not cwelled thy father now fuccan cwell him cilde for all this was thy thought

tofe locs down at this ingenga again and now he is not talcan of cwellan and grene men and feohtan. now he is lic what he is a small cilde from a fenn ham

he may be a good man in his own land saes tofe

what is this i saes what is this scit cilde. this is not a fuccan game a good man a good fuccan man tell that to thy father to my wifman tell that to harald cyng cilde

i tacs the scramasax from him then and i gan down on one cneow and i stics it into the frenc mans throat deop and he gasps and calls then and his arms and shancs they mofs to try and cicc me away but i has my cneow on his breost and with my scramasax i saws up until his throta is cut and blaec blud then cums roaran out lic gathran wind and he claws and cocs and his eages is on on mine first wid then dim then gan

i stands and i gifs the scramasax baec to tofe all wet

143

with blud and his sceacan hand i macs to grip it. he is
hwit now this cilde and grimcell who stands there is still.
along the blaed of the scramasax i runs my hand until my
fingors is all in frenc blud and this blud then i smears on
the nebb of this cilde tofe and though he starts he does
not stop me

has thu seen the hafoc feohtan with the craw i saes.
all of the world is blud cilde it is wiht agan wiht will thu
be hafoc or craw will thu be fugol or wyrm will thu be
anglisc or frenc will thu hang or be hanged for there is
naht else now in all this world

thu has thy wergild now cilde i saes now cum we moste
mof him

i had thought to mof the scucca from the straet and
leaf him in the holt for the craw and the fox and to tac his
hors what was a good hors. but none of this cum to be
for as we gan to tac him betweon us to mof him two men
on hors cum down the straet and these two men they
was frenc also. it seemed to me that these men they was
with the thegn for their frenc clothes and haer was lic his
and they was cuman not so far behind him. well these
men they seen us they seen their man on the ground all
in a mere of blud and his hors standan locan and these
men they calls out and spurs their hors and they cum
down on us and in their hands i sees they has frenc sweords

but here is the thing about these frenc they lufs their
hors. seldum does thu see a frenc man who is not on the

baec of a hors sittan or walcan. they specs on hors they etes on hors it may be they sleeps on hors. i does not cnawan if this is what they does in their own lands or if they stays on hors only in angland to cepe safe from anglisc folcs but all i does cnaw is that sum times it seems frenc folcs was born on hors

this was good for us now for we seen these two men cuman down on us and we ran all three into the holt. the holt in these parts was thicc the treows old and near the ground thicc with grene and with many small treows also growan in all parts. we was men of the fenns and we cnawan how to mof in these fenn wuds but this was not ground for hors. locan baec i seen these men cum to the treows on hors and loc in and i seen them get down and tie their hors to treows and begin to cum in but it colde be seen that they wolde not cum far. they mofd slow and cept locan baec at their hors for fear of losan them and they did not cnaw what was in the holt in the deorcness. for all they cnawan there colde haf been a great fyrd of anglisc folc waitan for them and so it was not long before they teorned baec to the light on the straet and the bodig of their dead freond

we cept mofan goan south in to the holt and we did not stop until we was sum way from the straet and we had cum to a place where we colde see all around and hiere if any man cum in to the wud. a clene daeg it was and the holt was alyf all with the sounds of small things rustlan in the leafs and in these wuds in these treows a man colde sitt for micel time and breathe deop and it colde seem that angland was all still and that no great sicness was upon her


the night after that daeg i gan to sleep in the small hus in the holt with the swine and with tofe and grimcell slepan near and again i was dreaman of the fyr scip. i stood on the strand and the great scip was before me right by me and the fyr was so hot it was macan me want to go baec and scaps mofd again in the fyr and i did step baec and then from the fyr cum a man and he stood before me and this man was my grandfather

i woc early with this dream still in me and i lay on the ground in the deorc for the daeg had not yet cum up and i thought then of the last time i seen my grandfather. i was a yonge man as yonge as my dunstan had been when he was tacan by the frenc and my grandfather he was eald he was ealder than any man in the fenns and there was those saed this was due to his wicce craft for he was not with the crist and that he wolde go on his death to hel. this is the scit what folcs specs if they is left to them selfs and it is why they sceolde be loccd ofer by greater men

well my grandfather when i was a cilde he had been a great strong man but now he was weac and colde not hardly efen walc without stics and efen then not long. his cenep was thynne and he was small but still in his eages there was a great fyr and efen my father wolde not spec

146

ill to him if he colde be in sum other place. it was in the sumor that my grandfather died on a daeg that was high and clene lic his great sawol had been

sum daegs before this my sistor aelfgifu and i had been sittan with him in the sunne by the great hus what later becum my hus and then was gan in frenc fyr. he was sittan on a stool what he had macd many years before and my sistor and i was sittan by him on the ground for he licd to be abuf us when he was specan. he was specan now but his words was not always clere and his heafod was mofan around lic it was mofan itself

i will be gan soon he saes gan to eorth and erce

i saes this is not so

bury me in a scip he saes

i saes what

a scip a boat bury me beorn me in fyr put me in my boat with welands sweord send me baec to the eald folc. they was buried in their scips he saes in their scips and sum of them was beorned in them

of who is thu specan grandfather saes aelfgifu. she was a girl of great beuty her haer gold her bodig thynne and scapd well and her words was soft lic her heorte when she locd at me

in their scips he saes the eald cyngs deop in the ground

what scips is these i saes. i was sad to hiere my grandfather spec lic this for it seemed he spoc lic a cilde

cilde he saes i had thought i had telt thu of the eald times does thu cnawan naht after efry thing i has done. not so far from here cilde in the land of the eald folc of

147

the east there is a wide feld cilde and this feld is full of
hylls and eacc of them macd not by erce but by man. they
is great hylls cilde i has seen them erce breathes through
these hylls there is great strength in the land at this place.
under these hylls is buried many great scips and in eacc
of these scips is a great cyng buried with gold with sweords of great craft with helms of seolfor and with hors.
there is great halls under these hylls laid out with foda
and cuppes and plates of gold and whole scips cilde scips
of the eald times scips of the cuman. this is what we is
cilde these is our folcs the eald cyngs cilde the eald gods
beneath now all beneath and waitan

   cyngs is blud i saes grandfather thu saed this

   sum cyngs is blud sum cyngs is good the eald cyngs
was great men. it is cyngs now what is low lic wyrms

   i does not trust cyngs i saes

   this is a good thought cilde a good thought but there
was times when cyngs was gods

   cyngs is men

   triewe anglisc cyng cilde is of wodens blud i has telt
thu these cyngs we has now they is men only their blud is
not triewe we moste go baec cilde go baec

   has thu seen these great scips grandfather these great
hylls

   i has seen the hylls cilde i seen them when i was yonge
lic thu but what is under them no man lifan has seen.
only i lic others has heard the tales and tales succ as these
they is not lies. ah i wolde be buried in my boat in my
lytel boat only or laid on the fenn in it and set afyr to

148

drift on these waters to my cynn folc who is waitan waitan

aelfgifu she locs at me then for grandfather is mofan bacc and forth and locan at the heofon and he seems so old so old

cilde he saes when i go cilde thu moste spec to the land for i no longer can

the land grandfather

cilde i has telt thu how the land specs and thu has seen in this ham how folcs has teorned from it to the hwit crist and this has been the brecan of angland cilde. it is not in the words cilde it is not in bocs thu moste go to the holt to the fenn sleep by the waters cilde in the wuds in the regn do not spec and thu will waec one daeg and the land will be in thu and thu in it and thu will feel as it feels and all that it has will be in thu cilde and in this way the eald gods will return cilde they will return in thu

grandfather saes aelfgifu gently wolde thu lic mead or wolde thu maybe lic to sleep in the hus

fecc me mead girl saes my grandfather and though i is eald i is not a dumb esol i will sleep when the gods calls me and then i will sleep long

my sistor then she gan to the hus to fecc mead and loccan baec at me gaf a smerc

cilde saes my grandfather when she is gan a boar spac with me

a boar grandfather i saes and i wysces aelfgifu was still here

a boar cilde i was in the holt i was in the brunnesweald

149

thu does not cnaw this holt yet cilde but thu will it is a great wud thu moste cross it to leaf the fenns to go to the west i was in this wud cilde and

aelfgifu cums baec here with a cuppe of mead and she puts it in my grandfathers hand what is sceacan but he does not stop specan he does not efen loc at her

i was lifan lic i has saed to thu i was a yonger man i had gan to the holt to cepe away from men to cum to the wilde and for many daegs i saed naht only lifan and etan and mofan in the holt. i seen the fugol and i mofd lic the fugol and it cum to me. i seen the fox and i mofd lic the fox and it cum to me. i seen the brocc and i mofd lic the brocc at dusc and it toc me for its brothor. and one daeg as dusc was cuman on the holt i stood in a wid part of the wud and a sound cum and cum nearer and in to the lea cum a boar

well this boar locd at me and it colde see that after so many daegs in this holt i did not loc nor seem nor smell lic no man. this boar it mofd its heafod and i mofd my heafod the same. i locd at it and i was in this boar. when it breathed i breathed when it mofd its scanc i mofd my scanc. i was boar i was the eald boar of the holt cilde

i did not say naht for i colde not

all was still cilde all still in all places and then this boar in my heafod and in the holt cilde this boar spac to me

grandfather what did it spec

it saed cepe it

cepe it

it saed cepe it. this is all cilde it saed cepe it and then
this boar teorned cwic and i was man again cilde and it
ran from me and i cnawan i moste go baec to the ham

cepe it saes aelfgifu

cepe what i saes but my grandfather he is dreanan his
mead and he is tired tired lic the waters after the regn


well these swine of tofes they was not specan to no man
only walcan and gruntan about in the holt all of the
daegs. that mergen when all was wacend we broc down
our lytel hus of stics and leafs so none colde see and we
ciccd ofer the aesc of the fyr and we went to mof on. but
we was hungered we was three men needan sum foda
what was mor than leaf or root or berry and all we had
was these swine. i had ate all the mete from my own
swine with out tofe and grimcell sean for there was no
reason for them to see this and now i was hungered also

well we had brought along this cilde and his swine and
it wolde haf been a cwic thing to cwell them and mac
them ready but while we colde haf coccd sum mete we
colde not cocc it all. we was goan to need to cepe sum for
sum daegs for a good swine macs micel mete and to let it
be eatan by wihts wolde haf been a great synn. we
thought about smocan it but how colde we smoc it we
wolde need a great fyr and a place for hangan for sum
time and we did not haf neither of these things. it seemed
then that we sceolde salt the mete for though we colde

not do it well lic our wifmen did at least saltan it wolde cepe it for sum small number of daegs and in this time we colde eat

but of course none of us had salt and there was no pans here for we was not near the sea. whether saltmen wolde efer cum again now after the frenc cum we did not cnaw but they was not here now. any salt there was wolde be in the hams and we thought to go to langetof before we left this holt to asc for sum. grimcell was agan this he thought we sceolde go now he thought the frenc may be in langetof after the thegn was cwelled he saed there was no tellan what folcs wolde sae of us or do. tofe saed to him that we was great men hafan cwelled this ingenga and we wolde be wel cum in the ham lic gods and this thought i licd though in triewth i was thincan it wolde not be so

well what we done we gan through the holt to langetof and we cept in the treows where we had been before where we colde see the ham. i was at first blithe to see that the ham was still standan that folcs was there that the ingengas had not beorned it for then this war it wolde haf been greater efen than it was. the ham was still here and we colde hiere anglisc folcs specan but their words seemed the words of fear and there was callan and wepan cuman from the ham at a place we colde not see

well we mofd in the holt we mofd along the ecg and soon we seen a sight not to be forgot. all folcs of the ham it seemed was gathrd in the straet and before them was the two frenc scuccas we had seen cuman after us when we cwelled the ingenga who called himself our thegn. they was on hors as i was saen frenc is all times on hors and again they was with sweord and they stood before the folcs of the ham who was on their feet callan to them for mildheortedness. the ingengas nebbs was set lic style and before them they held an eald man

this man his haer was hwit and he was eald and one of these ingengas on hors he had a line around this mans necc and was pullan him so this eald man stood on his toes only and he was gaspan and clawan at his throta and he loccd to me lic the ingenga thegn before i cwelled him

who saes one of these ingengas to the folcs of the ham

o none they all calls it was none of us we has telt thu we telt thu yesterdaeg do not tac another of our men it was not us it was ingengas what done it

ingengas i saes to tofe ingengas they saes

who saes the frenc man again to them and he pulls on the line again so this eald man he is almost off his feet now and the other ingenga he raises a sweord

at this the ham folcs calls efen louder and they mofs to go to the frenc but the sweord man he wafs his blaed and they dares not. father cries sum man in the crowd o father o cepe him he is an eald man and good

it was not us saes a wifman o great thegns it was not us we nefer seen it we wolde not we is good folcs o spare us. well the sound is great by now but these ingengas they seems not to lysten or i thinc to cnaw the anglisc words who cwell thegn saes the ingenga with the line and he is mor ired now efen than before. gif or we cwells

no cries the folcs in the ham again no it was not us it was ingengas

well maybe it was the word ingenga what these frenc hierde and thought was an meant for them or maybe they was ired or maybe they did noy belyf but it seemed they had seen and hierde enough now for the man with the line he lifts this eald anglisc man as high as he colde ofer his hors and the other ingenga he brings down his sweord scearp and strong and he cuts his throta so deop that his heafod near cum off and blud gan all ofer the ingenga hors and there is a great roar from the folcs and the ingengas then they lets the man fall to the ground and all runs to him and a man tacs his bledan heafod in his hands and saes father father but his father is hearan naht no mor and will nefer

tomergen saes the first ingenga to the folcs as they teorns their hors away. tomergen one mor. efry daeg not tell one mor. he specs anglisc lic a cilde but they cnawan what he saes. then they spurs their hors and gan down the straet leafan the folcs of langetof wepan all in blud and water

i locs at tofe who is hwit and grimcell who is saen naht only locan on and locan grim

well i saes i thincs these folcs will not haf salt for us. grimcell he locs at me lic he is both sad and in ire

this was our doan he saes it is lic we cwelled this man

that is scit i saes scit frenc ingengas cwelled this man lic they has cwelled all our folcs

these folcs is bean cwelled for what we done saes grimcell it is wrong

then go and gif thyself to ingenga sweords i saes go and walc in the straet with thy heafod down while ingengas fuccs thy folc and thy land. there is no way to be without blud now grimcell we is all in blud now we can only asc whose blud is on us anglisc or frenc

this is anglisc blud saes grimcell that is on us

they is scuccas saes tofe now and he locs lic he will weep scuccas all they lufs is cwellan o who has sent them

our bastard cyng i saes our bastard ingenga cyng

we moste go saes grimcell

where saes tofe

to a place where there is no ingengas saes grimcell to a place in angland they has not cum to a place where there is stillness

thu is an esol i saes there is no succ place. ingengas is in all places they has tacan efry aecer of angland for their own there is nowhere free of them

the holt is free of them saes tofe

yes the holt is ours i saes the holt is the place of eald gods and eald wihts and free folcs but they will cum for the holt also in time. we cannot hide now thu has seen we can only feoht

for efry ingenga we cwells saes grimcell they cwells a ham. we digs our graefs

i wolde sooner dig my graef i saes than haf sum ingenga dig it. at this tofe smercs a lytel lic he has been made
strong by my words

yes buccmaster he saes thu is right we moste fight
them for they has tacan all things from us is this not so
grimcell. grimcell locs at him and then ofer towards the
ham and then up at the treows

they has tacan all things he saes soft all things. he locs
down then and saes naht mor


this cilde this cilde tofe at this time if i is bean triewe i
wolde sae he helpd me to lif. for this cilde he loccd up to
me as a great man and this i needed at this time for there
was sum daegs i loccd on my self as a lytel man. great
weland he spoc to me at this time and he telt me to feoht
he cum to me from the ealdors with words and he cum
to me from my grandfather. great weland he telt me my
grandfather was with him locan down at me and this
macd me feel a lytel man in triewth for if he was locan
then all my folcs was locan all anglisc folcs of the eald
times was locan and what wolde they thinc of me. i was a
small man in the holt with an eald sweord not swung i
was eatan leafs and slepan on the ground runnan from
ingengas in my own land a small man a weac man

but this cilde he colde see what i in my weacness colde
not at all times he colde see the greatness in me what had
been seen also by weland and the gods and what had

156

been seen by my grandfather. he colde see what i had
been ceosan to do what i had cum for he colde see the
freodom in me for this was the freodom of all of angland
here in my heorte and this frenc ingenga scucca he had
been gifen a fuccan taste of this and he wolde not be the
last for i was cuman with my sweord now with my werod
i was cuman yes lic the eald cyngs to tac baec my ground

tac baec thy ground

i sceal

thu is worthy only be triewe

to this land

to its folc

to the eald hus

the sunne gan down the sunne rises

we will rise


well tofe he gaf me sum strength at this time but also
strength was gifen me by thoughts of my grandfather
and what he had telt me in his last daegs. i thought of
what he saed about goan to the holt and lifan without
specan and about the wihts what spoc to him and i seen
that to be in the holt lic us to be grene men as this cilde
was callan us well this was not a thing to mac a man feel
small. for these was the wuds of angland the wuds of our
folc of our land and my grandfather had saed to me he
had saed thu moste spec to the land cilde for i no longer
can

it was triewe i had lost my hus and my wifman and my oxgangs and my swine and my seat on the wapentac and all but when our folcs first cum to angland they had none of these things. it seemed to me then that i had been a soft man that i had been macd soft by the great things i had done and had been and now the gods had toc me to the eald holt and left me there with naht and was saen to me now buccmaster of holland now thu sceal lif lic a triewe man now thu sceal lif lic the eald folc now thu sceal lif lic us

i was thincan of this as i was walcan through the brun-nesweald with tofe and grimcell that mergen a mergen when the heofon was graeg and no wind was cuman and the wud was still with lytel sound i was thincan of this and i felt strong again. i cnawan i was ceoson and this cilde tofe this lytel denisc cilde becum anglisc he colde see in me a great strength and the gods and great weland i seen now they had sent me to the holt to spec to the land to lysten to be a man in the wilde places lic all ang-lisc folc sceolde always be and now i seen the greatness of what i colde do. i had seen what these ingengas was doan to our folcs all ofer i had cum down from my place in the ham to my place in the grene holt and my werod now i was gathran and a war it wolde be a war agan the deofuls what was cwellan our folc and tacan our land

thu swam in the mere

i went to the treows

thu was there

with my hands i gripped them

*they cum to thu*

they cum

*now they is here*

i sees them i feels them

*tac thy sweord buccmaster*

we is risan

micel walcan wolde we do from that daeg micel walcan
in the great holt the brunnesweald but though we walced
for wices months years though this holt becum ham to
me for so long still we did not see efen a small part of it
so great was this deop eald wud. so great was it that
many things dwelt there what was not cnawan to man
but only in tales and in dreams. wihts for sure the boar
the wulf the fox efen the bera it was saed by sum made
this holt their ham. col beorners and out laws was in here
as they was in all wuds but deop deoper efen than this
was the eald wihts what was in angland before men

here i is meanan the aelfs and the dweorgs and ents
who is of the holt who is the treows them selfs. my
grandfather he telt me he had seen an aelf at dusc one
daeg he seen it flittan betweon stoccs of treows thynne it
was and grene and its eages was great and blaec and had
no loc of man in them. well he was blithe to lif after that
for oft it is saed that to see an aelf is to die for they sceots
their aelf straels at thu and aelfscot is a slow death

but when we left langetof we was not thincan of aelfs
we was thincan of mete for we was still needan to eat and

we had no salt and in triewth we did not cnaw what to do. grimcell and i our wifmen wolde mac all our mete and foda and though we as men cwelled the wihts on our land they as wifmen wolde mac them in to foda and for tofe it was his mothors sistor wolde do so for this was wifmans worc. i cnawan that salt cept mete and that smocan cept it also but i had not done these things for i was worcan in the felds and in the barn

so here is what we done we walcced from langetof for one daeg deop in to the brunnesweald to the west and we cum to a place what seemed to be far from any ham or tun and we found a lea in the wud what had been cut for col and where the stoccs of treows was small and thynne and many was cut. here was macd a hus of stoccs and leafs for now it was thrimilci and things was grene again and we macd a fyr. we macd this fyr wid and deop and we macd it with berc treows what was growan there for i cnawan that the berc is used by wifmen for smocan mete and smocan mete was what we thought we wolde now do. we macd this fyr under a great treow and on this treow we tied sum line the same line what we had used to cwell the ingenga

tofe had brought his three swine to the lea and tied them also with line to another treow. we toc the ealdest of these swine and untied him and i got my scramasax and i telt tofe and grimcell to grip this swine hard. this they did and i gan to him then and i cut his throta lic i had cut the ingenga and the ingengas had cut the eald

160

man. only the throta of a swine is thiccer than the throta of a man and this scramasax it was not sharp for i had no stan and my cut it did not go deop enough. this swine then it called and called long and loud and it teorned and pulled and it gan away from tofe and grimcell and it ran in to the treows with blud cuman from its throta and we three men runnan after it cursan. swine is not dumb and the other two had seen this and was now teran at their ropes and callan also from fear

well i was glad we had gan deop in to the holt but still i was afeart at the sound for it colde not be cnawan where ingengas was or where was anglisc men who might hiere and tell it to them for gold or fafor. these swine was callan and callan lic yonge cildren and we was runnan through the wud after this swine what had gan away and it was hard to see though it colde be hierde before us. we ran for sum time and grimcell who was a big man he was slowan and fallan baec but the swine slowed now also for his throta was cut and he was wearyan. we cum to this swine by a big ac treow and he was gruntan and callan but his call was smaller now and he gan ahead of us but slow lic he cnawan it was ofer

i sceolde not haf done it i cnaw now but then i was tired and dreaned and this swine had ired me and my scramasax was blunt lic a maedens cnif so i toc my sweord what was always at my side and i gan to this swine and this sweord i throste into his heorte under his scanc and the swine he fell dead then without no mor

161

sound. i toc out the sweord what was wet with the blud of this swine and i clened it on the leafs of treows lic it was a good thing to be doan but in my own heorte i cnawan deoper and deoper as i stood there that i done sum thing wrong for this was welands sweord my grand-fathers sweord it was a great thing for great men and great deeds it was not for cwellan wihts for mete

it toc us sum time to tac this swine baec to where we had macd the hus and the fyr all three of us draggan it and it toc us time also to cut it and tac the bits we wolde cepe and tie them to the treow ofer the fyr. then we light-ed the fyr and we coccd what mete we wolde eat then and the next mergen and the rest of the mete we smoccd for the night ofer the grene wud on the fyr. we ate swine mete that night and dranc good water from a small ea in the holt and we spac well but all the time i loccd ofer to where i had put my sweord and it seemed this sweord loccd baec at me and was ired


in the mergen i was waecend by the sound of wind in the treows and a great wind it was. blowan from a great height blowan with the strength of thunor this wind it mofd the great treows baec and forth and the sound was grim to hiere. i cnawan this was a sign of sum great thing that had been done or was cuman but i cnawan not what. i cum out of our hus of stoccs and leafs and i seen that the mete we had tied ofer the fyr had cum down in the wind and was all ofer the ground. i seen also that micel of it was gan tacan by wihts and i cursed the wud then as i toc up the mete that was left and clened it of aesc and mudd. it smelt smoccd and this seemed good and i hung it again from the line in the treow to cepe it clere of the fox and the wyrm

always in the mergen i waecend before tofe before grimcell and oft i waecend not cnawan where i was or who. i cum up from sleep thincan i wolde be in my hus in my bed by my odelyn with the stenc of last nights fyr in the hus and with the sunne cuman through the slits and with the sound of the fenn and my scepe and my sons and my geburs worcan or eatan. but i cum up instead to a small hus of stoccs and wet leafs in a deorc holt what i did not cnaw with a man and a cilde who was not of my cynn and all that i cnawan beorned away. hard it was and bitter and i wolde lie locan up at the heofon through treows and stoccs of treows and i wolde thinc that a great wrong had been done to me

well now that all this is gan there is yonge folc in this land who is forgettan already how things was. there is yonge folcs in angland now who nefer cnawan a time before there was frenc ofer them nefer cnawan a time when our cyngs and our thegns spac with us in our own tunge nefer cnawan what it is to lif in a land where all the ground is not tacan by one man and this man an ingenga. thinc on this thinc on it for yonge folc born today in angland they does not cnaw what freodom is. all their lifs they has been under ingenga folcs who tells them where to worc and when and whose laws is ingenga laws the laws of thiefs and the cwellers of their cynn but for these yonge folc all of this seems to be only the way things is and has always been

well in the brunnesweald in those times i did not cnaw how fast folcs colde forget what they was i did not cnaw how time worcs did not cnaw that when a great storm cums lic it had cum upon angland then all the feohtan and the ire in the great world cannot put things baec to how they was and sceolde be. ah i did not cnaw how small man is how weac i did not see that a broc thing can not be unbroc only through wantan. but i did see what many folcs now does not see and what yonge cildren of angland now with their frenc haer and frenc names did not efer efen cnaw

i seen that the names of the folcs of angland was part of anglisc ground lic the treow and rocc the fenn and hyll and i seen that when these names was tacan from the place where they had growan and cast down on other ground and when their place was tacan by names what has not growan from that ground is not of it and can not spece its tunge then a great wrong had been done. then sum thing deop and eald had been made wrong and though folcs wolde forget cwic the eald gods and the eald places the eald trees and the eald hylls these things wolde not forget what had been broc and how things used to be and sceolde be and one daeg though not in our lifs one daeg all will be made right again

164

well i will not tell thu how many mergens there was lic this in these wices nor how much walcan we done in the brunnesweald and in the land around it. we three men and our swine we gan through these lands cnawan them and cepen loc out for frenc and for anglisc also. we saw few folcs for we cept to the deop holt and in the deop holt far from any ham and far from any frenc we macd our selfs a place to be what was stronger than the small hus of stics and leafs what we had been slepan in before

ofer sum wices we macd this place together for it seemed now that we wolde be together for sum time and though i was not blithe at this i colde not see no other place to go. also it seemed to me that i was leadan these men and that they neded leadan for though there was sum strength in them they did not cnaw how to use it well for them selfs and their folc. so together we macd a strong hall in the deop wud a hall that colde tac many folcs for others may cum we saed and i had in mynd to see that they did. we macd this hall of strong wud and thaeccd the roof and by the hall we macd another small hus of wud and thaecc for cepan things and we had a place for a fyr in the lea of this wud and logs for sittan on by it and when we had done after sum time this was a good place to be and though still rough it was dry and strong and a place to cum baec to from where efer we gan

well i cnawan now that i stayed too long but then i did not cnaw what to do. we had cwelled a great frenc man and this was good but no war had begun and no others had cum to us and in the brunnesweald few other folcs we saw though tofe and grimcell had talcced of these grene men this anglisc fyrd gathran agan the frenc. well i did not see this we saw few folcs for sum time and now that we had a hus i wolde go eacc daeg in to the wud alone and i wolde spec to the wihts and i wolde spec to weland

this of course was what my grandfather had done and it was what he telt me to do loc ofer the land cilde he had saed but the land it wolde not lysten. no wihts cum to me and when i cum to sum hara or boar or fugol it ran from me i colde not be the land the land wolde not lysten. naht gan right at this time for weland wolde not lysten neither and though i wolde spec with him and asc him what will i do now where sceolde i go he saed naht to me and i cnawan why

and so efry daeg i wolde walc the holt and tofe and grimcell they wolde go huntan and we wolde coc together and in the nights around the fyr we wolde sitt and we wolde spec of what had been and also of what was to cum. ah we wolde spec micel of this grimcell he wolde spec of when the frenc was gan drifen out and his hus built again in our ham and him in it and of findan a new wifman and lifan again on his ground. tofe wolde spec of great feohts and of an anglisc fyrd risan from fenn and holt to cum down on the ingenga in blud and of succ deorcness and blud wolde he spec that it colde be thought he was an eald feohtan man and not a yonge cilde who colde not efen grip a scramasax without pissan himself me i wolde not sae so micel though i colde see both thoughts and feel them both in me but i was still thincan of all that had been and not cnawan what was to cum and efry mergen i wolde rise again and eat at the fyr and then go walcan. in triewth there was sum thing i licd about this place for efen though all was broc the hus and the fyr cept a small part of me baec on my land with my cynn and my geburs and what man wolde not want this. also i saed then and i sae now that he wolde not cum he wolde not cum and so if i was lost for a time this was on him and not on me

well one daeg when we had been in the wud for sum time tofe cum to me in the mergen as i was eatan and before i colde go walcan. tofe had ascd me efry daeg in the mergen if he colde cum with me thincan that i was doan great things in the holt and efry daeg i saed no cilde and this macd him thinc only mor of me. but after sum wices i colde see he was thincan less of me and our place here and on this daeg i was thincan he wolde asc again to cum with me but he wanted sum other thing

buccmaster he saes i wolde lic to cnaw what we will do now

i is goan to the holt cilde i saes i has telt thu there is things i moste do there and thu can not be with me

i does not mean this daeg he saes. i locs at him and it seems he is tryan hard to be strong. i means in this holt he saes i means our worc

worc i saes

our worc he saes our war with the frenc. it has been many wices since we cwelled the ingenga and yet we has not brought our war to others

lysten cilde i saes this war thu specs of it is all around thu. if thu leafs this holt thu will see it in all hams and tuns if thu wants frenc go to them with thy great strength

buccmaster saes tofe thu saes thu is leadan us thu saes thu is ring gifer. in my ham before i cum to thu there was micel specan of the grene men and all cnawan they was gathran in the brunnesweald for it is the greatest holt in angland and folcs who is free and is agan the ingenga cum here to gather and spec of war. when i cum to thu i cum for this and yet there is three of us buccmaster and no war

cilde i saes this is no way to spec to me

i does not mean naht by it saes tofe i does not mean to sae thu is wrong but i is only ascan that is all when we will gather when others will cum for surely there moste be a great risan lic folcs was saen in my ham there wolde be lic there will be soon in elge

in elge i saes

tofe locs at me lic he has saed sum thing wrong

in elge he saes

what of elge i saes what of this place

oh it is only tales he saes cwicc tales that is all has thu not hierde them. in elge on the ealond on the fenns there is men gathran it was saed under an anglisc ealdor namd hereweard and they is lic us they is grene men they is

168

standan agan the ingenga lic we will lic thu is leadan us

i stands up at this point for i has eatan and i locs down at tofe who now feels small i can see and i saes cilde wait for me that is all. thu will see i saes thu will see and now i moste go

well i was blithe to go for this cilde had ired me and this was not good and in triewth i cnawan nuthan but that i had foda in the holt for the last of the swine still lyfed and there was water from a small ea and a hus now also and i colde not see why i wolde go any other place. of course i colde haf lifd there i colde haf saed to this cilde and this cottar grimcell i colde haf saed go then go in to the world and leaf me. micel of me wolde do so and yet i did not and now i gan in to the holt tellan myself i loccd for wihts and weland but in triewth i was walcan only and walcan and walcan for want of any other thing

and now when i was not specan to him he cum to me and he cum in a sound lic a great wind in treows lic a roar of water lic a red ea red with blud

*another is cum*
i has called for thu i has spocan to thu

*there is cum a greater man*
why has thu not cum

*this other he ascs naht only cwells only feohts*
what other

*thu has been a small man buccmaster a weac man*
i is not weac

*weac lic a wifman in thy warm hus eatan and slepan while*

169

                              *angland beorns*

i cwelled a frenc thegn

                              *and then thu slept*

i is not slepan i is thincan

                              *thincan is for wifmen*
                    *they is thincan while weafan and reapan*
          *thincan while bean fuccd up the arse by frenc men*
                              *thincan their men is weac*

i has ascd thu

                              *is thu sum cilde*

who is this other

                    *he will gather men they will follow him*

i will gather men

                    *he will tac down the ingenga he will be thy cyng*

where is he

                              *he is cuman*

who

                    *he cepes his great sweord for great things*

we neded mete

                              *mete is all thu is*

i will use it well i will use it well

                              *the time for that is gan*

the time is here i will gather my werod i is ready

                              *he is in the holt*

in the holt

                              *hereweard is cum*

oh i had cnawan he wolde be ired for what i done with
his sweord his great sweord what he macd for my grandfather and what i had used in a low way and now he
had telt me what he wolde do. now he had telt me there
was another in the holt a greater man and triewe to the
sweord and he telt me i was weac and i was not weac i is
a socman i is strong. well for a small time i was in ire and
fear thincan i was lost but then i seen what he cum for
and why he spac. for if he had left me for another i was
thincan he did not need to cum to spec to me and yet he
did and i cnawan why

great weland had cum to try me lic the eald cyngs was
tried he had cum to sae to me buccmaster there is another and to be triewe thu moste be greater than him. well
this other this hereweard i did not cnaw him nor cnaw if
he was efen a man but i cnawan now what i moste do to
be triewe and for the first time since i cum to the brunnesweald then i felt strong

i gan right baec then to the hus and the fyr where
grimcell and tofe still was sittan and talcan and when
they seen me they loccd up for they had thought me to
be gan a long time

grimcell i saes tofe we moste go

go saes grimcell

i has been gifen a sign i saes now we moste go

a sign saes grimcell

it is not for thu to asc i saes i is tellan thu now there is
worc to do

worc saes tofe is we gathran buccmaster is we gathran our werod

cilde i saes we moste go huntan

what will we do saes grimcell always he is ascan

always ascan i saes always what and why and where grimcell lysten to me man there is worc to do

for wices we has satt in these wuds saes grimcell and all has been still and now thu wolde feoht all the ingen-gas in angland

grimcell i saes thu is an anglisc man a man of holland now thu will lysten to me. we is goan gathran we is goan huntan we is goan to gather a werod and we is goan to feoht. thu will ceose if thu wants to cum but this cilde and i we is goan now

i is ready saes tofe

grimcell locs at me and at the cilde and he locs around and well what will he do here alone. he stands


it was lic this i woc in the mergen sum three daegs after i had hierde from my grandfather of the boar who spac and sum thing was not the same. it wolde not be the same efer now i seen as i locd at my father stridan about specan low and my sistor aelfgifu wepan and wepan. well i seen before any folcs colde spec i seen what it was for in the night while i had slept my grandfather he had gan to the other world

it was still early in the mergen but in the great hus of

my grandfather the wifmen of the ham was layan him out. i stood outside the hus for sum time for i was not strong enough to see him gan to see him laid down cold but soon aelfgifu cum for she colde see what was in me and she toc my hand and in the hus we went together

the hus was always deorc with the stenc of smoc but this daeg there was also the stenc of beornan wyrts. my mothors sistor agnes was leadan for i had no mothor she was with two wifmen from the ham one was annis who was later to be my wifmans gebur though she was yonge then and the other was her mothor. they was doan what wifmen does at death they was beornan the wyrts and singan the eald songs as they laid out the great hwit bodig of my grandfather

he was laid out on his bed with blosms around him and with leafs also for it was sumor and he was in a scirt of hwit and blaec brices and his great eald boots what i had seen him in efer since i was a small cilde. he was clene his great beard hwit though thynne and his eages scutt now for efer and in sean this i colde not be strong no mor and i wept lic a maeden and aelfgifu she held me until i was strong again. all this time these three wifmen they spac naht to us only busy macan the place right and singan the songs

aelfgifu my sistor and i we went out again in to the sunne for the daeg was high and clere and of great beuty and this was right for the daeg when my grandfathers sawol had gan to find his cynn folc. but i cnawan what was done in these parts when a man was gan and i was afeart

aelfgifu i saes what will they do. she cnawan what i is thincan right then

i does not cnaw she saes but i thinc it will be the preost and the circe

they can not

thu cnawan our father thu cnawan how our grandfather was seen

no preosts no circe

all i cnawan she saes is how it is done. he will be in the hus for two daegs while folcs cums to see and to bless and spec and sing and then in the dawn he will be tacan along the blaec trac to bacstune and to the circe and there his graef will be macd and the preost will send him under and abuf

this can not be

then what brothor

bury me in my boat sistor he saed beorn me in my scip

brothor these is not the eald times

i moste spec to him

he is gan

no i moste spec with our father

lysten i has telt thu i will not spec of this man well thu will see why thu will see for my father was yfel. oh strong he was strong and tall and was thought of by sum in the ham as a great man. ascetil of holland thu wolde hiere folcs saen lic they was talcan of a thegn or a cyng well for me he was not great all he gifen me was fear this man all he gifen his cynn was fear

no esol was he and he wolde let no man spec ofer him for he moste always be right my father he moste always be cyng. all that he cnawan he seen as the triewth for all men and there was none colde spec agan him and if thu was his cilde thu wolde cnaw it. well i was his cilde but i seen things that this man had not seen

my father raised me in the circe of the crist as all did in those times for all was blind lic the frenc is now macan us blind. anglisc folcs has had their sawol eatan i saes eatan first by ingenga god and then by ingenga cyng and now what is angland but an ealond in the mist seen when the heofon mofs but nefer reacced again. my father he raised me under his hwit god under his man god but i left him for i hierde the call of the mere and my grandfather who toc me there was now gan lic the land we haf been

well this daeg i gan to my father i walced to his side where he stood in the hus locan down at the hwit bodig of my grandfather saen naht. oh always i wanted to spec to my father to tell him how things sceolde be to feoht him to say father i is man and as man i will do as i wolde. but always when i cum to him when i locd in his eages i colde sae naht for his strength was all in his bodig and to stand agan him was to stand agan the rocc or the water

well this daeg i gan to him as he stood there with the

wifmen frettan all round him and as i cum up by him he
teorned and he locd at me and in his eages i did not cnaw
what i colde see

father i saes

son

thy father is gan

thy grandfather

he was a great man

he was a man

for sum time i colde not sae what i had cum to sae and
i thought to go but i cnawan that if i did not sae naht
now i wolde nefer sae naht

what will cum now father to him

what will cum he will go to his graef son he will not
stand and sing for thu

his graef in the circe

in the circe yes. here my father locs at me for he cnaws
what i is thincan

father he

i will spec to thu now son of this and will not spec of it
again. thy grandfather was of the eald hus and this brings
great sceomu on me and on thy cynn. thu has seen how
folcs locs at us in the ham and in the circe thu has hierde
what is saed. my father was an esol who lifd in dreams of
times gan and the deorcness and sceomu he gaf us will
go to eorth with him. he will go to the circe cilde and his
graef will be there and in this way we will tac baec our
name

well i saed naht for what colde i sae once mor i had
been brought to nuthan. now my father he loccd at me
strong and i loccd at my grandfathers bodig for it was a
better sight than my fathers eages

son saes my father this will end here there will be no
mor of this in this hus for we is men of the wapentac
men of strength in this land. there will no mor cildes
tales to bring sceomu and synn upon my cynn there will
be no mor. he cepes locan at me then and i cepes locan at
my grandfather and i cnawan my nebb is red lic the
sunne. then my father he teorns and he is gan from the
hus


i is thincan of my father as i is walcan through the brunnesweald with tofe and grimcell thincan of what he saed
that daeg there will be no mor of this cilde no mor. always
there has been men lic my father who wolde throw out
the eald thincan it is no good but not sean what the
triewe good efer was. i was leadan my men south they
had not ascd where we was goan or what we was doan
and in triewth i did not cnaw. we was in a part of the holt
now i did not cnaw and they did not cnaw so all we was
doan in triewth was walcan and waitan to see what we
wolde cum to

well soon enough i seen sum thing though it did not
loc lic no great thing then. we cum to a path in the holt at
a place where haesel wud was bean tacan for worcan so

we was locan and tacan care for we did not cnaw who was here. well we hierde none but fugols callan in the treows for it was late sumor now and all treows was grene with leaf and wolde soon be teornan. but when we cum on to the path we hierde the sound of a man specan and he was specan to me

buccmaster of holland he saes and grimcell of holland well what is this we has. well we locd but we colde see no man and this was not the sound of weland specan it was the sound of a man of this eorth and an anglisc man

i had not thought to see none from thy ham again saes this man and now he cums from behind the stocc of a great ac treow and i sees that i cnawan him. this is the gleoman who cum to our ham so oft before the beornan with tidans and tales. when i last seen him he was thynne and weac and in fear for he brought tales of the great woe of angland and the cuman of the bastard but it seems now he has cum up from his low place and though an eald man he has fyr in him again

it is ulf the gleoman saes grimcell ulf the scop i had thought thu cwelled my freond. grimcell seems blithe to see this man they is both low folcs after all

ah i has the fleetness of an aelf saes this ulf smercan no frenc man can tac me before my time

where is thu cum from saes grimcell

i is cuman and goan in this holt goan from ham to ham as i does saes the gleoman and doan so cwic for it is not cnawan from one daeg to another who thu will find in this place

but i seen what cum to thy ham saes the gleoman now
not smercan no mor and thu is not alone in this for i has
been to many places since the cuman of the frenc cyng
and there is fyr all ofer the fenns and all ofer angland in
these times

i has hierde the cyng is gan saes grimcell

gan yes gan baec to his frenc lands to feoht his own
folc they saes and in his place is biscops and frenc ealdors
and these cnihts on hors and they is tacan what they can
while their mastor is gan. but now what is thu folcs doan
walcan in this holt in these daegs

we is grene men saes tofe now. he has not spoc yet but
now the gleoman locs at him. tofe he saes it is tofe of
bacstune is it not

we is gathran saes tofe and he does not smerc we is
gathran men to feoht the ingenga

well now saes the gleoman and he locs at me well now

we will haf our wergild i saes locan at him and with
my eages saen do not smerc at us gleoman

wergilds he saes wergilds well now there is many who
specs lic this and yes there is grene men in these wuds
and sum of them i has met and spoc with

thu has met the grene men saes tofe now lic a cilde
again

well now i has met sum mor saes the gleoman yes
there is worc bean done. to the west there is men risan in
the hylls and in the north there is micel talc of tacan baec
the land and in the holts there is grene men all about
they is specan and thincan and sum times they is risan to

cwell frenc folcs. perhaps as grene men then thu has hierde of this man hereweard

hereweard saes tofe yes

hereweard i saes but i saes it cold

hereweard they saes is a great man of angland saes this gleoman. i has not seen him but he is spac of in these lands now with fear and with fyr. hereweard is son of a great thegn of these parts and he was in gan in flanders for sum time but his cynn was cwelled and his land was toc and he is baec now they saes baec to lead men agan the frenc. when the bastard cum this man hereweard hierde what had cum upon angland and he cum baec to see what was becum of his folcs. well he cum to his hall what had been the hus of his father a thegn and his mothor and this hall it was all gan in fyr and all his cynn folc in it. then he gan to the hus of his brothor but folcs telt him that frenc had cwelled his brothor also and toc his hus and toc also his wifman who they now used for their games

well hereweard he is a great feohtan man he has been feohtan in fyrds all ofer in scaldemariland in flanders efen in the eastern lands where there is no night. this man he toc his great sweord and he gan to the hus of his brothor where ten frenc men was sittan eatan his brothors foda and drincan from his brothors cuppes and bean gifen mete by his brothors wifman and a sad sight this was to see. well these man was not thincan to hiere from another man of this cynn for they thought all was cwelled

180

and soon they all was cwelled also for hereweard he gan in cwic lic lihtnan and he spared none he cut them down and their heafods he put on the hege of his brothors hus all ten of them in a grim line and this to say to frenc folc that this is what wolde becum of them in angland

hereweard then he toc his brothors wif from the hus for he cnawan what wolde becum of her if she staed and they went in to the brunnesweald and it is saed they is here now gathran folcs for the feoht for the great feoht that is cuman for the time when angland rises agan the frenc and drifs them baec to the sea

well at this of course the dumb cilde tofe is leapan around lic a frog in a fuccan croc. he teorns to me with light in his eages and he saes buccmaster this is the man i was tellan thu of that folcs spac of in our ham but we did not cnaw if it was tales only. buccmaster we moste find this man and feoht with him for together there will be no stoppan us all

who is thy fuccan ealdor cilde i saes for i is not hafan this. tofe he stops then for this is not what he was thincan to hiere from me

who is thy fuccan ealdor i saes again i sees this eald gleoman loccan at me

thu is my ealdor saes tofe his words small now his bodig still

i is thy fuccan ealdor cilde i saes that is right not this hereweard not any other man

i only

it is me tofe it is me this is my werod if thu wolde go to sum other then fuccan go cilde fuccan go now but do not cum baec to me efer

he saes naht locs at the ground

this is my werod and we has worc to do and this other man this great cyng this fuccan hereweard he may do his own fuccan worc but i will not hiere naht of him again for it is not our worc cilde it is not our worc

none saes naht then tofe locs at the ground small and the gleoman locs at me and grimcell locs at me lic he oft does with no loc in his eages at all

well then i saes lic naht had been saed well then we moste go from this path for sum may cum here who does not wysc us well. we is goan south

cum saes grimcell to the gleoman and he saes it strong he does not asc me does not loc at me. the gleoman locs at him

where was thu goan saes grimcell to him cum with us for sum time efen if the time is only a scorte one. gif us as we walcs tales and tidans from the land

the gleoman locs at him for a scorte time then at me and tofe and he saes well i will cum then i will cum with thu for a lytel for i wolde cnaw where thu has been and what thu has seen and many things i has to sae what thu may find good to hiere

*now thu has hierde*

who is he

*thy brothor and thy enemi*

i is stronger

*upon a hyll stands a treow but this treow it has no stics no leafs. its stocc is gold on it is writhan lines of blud red it reacces to the heofon its roots is deop deop in the earth. abuf the hyll all the heofon is hwit and below all the ground is deorc. the treow is scinan and from all places folcs is walcan to it walcan to the scinan treow locan for sum thing from it. abuf the tree flies a raefn below it walcs a wulf and deop in the earth where no man sees around the roots of the treow sleeps a great wyrm and this wyrm what has slept since before all time this wyrm now slow slow slow this wyrm begins to mof*

well because we is grene men and because we is as great as any fuccan hereweard we walcs now down the straet and not in the treows lic hunds. we walcs all of us and with me leadan and with my sweord on my belt we walcs tall lic we is the fyrd we is goan to be

where does thu go to ascs the gleoman as we is walcan. this one he locs at me lic he is all the time smercan it seems lic he is all the time smercan yet there is no smerc on his nebb

what is the ham that is most near i saes to him
creatas tun is two miles on this straet he saes
then we will go to creatas tun and there we will spec to

the folc and we will tell them we is men of the holt and we is gathran to mac a fyrd agan the frenc and we will asc the men of the tun to cum with us

it is a small place there is not many folc

many small places will gif us many good folc

yes saes tofe yes we gan gathran and he is blithe as a man who goes gathran a wif in litha

is there frenc there saes grimcell to the gleoman we does not want to see frenc

thu has seen too many frenc yes saes the gleoman and cwelled one i thinc

who telt thu this i saes

folcs specs saes the gleoman and folcs thincs the frenc thegn of these parts sum wices ago was cwelled by folcs from the holt

and what does thu thinc gleoman i saes and i saes it strong but still he is smercan it seems to me

i is only a gleoman he saes only a scop what does i cnaw

what does thu cnaw

if any was to asc i wolde sae that to tac and cwell a yonge frenc thegn in the holts of angland is a great thing and that many folcs here specs of it when there is no frenc near them and they is in awe of the folcs who done this though also in fear. for of course it is also a dumb act an act of blud but at a time when all angland is in blud who can spec of this in succ words

folcs specs of it saes tofe folcs of these wuds. he is in a great thryll now

i has hierde folcs in hams spec of it saes the gleoman
and i has hierde frenc also spec of it they is in ire and
perhaps also in sum fear

fear saes tofe the frenc in fear

of course they does not cnawan who to fear saes the
gleoman and the folcs of the hams does not cnawan who
to thanc

none cnawan naht saes grimcell

sum saes this thegn was cwelled by aelfs saes the gleoman

aelfs i saes aelfs with lines

but most saes the gleoman is thincan he was cwelled
by hereweard

hereweard i saes fuccan hereweard. o i is in ire to hiere
of this again who is this fuccan hereweard hereweard
always folcs is lic sceop

he ires thu saes the gleoman to me

thu fuccan ires me gleoman i saes with all thy words all
thy specan of fuccan hereweard it was not he cwelled the
thegn it was us it was me

well saes the gleoman well

with a line saes tofe

ofer his fuccan frenc throta saes i

well saes the gleoman

is thu fuccan smercan

smercan saes the gleoman well no i is not smercan

fuccan hereweard i saes who specs of him why does
folcs always spec of him

folcs is folcs saes the gleoman they needs tales of great

men it cepes me eatan

tell them tales of us saes tofe tell them tales of us cwellan the thegn

do not saes grimcell do not. does thu want to feoht one hundred frenc men tofe do not spec of us lic this we is men only

we walced on we walced towards creatas tun but i was in ire thincan of this hereweard and of all this specan of him and of how a socman with three oxgangs can cum to be lower than a gleoman sleepan in the fuccan holt lic a brocc or a fox. well i had to thinc of weland i had to thinc of his words always for i cnawan i was ceosan i cnawan i moste be triewe

the daeg was wanan and i was needan to thinc on what had cum and on what wolde cum now and so i telt my werod to stop that night in the holt and when the mergen cum we wolde go in to creatas tun and we wolde tell them of our greatness of our deed with the frenc thegn and we wolde call on men of that ham to cum with us to feoht. i wolde gather many folcs and what moste be done then wolde cum to me or weland wolde cum to me and gif me my lead when my werod was great and my sweord again free for feohtan lic my grandfather had meant it to be

we macd a fyr then and we satt and we ate sum of the last of tofes swine what we had cwelled and smocd sum time before and also we ate sum swamms what by now was growan in the holt. after this we wolde be needan mor foda and we moste thinc on this if we was not to be eatan bits of fugol and fox and the leaf from the treow

well when thu sits a gleoman by a fyr and gifs him foda he starts to spiw out raedels and soon enough this ulf he was doan so. tofe and grimcell they was laughan and grimcell well i had not seen him laughan efer

a yonge man saes the gleoman macs for the ecg of the hus where he sees the thing he wants and with his hands he lifts up her gyrdel and under it he throsts sum thing long and hard. well this yonge man he worcs his will and the both of them they shacs then this man he cwicns and then is tyred. he falls baec but his worc is done and under the gyrdel sum thing is growan what this yonge man will be blithe to see in times to cum

tofe and grimcell they is both laughan now and the gleoman this time he is smercan for real. i does not cnaw of what he is specan

buccmaster calls the gleoman tell us what was this yonge man doan

no gleoman i saes i does not do games

tofe cilde saes the gleoman thu can tell us can thu not for thu is a great man of this world. tofe then he is gan red lic a berie and only laughs

ulf saes grimcell thy raedels runs out this one i has hierde before the man is ceornan buttere

buttere saes tofe and he almost falls ofer laughan. nefer has i seen why men pleges lic this when they sceolde be strong. i is sat around this fyr for the heat but i is clenan my sweord not plegen. well at this time i was needan a piss so i left my sweord and i gan in to the holt and when thu gan from a fyr in to the deorc of the holt the deorc seems deoper than at any other time and hard it is to see any thing. as i gan in to the holt sum small way i hierde a sound near me and i was thincan i sceolde not haf left my sweord by the fyr that again i has let weland thinc small of me for always he is locan on

but the sound was small it was not the sound of a man i locd down as my eages began to see in to the blaec and i seen a fox mofan away from me in to the holt. i thincs naht of this only that he had seen our swine mete and now had seen me and was runnan but as i cum to a treow and begun to piss i seen this fox stop walcan. this fox he stopped walcan and he teorned and he locd at me and in his eages there was sum mad thing. this fox his eages was not the eages of a wiht they was the eages of a man and it was a man i had cnawan but what man i colde not sae. this fox he stood and locd at me for sum time it was lic he cnawan me lic he was locan for me lic he wolde spec to me but then he teorned and he mofd in to the blaec holt and was gan

well i gan baec to the fyr then and i was in deop thought and i hierde the gleoman specan to tofe and grimcell as i cum and he was specan soft

he is waecnan saed the gleoman he is waecnan while others in angland sleeps and it is saed by the folcs of these parts that he is cum to waecen us all and lead us agan who i saes cuman up to the fyr. well the gleoman locs at me then and in his eages this time there is no smercan but his eages mofs cwic at sean me

of who is thu specan i saes. tofe and grimcell only locs at the fyr

sitt down buccmaster my freond saes the gleoman now his words cuman again sitt down and i will tell thu of eadric the wilde

eadric the fuccan wilde i is not an esol i cnawan of who these folcs was specan when i was gan i cnawan what they was doan that they was not triewe to me. but at this time hafan seen this fox and wundran on what this thing was i saed naht but i did not forget no i did not

tell us of eadric saes tofe

eadric is a great wilde man saes the gleoman a great wilde man of the west. i has met folcs from the west of angland from the lands near the wealsc lands for this is where eadric was bred. on the ecg of the wealsc lands is great duns and hylls what gan so high they is in the heofons and thu can stand on these great roccs and under thu is cloud and abuf thu only the sunne in the heofon

how is this saes tofe in wundor

well lifan in these fenns cilde thu has not efer efen seen a dun saes the gleoman but o great and high they is with great hwit eas what foams down them so wide and fast that no man efer can cross them. on the other side of these great roccs and eas is the lands of the wealsc and good it is that these duns and eas cepes them from us for they is a deorc folc lic dweorgs they is full of blaec yfel

189

and mad ways and ire against all anglisc. well in these duns and by these eas and in the great deorc holts of those lands this is where eadric lifs

this eadric a man of parts he was in his lands yes a little lic thu buccmaster of holland a man with a great hus micel thought of. a great thegn was eadric it is saed but he wolde not gif in to the laws of the bastard and so the frenc cum and they toc his lands and his hus and he gan in to the holt and he sworn he wolde tac all baec. well eadric he has been gathran a werod yes lic thu buccmaster micel lic thu and this great werod he has been leadan out from the holt when none cnawan he was cuman and micel frenc blud has he spilt. many frenc folcs he has cwelled on the roads and sum of them great men sum of them efen cnihts he has cwelled them and their hors

o saes tofe then there is grene men all ofer

o all ofer yes saes the gleoman great werods of grene men lic thu yes and this eadric well it colde be he is the greatest of them all for sum wices ago he beorned a frenc castel

a castel saes grimcell what is a castel

if thu moste asc this saes the gleoman then it is good for sean one of these things wolde fill thu with fear. he is talcan it up again as gleoman do here i is clenan my sweord to cepe from specan at him scarp lic

i has seen a castel near these parts saes the gleoman at stan ford where the frenc has macd one and it is a fearsum thing. a great hyll they macs from the eorth they

190

macs anglisc folc build it then on the hill they macs a great tor and round it a wall and gates high and strong and in this castel is cnihts on hors and all the land near them they can see. and if any anglisc specs agan them or does not gif geld or does not gif their land or wifmen to the frenc when telt well these cnihts they cums out with sweords and floods the land with anglisc blud

these ingengas they is deofuls i saes deofuls

this is an yfel thing saes tofe

well eadric saes the gleoman he seen also this yfel and in the night he toc his men to a castel near his lands and they put fyr to it it and in the castel many frenc cnihts beorned. well the frenc now they hunts eadric all ofer but he is in holt and on hyll and they can not find him for he cnawan his land and they is afeart of it and now of him

then it is true anglisc is risan saes grimcell it is not only words. as he specs he seems to lif lic he has not done for sum wices efen since he put ecceard in his graef

anglisc is risan saes the gleoman they is risan all ofer but they is awaitan an ealdor. harald cyng his brothors his eorls many thegns all is cwelled or fled so who will lead us now. all ofer men locs for a cyng and when a cyng cums well then they will rise lic the winter sea and then it may be there will be no mor frenc castels in angland and no mor frenc cnihts not efer

in the mergen it was lic i had gan baec

in the mergen we woc we lit the fyr and we ate and spac about what we wolde do. when we had spac and when i had telt my werod what we sceolde do in this place and why we was goan then we cyccd the fyr ofer and we macd our way through the holt and out to where the light cum in around the ham. this was a small ham smaller than ours but still it toc me baec to the eald lif for this ham was worcan and lifan

we cums from the holt and to the ecg of the ham and we cum past swine rootan where the treows gan smaller and then through felds of beans lic what i was growan in my felds and peas also and leacs. there was aeppel treows then and a small ea and the heofon smelt of ealu and smoc and treows and folc. there was eight hus there small for small men but still it macd me loc baec on what i had been and what had been tacan

and what i was felan then well it was felt mor deop when i seen what was in the ham for it seemed that the haerfest mass was happnan. long had we been in the holt and hard it was to tell the passan of the year in the treows but now here i colde see it was haligmonth the month of the haerfest and it was lic a spere in my heorte. then i colde feel deop the need for my land the need to worc it and be with it and i colde feel deop what was tacan from me. what had cum to my land i was thincan was it now becum treows again was it still blaec with aesc did sum other man cum to tac it was he frenc or anglisc. was there any left in my eald ham did any lif there. ah succ wundor there was in my land what had been the land of my grandfather and of his so micel worc in that ground so micel of my cynn and now

well now i loccd at tofe and at grimcell and at ulf the gleoman i loccd at us all standan in the ecg of the wud there not seen by the ham folcs and we men we was lic ghasts from the deorc. all of our clothes blaec and filthd our nebbs deorc and all of us stincan lic a byr and us locan there at these folcs of the ham and they was laughan and singan for the baerlic haerfest was cuman in and here in this small place in the holt it was lic angland for sum small time was all alyf again and i felt small lic a weac weac man and i felt my father locan at me saen this cilde was always small and my grandfather locan at me saen cilde thu is no good

in the straet betweon the hus there was sum folcs cum from the felds and they was cuman with blitheness. the sunne was high in the heofon this mergen the heofon lic flax and from the felds was cuman men with sithes and wifmen with sicls and they had baerlic sheafs and these they put on a waegn what was tied to a small esol. this waegn it had leafs of ac and aesc wound around it lic the haer of a wifman on the daeg she was wed and on the waegn was a wifman but she was not lifan. this wifman she was macd of baerlic sheafs and her haer was macd of leafs and blosms was her clothes

this cwen of the haerfest she was passan through this

small ham as folcs put mor baerlic on the waegn and threw blosms at her. there was a cilde plegen a harp and also a cilde with pipe and they was macan songs what sum folcs was steppan to as they gan after this slow waegn what was mofan to a barn at the end of the straet. well this waegn it went in to this barn then and folcs followed it and from in the barn then cum the sounds of blithe lif

i telt my men to follow me and to this barn i walced and i walced tall. in this gathran of folcs there was wifmen and boys and eald folcs but there was also men of good age and sum of these i was thincan wolde cum to us when they cnawan we was gathran a werod to stric agan the frenc. in to the barn we gan and we gan tall and in the barn we seen the waegn and around it folcs singan and leapan and there was drincan of ealu and pipes and harp plegen and micel blitheness

soon enough this stopped when we was seen standan at the door. music stopped and singan also and folcs loccd at us in sum wundor and also in fear it seemed for they did not cnaw who we was we might haf been ingengas

so what i done i spac to them as they loccd at us and i spac cwic before sum folc spac to us. anglisc folcs i saes good anglisc folcs of creatas tun do not be afeart for we is not nightgengas or wihts of the holt though it is triewe we has been lifan there. my men and i we is grene men

there was sum specan low at this and this macd me feel strong we is grene men i saes again we is risan agan the bastard cyng geeyome and the frenc what has toc our lands and our freodoms and the eald ways from us. all ofer angland grene men is gathran there is great fyrds of us and we has cum here to tell thu of this great thing and to call on any folcs who lufs freodom in this ham to cum with us that we may drif the frenc in to the sea lic the wihts they is

here two or three folcs seemed to mac sounds lic they thought this was good but most only locd at us still. lic hunds they was only locan. well i had thought that this tale of feohtan and freodom wolde mac men cum to us but all only stood locan lic we was aelfs macd flesc

then a man cum from the folcs to us he was a yonge man with bright eages not an esol he cum up and he spac to me

what is thy name he saes

what is thine i saes cwic

he loccs at me for sum small time and i sees him also locan at welands sweord what i is wearan on my belt and what is scinan bright after i has clened it

i is harald he saes i is gerefa of this ham

i is buccmaster of holland i saes and i is leader of this werod

werod he saes smercan locan at us well this is sum small werod i can see why thu locs for mor men

we locs for men who lufs freodom saes tofe

men who wolde lif saes grimcell without frenc fyr and theft

fyr and theft saes the gerefa well we has had none of this here thu can see folcs in this ham is blithe. none will be cuman to the holt with thu for there is worc to do here

does thu spec for all men then i saes has folcs not tunges here

all has tunges saes harald and specs then to the folc in the barn. men he saes men of creatas tun if thu wolde go with these wihts of the wud then go now. well he waits but none cums to us and he cnawan this wolde be so

thy tunge gerefa i saes is sic we is not wihts we is men feohtan we is men who has lost land wifmen all things to the frenc hunds and yes we has lost all of angland to them also it seems thu thinc this is sum small thing

it is no thing of ours saes the gerefa that is all no thing of ours. we has gifen geld to the frenc and done their biddan and thu can see they has left us free as efer we was if thu does their biddan they is good to thu

good i saes fuccan good well i is ired now my wifman in the ground and this hund specan of good frenc folc. good i saes i has lost all things there is men rottan in the ground all ofer angland and thu tells us of these great frenc men

this gerefa he locs at me then and at my sweord again and he saes so tell us grene man what will thu do

we will feoht saes tofe we has cwelled a frenc thegn and will cwell many mor. well at this there is sum mofan in the barn then thu sceolde go now saes the gerefa for cuman here will be bad for us thu moste cnaw this

now lysten i saes lysten angland is bean cwelled all ofer by ingengas while thu is singan and drincan. does thu thinc this is good does thu thinc this is right thy anglisc cyng harald godwineson and all his thegns was cwelled by ingengas our land was toc and all things anglisc now they is goan up in fyr. these castels is bean put up with frenc cnihts in them anglisc gold is bean tacan to the frenc lands all things we had was gan our cildren will haf frenc names they will spec frenc words all that we is is bean tacan from us

the gerefa then he wafs his hand at the barn and the waegn. this is all that we is he saes and it is the same as it was and it will cepe bean this way no frenc has cum here to mac us do frenc things. before the frenc cum this was a wilde place there was out laws in these wuds now there is mor laws from abuf and there is no out laws. thy harald cyng he did not cepe us safe yet this frenc cyng does now what does thu grene men say to this

scit saes grimcell this is scit let me tell thu how safe my wifman is she is in the fuccan ground

well i is sad to hiere this saes the gerefa but in this ham thu can see that all is well

so thu wolde cepe to thyself saes grimcell lic there was no place outside

we wolde cepe to our ham and to the laws of angland saes the gerefa that is all then thu will be thralls i saes fuccan thralls all of thu

at this the gerefa he is ired for the first time since i has seen him. thralls he saes thralls thu saes well we is all thralls my freond all the time and has always been in angland. thralls there has always been here and ceorls and geburs tell me my freond how is these folcs free. when their thegn ascs of them three daegs on his land efry wice or a winters harrowan when he ascs for a score of hens efry sixmonth or fifty carts of their own wud when he wolde lic the fyr higher in his hall. or when the cyng cums through and calls up the fyrd and they is tacan from their wifmen and their cynn with naught but stans and sithes to sum feld to die in a dic for his war with sum denisc cyng. tell me buccmaster of angland where is it that thu can see the freodom thu wolde haf us feoht for

well what is this scit i thincs what man wolde spec this way. thu is a fuccan hund i saes i is a socman of holland a man of the wapentac i has three oxgangs i answers to none

there is not so many lic thu saes the gerefa not here here we worcs for thegns and is these thegns anglisc or frenc well these is names only. thralls for harald thralls for geeyome if we can bring in our baerlic and sing for the gift of it we does not asc why

fucc saes grimcell and i locs at him now for i has nefer hierde him spec with ire lic this. fucc man he saes does thu not cnawan what these frenc has done to thy cynn folc

198

my cynn folc is here saes the gerefa the frenc has done naht

loc i saes and i saes this now not only to this scucca of a gerefa but to all folcs in the barn who is all gathran round. loc i saes at this yonge man this yonge cilde and here i tacs tofe by the sceoldor. this yonge cilde i saes this yonge anglisc cilde he seen his father and his mothor cwelled before him by the frenc hunds thu gifs thy geld to. they cum in to his ham on great deorc hors one daeg lic this daeg now and they toc this boys mothor and they fuccd her on the ground before him in the straet before all his cynn folc all these frenc hunds they fuccd her in the dirt lic a wiht and then they slit her cunt with frenc style and she bled there before her son

there is gaspan and whispran at this and tofe he mofs lic he wants to spec but i locs at him and he does not

and this yonge boys father i saes well he toc on these frenc hunds with scramasax as any triewe man wolde and sum other men of this ham they done so also and they cwelled many but they was cut down too then they was gelded alyf and hanged before all the folcs of the ham as a warnan to all anglisc folcs of who was their mastors now. well tofe now he locs small but the folcs of this ham they is triewely ired to hiere this

well now gerefa i saes it seems thy folcs is not so in luf with these fuccan ingenga hunds as thu is. colde it be that thu is tacan frenc gold colde it be that lic all gerefas in all hams thu is a fuccan little hund who tacs what he is gifen by his mastors as long as it cums also with gold well at this there is sum smercan from sum folc behind the gerefa who is locan ired with me mor

tac thy flocc of wud wihts and leaf this ham he saes for by bean here thu is bringan all these folcs to hearm. does thu thinc i does not cnaw this we has all hierde the tales but we is cepan to our ways and doan our worc and gifan our geld and this way all men has wifs and all wifs husbonds and all cildren has fathers and mothors. if thu wolde tac thy one sweord agan all of the frenc then do this but no men of this ham will cum to thu

thu is a hund saes grimcell that is all a hund

it colde be that i is a hund saes the gerefa but my folcs is alyf and free as efer they was

i locs around but no men cums to us well what can we do there is naht else

cum men i saes to my werod there is no free folcs here only thralls

thralls saes tofe and him and grimcell and the gleoman who has saed naht only locd on they cums with me out of the barn in to the light


well when we got baec in to the treows i sat down by the aesc of the fyr and the others sat with me

these men saes grimcell is all esols. i has not seen grimcell ired and specan lic this before and it is good

esols saes tofe yes esols and dumb hunds. my men i thincs they is men now for sure they is men of my fyrd of my werod it is good to see it macs me strong

gleoman i saes thu has saed naht tell us thy thoughts
on this

well saes the gleoman they is men and they wolde lif
that is all. many hams there is all ofer angland lic this
they has been spared spere and fyr why wolde they asc it
in

esols saes tofe again

afeart saes the gleoman that is all afeart and hidan
from the storm

then the storm will tac us all down i saes

a storm saes the gleoman cums from heofon it cannot
be feoht only lifd through

this storm can be feoht

by thu

by us by others

well saes the gleoman there is many who wolde thinc
these great words

*well this is sum thing*
thu

*what will thu bring now*
bring

*what will thu bring to this ham what has moccd thu*
they is afeart

*thu is afeart*
nefer

*anglisc folcs who wolde be frenc what is they worth*
naht

*their barn is full of baerlic and thu eats leafs*

they moccd us

*moccd the gods*

they is not anglisc

*all angland sleeps while thy lif is dreaned*


men i saes we is goan baec

baec saes tofe

baec to this ham i saes these folcs they moccd us moccd the grene men moccd the holt moccd angland. they is worse than frenc these folcs and if they will not feoht they will gif us geld for our worc

this is good saes tofe

geld saes grimcell

foda i saes foda ealu waepens things we need. if they will not feoht with us they will gif us means to feoht and lif it is only right we feohts for them all

well saes grimcell it colde be

i will stay here i thincs saes the gleoman for this feoht is not mine

it is the feoht of all folcs in angland i saes to him in ire and he bows his heafod sum small way and saes o yes buccmaster this is of course triewe but i is not a feohtan man and so i will stay here and tend this fyr for when thu cums baec

well i does not need this esol with his smercan and his stillness so tofe and grimcell and i we gan baec in to creatas tun where the barn is still loud with song and the sunne is still scinan in the heofon and in to the barn we gan again and as before stillness cums down as we is seen

folcs of creatas tun i saes and i saes it strong. we has ascd thu to cum with us to feoht with us to feoht for angland and all thy folcs and thu has saed naht thu has staed here steppan and singan and drincan while anglisc men lies in their blud rottan in felds and in holts. well if thu is esols and small folcs this is well for we does not want thu feohtan with us but thu can at least feed thy fyrd. we is needan foda and ealu and boots and line and fyr stans and thu can gif these things to us if thu will not gif thy arms and sweords

well for a small time there is no sound but then the gerefa he cums from the folcs and this time not alone this time he has three men with him big men of the ham and he is ired again and he cums to us cwic. well i tacs my sweord from my belt cwic and i mofs it about so that the light of the sunne what cums through slits and through the door of the barn is tacan by the blaed and sent in to the eages of folcs and there is sum gaspan at sean my sweord with runes and wyrms and the carfans of the eald times upon its blaed and this is good this feels good and now i seen it i seen it

this is welands sweord i calls macd for me and my cynn by the eald smith of the beorgs so that we may feoht for angland in deorcest times. the gerefa and his freonds then they stops before us and i seen that tofe and grimcell has scramasaxes in their hands and that these men from the ham they does also

i has telt thu go from here saes the gerefa go

thu will gif us geld i saes for thu is a scucca and angland is in need

thu is not angland i will tell thu again go or we will send thu away

will thu send this sweord away gerefa will thu send weland away

i will asc thu again it is the last time go

gif us geld

well things mofd cwic then and i can not sae now how things was for i was not thincan not doan and weland it seemed weland toc my sweord from me then and done with it what sceolde be done. the men from the ham cum to us with scramasax to mof us from the barn and tofe and grimcell they gan for them and weland he gan for the gerefa and a roar there was in the barn succ as there had nefer been and the gerefa fell with the sweord in his heorte and he did not mac a sound only fell and was still then for efer. and sean this the other men of the ham they ran baec and i seen tofe was hearmd his arm bledan and his nebb hwit but these folcs they was small folcs and when they seen what my great sweord done they was hwit also and they gan baec from us

i telt thu i calls i telt thu what wolde cum of moccan the grene men now thy esol gerefa is cwelled by welands sweord by anglands sweord for thy fear and thy greotan.

o they was wepan now and fearan they sceolde haf lystened to us to me

gif us foda i saes gif us loafs and mete gif us boots and fyr stans and line and we will leaf thu to thy singan and thu may thinc on what thu has cum to

well we was baec in the holt with the gleoman soon enough and with us we brought mete and loafs and fyr stans and a line and also sum ealu in flascs and i had been gifen boots what had been this gerefas. two men had tacan us around the ham and gifen us these things in stillness my sweord still out and still wet and we had tacan them and this was right for now we had what we was needan to feoht and feoht we must. tofe he was cut on his arm but the cut was small and we had clened it in water and put cloth on it and now he loccd not hwit but strong with pryde

the gleoman he is only sittan on the ground there is no fyr he is sittan by a treow eages scut

ulf saes grimcell waec mac a fyr we will eat

eat

we has foda ealu many things

we has cwelled the esol gerefa saes tofe proud

cwelled saes the gleoman cwelled why

do not asc why i saes thu did not cum

he fell on buccmasters sweord saes grimcell he wolde not lysten .

cwelled saes the gleoman well this is bad is it not

it is good saes tofe for he was a hund

it is bad saes grimcell yes it is bad and he locs at the aesc of the fyr. so many is cwelled in angland and now there is one mor

and this one cwelled by anglisc folcs saes the gleoman not frenc

light the fuccan fyr gleoman i saes thu is with us only through our mildness of heorte thu has done naht for us. this gerefa was ascd for foda and he cum to feoht us well what was we to do but stand if he is cwelled he brought it to him self

well saes the gleoman the frenc will hiere of this and of the grene men in these wuds

then good let them cum to us let them all fuccan cum to us now light the fuccan fyr

well the gleoman lit the fyr and we coccd cycen what we had been gifen and dranc ealu and there was loafs also though i wolde not let us eat all this foda sum we moste tac with us. we had got melu to mac cicels and loafs and swine mete smocd and so we was blithe and was drencan and talcan. we had been hungord and when our guttas was full of coccd cycen and ealu we forgot the gerefa and spac of what we wolde do now strong as we was and growan

for sum time we satt there in the later part of that daeg the sunne ofer the treows warman the wuds where we was. tofe when he has dronc too micel ealu he starts talcan of the aelfs what lifs in the holt and how he is afeart of them and grimcell and ulf they is laughan at him and him saen stop do not mocc aelfs is to be afeart and this sets the gleoman on his tales again

aelfs he saes ah yes they is to be feart for aelfs is the ealdest of eald things does thu cnawan from where they has cum

tofe saes no though i wolde reccen he has hierde this scit before

ah well in eden saes the gleoman when adam and efa was the first folcs of all folcs it is saed that efa had many cildren so many that she was full of sceomu and she hid sum of these cildren from god she hyd them in fenn and holt. but the father he is great and can see all things and he seen these cildren and he saed to efa let them who is hydan from me be hydan from all men and these cildren then they growan to be all the hydan folcs of this world. sum becum aelfs the wud elf and sea elf and ground elf and sum becum dweorgs who lifs in cafs and in deorc places underneath and sum becum pucas who was lic aelfs but who lifs in all wuds and sings in the night to tease men

well gleoman i saes thu does not always spec succ scit as this it colde be that thu is druncen. this is all scit from the preosts i saes it seems to me that i can not go to any place in angland efen to the deopest eald holt where scit from preosts and their bocs has not gan. aelfs i saes is eald folcs lic we is eald folcs and lic the eald gods and all has been on this eorth since all time and all is macd to be in their place. the gods them selfs they has places woden is god of beorgs and duns thunor is of the heofon of the lihtnan and air frigg is of the grene holt ing is of the aeppel treows all has their place. aelfs place is in the wuds and in the grene places far from men dweorgs cums from under the ground ents lifs in the eald tuns of the brocn folcs from long ago before efen the wealsc and man is of the ham and the felds. other things there is too scuccas and deofuls and eorcas and they is of their own deorc places and will cwell men if seen

well this is a tale saes the gleoman

it is the triethwe i saes drencan mor ealu it is thy rot what is a tale the triewth is that all things and all folcs has their place what was set when the world was macd and when they gan from that place to others then erce is ired and the great tree of lif what binds all things to all other things then is mofd by its roots. and when all things is in places where they sceolde not be when aelfs has been drifen from the holts by men and dweorgs is ofer the ground not under it and frenc is in angland and ingenga gods is in our heortes then all is broc. then the treow will cum down in a great storm and all will be gan it will be man what has broc the land for efer

buccmaster saes grimcell who is druncen now too thu tells a good tale it was well cnawan in our ham

what was well cnawan i saes

thy tales he saes the eald gods thy cynn all cnawan of

208

the things thu wolde sae thu and thy grandfather

do not spec of him in this way i saes he was a great man

yes saes grimcell well i did not cnaw him but why man why does thu spec of the eald gods in these times in these times of the crist

the crist sceolde not be here lic the frenc sceolde not be here

the crist has been here since eald times buccmaster there is circes and preosts and folcs is all folcs of the crist now and we all has seen what the crist can do

has not the crist brought us blud for our synns saes tofe this is what is saed angland is in synn and now the crist gifs us to the deoful and these eald gods buccmaster and these aelfs and dweorgs they is deofuls worcan wicce craeft to tac folc from god to the deoful in hel

ha i saes ha well here we is anglisc men in an anglisc wud talcan lic our guttas is gan and it colde be they has for thu does not cnaw what thu is or from where thu is cum. this is scit spoc by preosts and cyngs spoc by all those who wolde put them selfs abuf us and tac our land and our sawols

sawols saes the gleoman our sawols wolde thy tac

lysten gleoman i saes lysten the eald gods they is land they is erce they is heofon and fyr and they is us folcs. these new gods they is ingengas this crist he is god of man he walcs lic a man he cums to tac our land and raise men up abuf the land and beorn it blaec. lysten i has been to the hus of the eald gods i has swam down my eages was open i seen it i seen them and lysten i seen the fugol what cum to warn us of this ingenga geeyome none wolde lysten none lysten to the eald and the words

and this i saes tacan my sweord and holdan it ofer the fyr this is the sweord of weland the smith

ah now saes the gleoman now here is a tale to be telt for sure

we has all hierde this tale saes grimcell

great weland saes tofe

well let me tell thu another and better i saes for weland the smith he cum to my grandfather one night in the holt near our ham grimcell thu cnaw this and he saes to my grandfather i has ceosan thu and thy cynn for great things and this sweord now i gifs thu to do these great things with so tac it my son and lead men

ah saes the gleoman is this what he saed buccmaster is this why thy power is now so great

gleoman i will haf thy guttas lic i has had the guttas of the gerefa

o saes the gleoman then i will still my tunge

was this a triewe thing saes tofe to me whose eages is now big

i does not spec of things what is not triewe cilde

welands sweord saes the cilde locan at my blaed in sum awe

and it was weland this daeg cwelled that gerefa i saes for i felt him mofan through me this is what he macd his

sweord for this feoht for angland for anglisc folc for the
eald hus for the eald times agan the ingenga

well let us hope it is a strong sweord saes the gleoman
for there is many mor frenc ones

it was at this time that we all hierde the sound of men
cuman through the holt near us. it was not fox not boar
it was men and we all stood as cwic as we colde though in
triewth sum of us was not good now on our feet though
not me i was strong. i toc my sweord and it was good that
i did for two men cum through the treows then and with
scramasaxes they stood before us

cum to tac a lif has thu i saes to them cum to get
wergild for thy esol gerefa well cum then lytel frenc hund
boys cum and tac what thu can

for a time these two men loccd at us saen naht. one
was a tall man his haer and cenep red lic a dene his nebb
thynne the other was scort and had lytel haer though he
was yonger. after a time the man with red haer spoc

we does not want blud he saes we has seen enough. i is
aelfgar this is gamel we is free men of creatas tun. we has
buried our gerefa today whose blud is on thy sweord

welands sweord saes tofe

this sweord lufs blud i saes

well we does not luf blud saes this aelfgar and his
words is strong but when blud cums to us we will stand
agan it

stand then i saes fuccan stand

not agan thu saes gamel but with thu

thu called for men saes aelfgar we is men

too many sings while frenc cwells their folcs saes gamel we has long thought so we will not sing lic our gerefa

we has been waitan for thu saes aelfgar

well for sum time there is naht saed. in triewth the ealu has slowed my tunge a lytel though of course i is still cwic. it is grimcell who specs first

gif us thy scramasaxes he saes let us see that thu has no mor waepens we will not sitt by the fyr with thu and be tacan from behind

thu will not saes aelfgar thu may tac them and he and this gamel they puts their scramasaxes on to the ground before us. grimcell he gan to them to see they has no other things but it seems they does not

well i saes well if thu is triewe thu is wel cum and if thu is not triewe thu is dead

at this aelfgar he seems ired

thu wolde cnaw if we is triewe he saes well let me asc thu man how many frenc thu has feoht

we has cwelled one saes tofe cwic before i can spec and he was a thegn

one saes this aelfgar thu has cwelled one. well thu sceolde cnaw that gamel and me we has cwelled mor frenc than there is in angland for on sanlac in the south lands we feoht with harald cyng agan the bastard

well this was sum thing and when we hierde this we telt these men to sitt by the fyr with us and drinc ealu and tell us of this great thing for these was men who moste be loccd at as men

   sanlac saes tofe sanlac then thu is great men

   great men saes grimcell

we is not saes gamel we is men only and we is lifan when many is gan

   tell us i saes

aelfgar then he sighs and he saes i has spoc so micel of sanlac that i feels i was not efen born before this daeg. loc i can not tell of it all again at this time not here to spec of it cwells my heorte

   this is triewe specan saes the gleoman for micel has i hierde of the sorness of this daeg

   i will sae only that it colde haf been ours that daeg saes aelfgar. these frenc thu hieres them sae that the daeg was theirs for they is great folcs with great hors well this is scit they was almost gan. we feoht when the sunne cum up in the mergen and all daeg we stood our ground on the hyll and soon it wolde haf been night and if we had held we wolde haf drifen the bastard baec to the sea in the deorc. we was almost there we colde see the deorc cuman ofer the waters but then the cyng fell and all was gan

   we colde haf toc them early also saes gamel for in the mergen we stood on the hyll the fyrd all along the rycg and behind us the huscarls with great axes and behind them the cyng and his brothors and his flag of the golden wyrm on the wind oh it was a sight. the frenc they cum up to the foot of the hyll in the mergen but they stopped

for sum time afeart of us for we was callan and singan
wafan sweords and axes and sithes we was castan roccs
down at them and scotan straels and callan out out out
out and they was afeart and they wolde not cum up

afeart they was saes aelfgar and then our harald cyng
he cum up to the front of us all on his hwit hors in his
golden scirt and with his flag of the golden wyrm and on
his heafod the most cyngly helm thu has seen with boars
ofer his eages and the raefn and wulf on his nebb and he
riden down the line with sweord in hand callan us to
feoht for great angland agan the ingenga and then he
stood before the line and he loccd down to these frenc
who had cum to his cyngdom and he called to them

what did he call saes tofe what

he saed cum then bastard and do thy will and thu will
brec on the strands of angland lic the weacest waef in the
sea

these is sum words i saes

harald was sum man saes aelfgar a great man a great
cyng the greatest since aethelstan and had he lifd now all
wolde be sweet in this land all wolde be well for our folcs

but now we is thralls saes grimcell thralls

and we colde haf toc them early saes gamel and not
been thralls for the frenc begun to cum up the dun they
sent men to scot straels at us and then they sent these
cnihts on hors for the frenc they feohts on hors lic wifmen not on foot lic men well they sent these cnihts on
hors with speres thincan they wolde mac us run but we

held the line and we toc many of these hors down with speres and axes all the time callan out out out and they fell baec the hors fell baec for they was afeart

it is triewe they was afeart saes aelfgar we seen it for we stood together in that fyrd and we seen their eages

and they ran saes gamel they ran these hors half the frenc fyrd they teorned and we ran also we gan down the dun after them we gan down to run them in to the sea and we wolde haf done so but for the cyng

it was not the cyng saes aelfgar scarp

he sceolde haf sent all his men saes gamel all of us then down the hyll we wolde haf run them all in to the sea

we wolde all haf been cut down saes aelfgar lic so many was

who was cut down saes grimcell

half the fyrd saes gamel we ran down after the frenc and many fell and we was thincan all the men and harald cyng was cuman too but they stood on the hyll

and then we seen him saes aelfgar we seen him call them to stand

seen who i saes

the bastard saes gamel the bastard on his hors

the cyng saes tofe

he is no fuccan cyng

how does he loc saes tofe how does he seem

he seems lic a deoful saes gamel. he is a great man tall and wide and he wears a helm lic that of harald cyng but when he seen his men flee lic wifmen he tacs off his helm and he calls to them he calls in his frenc tunge so i can not sae what his words was but they was yfel words i seen his nebb

thu seen his nebb

set lic style it is with no haer on it he is a strong man there is no luf in him

and what gan on

what gan on saes gamel well all cnawan what gan on the frenc hors they cum baec at his words they teorned and they cut us down. i was cut and i laid there my scancs was half gan now i can not run nor walc with ease

sum of us ran baec to the ricg saes aelfgar but most was cut down and that was half of the fyrd gan and the frenc now they seemed lic they had found their heorte

we colde haf tacan them if the cyng had mofd saes gamel locan in to the fyr

do not spec this way of the cyng

we colde haf cwelled the bastard then and all of his deofuls and wo did not and now we will be thralls for efer

not for efer i saes we will drif them from our land

all then locs at the fyr and there is no mor words for sum time. grimcell tacs the scramasaxes of these men and gifs them ofer and with no words they tacs them and puts them in their belts on a great dun a hwit stag runs the dun is high higher than all things abuf it only heofon under it all the clouds that stands abuf the eorth and all around it the sound of great hwit eas foaman ofer clifs that falls down down into the blaec of the world

on the dun the hwit stag stands and a cilde cums to this stag at the top of this dun and he locs in to its eages and the stag locs in to his

then the cilde he reacces out and he tacs the stag by its horns what is macd of gold and its heafod mofs in a small way and he specs the cilde he specs to the stag on the great high dun by the clouds and the hwit ea what is fallan down for efer into the blaec places of the eorth

when will i be free saes the cilde to the stag

and the stag saes thu will nefer be free

then when will angland be free

angland will nefer be free

then what can be done

naht can be done

then how moste i lif

thu moste be triewe that is all there is

be triewe

be triewe

the winter was longer than any winter there has efer been and deoper. we gan baec to the hus we had macd in the holt and this we macd warm gathran wud and cepan it in the hus cepan the fyrs high cwellan brocs and foxes for mete and for hydes. the foda we toc from creatas tun was gan soon and we toc to sendan tofe out for mor he wolde go to hams around the holt and loc for what colde be tacan for we thought that mor feohtan with anglisc folcs was not to be sought. sum times he cum baec with melu with baerlic or with smocd mete sum times with aeppels once efen with a sceop what he had toc from a barn and there was micel specan among us of whether this was right but it was cold cold that winter and wool and mete was dear to us

   all the time we was also secan frenc folcs to cwell and drif from this scir for now we was grene men triewe and growan in strength. ofer that winter we cwelled six frenc men we toc them from roads where they walced and from hams where they worcced we held them and we slit them and cut them all ofer and we spoc to them as they bled dyan on the ground we spoc to them of angland and its ways of our land and its folc of how they was fuccan hunds hunds and how their ingenga deoful folc wolde be sent to hel. it colde not be cnawan if they hierde us for they spac not our tunge but we telt them we telt them of their synns. when they was gan we toc from them clothes and any foda and gold they had and their bodigs we wolde leaf nacod in the straet or hangan from treows if we had line to sae to all frenc folcs go and to all anglisc rise

aelfgar and gamel was soon seen to be triewe for they was strong in cwellan and toc frenc lifs lic wihts in ire sum fyr beorned in them and tofe and grimcell they was lit by it. all this time i was leadan these men with my sweord by me always and they was locan up to me as their ealdor yes it was all in their eages in these times we was thincan we colde do all things efen tac the bastard himself from his fatt frenc hors and cut his fuccan throta lic a sceop

at this time all hams near the brunnesweald cum to hiere of us of the grene men in the holt and sum folcs wolde cum locan for us to spec or loc or tell us of where frenc was and how we colde tac them and cildren wolde cum to see these great feohtan men of the wuds. well tofe he lufd this and was macd great by it his heafod growan and growan and sum times i wolde need to tac him down from the heofon he had gan to. well i was hopan many folcs wolde cum to feoht with us but in that time only one mor man cum and in triewth it wolde be better if he had not for this man was dumb. a great tall man and wide and strong he was but of dumb ways he colde not spec lic other folcs and seemed to spec to the ground mor than he spoc to men

this man cum to us saen he was a man of the holt and lifd lic the treows and was scunned in his ham and he wolde feoht with us. in the mergen he wolde rise from by the fyr where we slept and gan to the holt and cum baec his nebb all blaec with aesc or eorth and sae i is of the holt and he wolde sae no mor for the daeg. his nama he telt us was was wluncus though i has nefer hierde an anglisc nama lic this it was as dumb as the man what held it

so we was six now six and the gleoman but the gleo-man did not stae when the cold began to cum he gan walcan again as gleoman does to places he colde get foda and ealu and warm fyrs and fuccan for his tales. he telt us he wolde cum baec in sum months when he cum through again and bring us tidans from other parts of angland but i did not thinc he wolde cum again and in triewth i was hopan not for this man was smercan all the time he was not a grene man he was not triewe

but he did cum baec and though i was not blithe it seemed grimcell was for him and this ulf they was fre-onds of old and this telt me that grimcell was a man who did not cnaw men and i seen again why i was ceosan. but in the winter on a cold daeg when our fyrs was high and wluncus was locan out for frenc men his nebb all blaec with fyr aesc muttran to the fugols the gleoman cum in to our part of the holt raisan his hand in gretan and bringan ealu. he cum from a place wluncus was not locan and this esol did not efen see so if he had been frenc we wolde haf been cwelled and i telt wluncus this in sum ire and he ran off then to the holt lic a cilde wepan triewely he was a fuccan dumb man

but the gleoman he brought ealu and so we macd the fyr high and we satt then and dranc for we had drunc no ealu in wices and the gleoman he telt us of what he had seen in angland. he telt us not lic a gleoman ridlan but lic a man specan and we lystened for his tales was blaec. the frenc he saed was in all places now and they was locan to see what they colde get from all anglisc men. they had raised geld in all places and they was macan men gif geld for all free things what had been their rights. geeyome the bastard he had macd a law gifen all the land in angland to him and nefer had there been succ a great synn done and micel of this land he had gifen to his frenc brothors and freonds and the scuccas what cum with him to cwell our great cyng at sanlac and now they was macan their new thralls bow to them

blaec these tales was for sure. tales of frenc men tacan the ceaps from tuns and hams and puttan them in their castels and tacan geld for efry small thing sold at them. tales of hams torn down to build these castels and of anglisc men macd thralls to mac them lic esols or oxen. tales of men gifan geld to walc their swine in their own

224

holt or to plough their own feld. many wifmen there was in angland now with no husbonds for they had been cwelled feohtan and these wifmen they had their husbonds land for this is the way of things in angland but frenc men was tacan these wifmen and weddan them at point of sweord so this land wolde be theirs in law. mynsters saed the gleoman was fillan all ofer angland with wifmen runnan from this deorc thing

   and men all ofer was bean thralld. all ofer the scir of lincylene saed the gleoman socmen who was free men who was the freest men in angland was hafan their land toc and bean macd to worc on it for the new frenc thegns lic thralls and this was puttan them in ire and in great deop sadness. one tale the gleoman telt of us a socman he cnawan well from a ham in the north who was a strong and good man worcan always for his folc but the frenc cum they toc his land and they macd him worc lic a gebur for his new lord. they toc his great hus what he had macd and macd him sleep in the byr with the oxen and this man he colde do naht and wolde be a thrall for efer. his yonge cilde a yonge son he died in the cold of the winter slepan in this byr and this man he colde tac no mor and his wifman cum in to the stincan byr one daeg and he was hangan from the beam lic a sacc of baerlic

   there was a great stillness after we had hierde these tales and triewely it was good that we had ealu. for this to cum to socmen of my scir this was a thing what macd my blud rise in my heafod it macd me tac my sweord in my hand there wolde be blud there moste be blud. then aelfgar he spac

what is being done gleoman he saed what is anglisc folc doan

well saes the gleoman they is doan many things thu cnawan does thu not what they is doan. sum is in the ground sum still on it rottan in the regn sum is gan from this land gan east of rome where they feohts in the fyrds of ingenga cyngs and dreams of angland. sum is gan north to the land of the scots where malcolm cyng bids them wel cum as free folc. sum stays in their ham and in their hus and macs best of what is gifen to them by their wyrd. then there is them what has ceosan neither to stay nor leaf but who is gan to fenn and holt and becum grene lic the leafs and the grass who lifs lic the fox and the wulf who is wilde lic the hafoc and the crow with teeth what tears from the enemi small bite and small bite and small bite until all the mete is gan

this is us saes tofe

these grene men saes the gleoman at first they was a small thing but now there is mor of them and great men of angland is specan as they spec. there is two anglisc eorls only left in this land they is edwin and morcar of northanhymbre and mierce and these eorls they is specan in stillness now of raisan a fyrd agan the ingenga

a fyrd saes tofe a triewe anglisc fyrd again

what men has they saes grimcell all their folcs was cwelled by hardrada they has scots men it is saed saes the gleoman for malcolm he thincs that the bastard will not stop at angland and they may haf denes cuman in scips for sweyn cyng of the north folcs locs also at angland with ire and fear. and many anglisc now wolde feoht with them there is men in holts all ofer angland waitan for a call to rise agan the frenc

there is sum stillness again then only the sound of men drencan

a great fyrd saes tofe a great fyrd again i wolde die for this i wolde die

tofe cilde saes aelfgar tell us why was thu not in the fyrd that gan to sanlac or to eorfic the fyrd what harald cyng called

they wolde not tac me saes tofe they was saen i was only a cilde though many in my ham gan what was not so micel ealdor

and thu buccmaster and thu grimcell saes aelfgar

i gan saes grimcell i gan in the first fyrd i gan north but harald he gan so fast that we did not get to eorfic before he had cwelled all the denes and we cum baec

and thu saes aelfgar to me thu and thy great sweord

well i was wantan to go i saes i was cene sore cene to go and to tac on the frenc but it was saed by our gerefa that i was a great man of the ham and was needed there for the wapentac for i was a socman with three oxgangs. but i sent my sons my two sons strong men they was and they gan to feoht for their cyng harald with my luf and

227

they nefer cum baec and there is not a daeg i does not thinc i sceolde haf gan with them and fought for angland no not a daeg

ah saes gamel if mor men had cum if the cyng had waited longer in lundun for mor men to cum from all ofer angland we colde haf tacan a fyrd bigger than any efer in angland and cwelled efry frenc man on that dun but the cyng he wolde run on fyr he was after tacan down hardrada it was saed he was thincan he was a god

it is gan now saes aelfgar it is gan gamel

we walced lic we wolde nefer stop saes gamel we walced lic hors all daeg and micel of the night. harald he had cum upon the landwaster when his men was slepan and he wolde do the same to the bastard but the bastard was ready he had men on hors locan all ofer and he seen harald and it was the anglisc who was tacan when not locan

harald saes tofe harald tacan that way

we cum on the bastard in the wrong place saes gamel there was a dun we seen it was the only dun near and we moste get to the top of it for the cyng wolde feoht with his huscarls and a dun was good for this so we gan to this dun what was named sanlac. on the top of this hyll was a small aeppel treow all alone it was and the cyng put his flag by this treow and we gathrd we macd a line but it was too lytel

the treow

the dun it was too lytel all men colde not hardly stand

on it we was so near we colde not mof it was wrong from the start we colde feel it was wrong

but thu colde haf tacan them saes tofe thu saed it

we colde haf we colde haf but we did not and on the dun they cept cuman and hard it was to cepe the line men was cwelled in the line and colde not efen fall to the ground so near was we all to eacc other dead men was standan

that is a hard thing saes grimcell

ah it is all a fuccan hard thing ses gamel all of it loc here we is sittan in the fuccan holt lic hunds all of angland is a blaec land now. so we has cwelled sum small frenc folcs in these past wices but the frenc will not efen see this we is fuccan gan we is gan from the eorth

this is not triewe i saes not triewe and we will not spec lic this here

o will we not saes gamel is this triewe buccmaster and who will sae how i will spec

thu will not sae these things i saes not here these is cildes words

thu will not stop me from specan any way i wolde spec saes gamel and there is fyr in him and i seen i will need to put it out

the frenc saes the gleoman cuman in to cwell the fyr the frenc they sees it well

how saes tofe

the frenc all ofer cnaws of grene men and is afeart saes the gleoman it is saed the bastard himself cnawan of the risans agan him and in these parts word is with the frenc of grene men in the brunnesweald

word of us saes tofe the frenc fears us they fears us

thu and others saes the gleoman

others i saes what others

there is other grene men in these parts saes the gleoman efen in this holt

there is hereweard of course saes aelfgar

we has not hierde micel of this fuccan hereweard for a time i saes not for sum time while we has been cwellan frenc what has he been doan this fuccan god

gathran men saes the gleoman he has near fiftig now they saes

all of them hunds and wihts i saes

has thu seen him saes aelfgar to the gleoman

no saes the gleoman and he is locan at me all this time no i has not seen him but he is near


*i is walcan through a beorg a grene beorg all light and grene sceadu walcan walcan though it seems not mofan yet sean sum thing cum nearer slow slow. what is this it stands on two scancs lic a man but is horned horned on its heafod grene light behind it i can not see it mofs it cums to me i can not see*

*all in this place is small things flittan flittan lic the bats through the cuman dusc steppan it seems steppan in hwit and grene small and thynne around this man who is cuman still to me grene and leafd horned and tall reaccan out to me specan now specan in the beorg of light specan my nama and all that i has seen and been is in this grene now and this light is all i is all i is i is i is*

as winter cum to spring as the holt gan from blaec to grene as the treows breathed again the buds cum up the ground sighed the fugols cum and sang as lif cum baec to the land lif was in me for i seen now where my wyrd wolde tac me. i seen now that i had been gifen deorc daegs deorc times lic the cyngs of old lic the gods them selfs lic great weland lic my grandfather and this thing i had cum through and strong now i was strong and ready for all the ingenga colde gif me

it was the gleoman had telt us about the castel at stan ford though we hierde it also later from other folcs in ham and holt. it was saed that the frenc was macan a castel in a ham to the south at the stan ford tun where they wolde put cnihts to loc down on the folc of the fenns and of the brunnesweald. tofe saed they done this for us for they cnawan of our feohtan and of our worc and our strength

well we talcd of this and of what sceolde be done and it was not long before we cum to spec of tacan it. all of us i sceolde sae cum to spec of this at once there was no man thincan other and this time now that i locs baec i sees that this time was when we was a werod triewe and no time wolde there be again lic this. for we had cwelled frenc men and now they was macan castles near to the brunnesweald and it was lic they had wafd a sweord at us and saed anglic folc anglisc men of the holt what will thu do

so we gan out and we gan south to find stan ford and to see this castel and what we colde do. the six of us gan and the gleoman saed he wolde cum for he had folcs to see on the straet and he colde tac us to earninga straet what wolde lead us to the tun. earninga straet was one of the eald roads macd in the times efen before the wealsc cum to angland. in many places it locd lic any other straet macd by men that is to say of eorth sincan in the regn and ricgd in the sunne but there was other places where it colde be seen what was under it and the straet was flat stan with stan dices for water to run in to and the straet was wide and long and straight tearan through the wuds ofer hangd with treows lic it was macd for ents to walc down in times before men

on a great straet lic this thu wolde pass many folcs for it gan down they saed right to lundun and up also to northern places. this was the straet what harald cyng toc to go north and cwell hardrada and it was the straet now what the bastard and his men toc to sec out anglisc who stood agan them and gif them blud. in the winter the bastard it was saed had cum baec from his frenc lands and toc angland again in his hands and he had seen that his biscop brothor odo had fuccd and cwelled the lands so bad that many mor anglisc was risan agan the frenc

and if the bastard will gif any thing to a biscop i saes this
is what he will get

but we cum on many folcs as we gan down this straet
the six of us we seen hors and we seen wagns we seen
folcs on foot alone and in gangs we seen ox and hunds
and sum times efen we seen frenc. when we seen frenc on
the straet always on hors of course sum was afeart though
not i. naht was done for in triewth none colde tell us
from ham folcs or tincers or beorners and since frenc did
not cnaw for sure what was done in these parts then
grene men colde smile and waef at them as they gan by
and they wolde not cnaw we was thincan of coccan their
beallucs ofer the fyr

in the holt time mofs in ways not lic those in the hams
but still it colde be seen that the world was teornan to
the light for the treows was buddan grene and the blosms
was cuman up on the ground. we gan down the straet
for it colde be three or four daegs and we gan by hams in
this time what was doan all the things of the month of
thrimilci when the cow is milcd three times in a daeg. we
seen dices bean dug and madder and flax bean sown and
harrowan bean done and all of this macd me thinc again
of my land and efry time a spere gan in to my heorte

sum there is who mofs and sum who stays it now
seems to me and i was one who stayed. i had my land i
cnawan my ham and my folcs i was a great man there i
had growan from that eorth lic a treow and then lic a
treow i was tacan up by the roots and cast on hard

ground. sum there is who wolde be cast all ofer sum who mofs lic the gleoman from place to place sum lic my dunstan who dremed of ingenga lands sum lic beorners or out laws who macs mofan their place but i was not one for i had seen what mofan was and mofan is sorness mofan is fear. stayan is right stayan where the gods has put thu if all folcs wolde stay then all things wolde be in their right place i telt this to my father

it was the third daeg of walcan down this straet and we was nearan stan ford. efry night we slept in the holt sum way from the straet and on this mergen when we woc the gleoman saes he wolde tac us to a ham what was near. we was needan foda and sum other small things and he telt us he cnawan of a ham what wolde gif wel cum to grene men for this ham was agan the bastard and all the frenc

can thu feel in the heofon what has cum this daeg saes the gleoman as we gan through the grenan holt

in the heofon i saes

it is litha he saes it is the first daeg of litha

litha saes the men litha this is good

will there be maedens in grene saes aelfgar in this ham

maedens with blosms saes gamel

maedens saes tofe

all ofer angland all ofer this world the cuman of litha is a thing to be sang for and sang to. this grene daeg is the byrth of the sumor and the beginnan of all the wundors that erce brings to folcs when the frost is gan when the daegs is bright when the ground is breathan and in its breath is the warmth of what is new

in our ham on the first daeg of litha there wolde be micel singan steppan drencan and lufan in the holts and the felds and for me this was both a swete thing and a deorc one. my grandfather had telt me about the eald ways of biddan the sumor wel cum in the times of the eald gods and the first folcs and sean what folcs done now i colde see micel of this still. i colde see the feccan of the grene in to the ham and the macan of the pal from a great treow what wolde be brought to the ham and folcs wolde sing by this. all of this had cum from the words of the eald gods from the luf of treow and holt what our eald folcs had but now it was a game only and a game what was locd ofer by the preost who wolde bring his bocc and bury the eald grene ways with the ingenga words of the crist

still it was litha and litha is grene and warm and for us men what had been in deorc wuds wet and cold and with deorc heortes for this long winter it was a thing to feel good for. we gan with the gleoman to where he toc us and we gan slow for we had been so long in the holt and was so wary of frenc and of anglisc who seen us as hunds or things to be feart that we did not thinc this ham wolde be as blithe to haf us cum as this gleoman had saed. but this time this last time the gleoman telt a truth for what we had when we cum to this ham is sum thing i will haf with me always we had gan away from the straet and down a path in to the holt. here the holt was light for it was worcd wud and swine wud so there was sum great acs and aesc treows but many mor small thynne haesels and lyms what was cut and growan again lic lines up to the heofon. many wyrmfleages was flutteran around and fugols was singan high and the sunne was cuman through the grene treows whose leafs was yonge and light there was sound all around and the holt smelt clene lic the lif of this land in the times before men. all of us was walcan lic it was a new year lic we was cum again in to this world

we cum to the ham after an hour on this traec it was a small place in a lea in the holt. eight or nine thaccd hus satt around a place where there was a cross of wud for the crist and his folc had been here efen here to the deops of this eald holt. there was small places cut in to the ground where holt had been and many swine mofan about free. hunds was sittan in the sunne and folcs was doan as folcs does. near to the ham there was an ea it colde be hierde runnan through the treows and wifmen was down there talcan as they talcs ofer and ofer. all of this smelt of smoc and the cuman grene

when the folcs here seen us cuman it was not lic in sum other hams where they gan still or mofd away no here they cum to us in blitheness. sean the gleoman then locan at us all blaec with aesc and the stenc of the holt and they seen what we was and was smercan at us when they cum. a gang of maedens cum mor lic yonge wifmen than maedens they was of beuty and good sceap and carryan leafs carryan the grene they cum to us and withigs they put around all of our throtas from the gleoman to tofe and i and efen to dumb wluncus withigs of grene of the leafs of the holt of litha

grene withigs for grene men they saes for sumor is in angland and angland will be again in sumor

these maedens is laughan and smercan at us and my men is laughan and smercan at them on account of hafan been lifan in the holt far from wifmen for too long they is weac they has not the strength what cums from the heorte. then we sees through them cuman a man not too old not too yonge but who seems strong. it is clere he is the gerefa here and that he is triewe not lic most

who is leaden these men he saes

i is buccmaster of holland i saes these is my men what of it

well buccmaster of holland he saes i is wulfhere who is called wulf i is gerefa of this ham and thu is bid wel cum here as men of angland as free men. this is a ham of free folcs we has not had sight of frenc yet for we is small and apart and we is still and this is how we will cepe it. but all here lufs freodom and stands agan the ingenga and we is blithe now that thu has cum to us for thu is the men who will mac us free again. now cum eat drenc plege with us for it is the first daeg of litha and lif is cum again to the land

i locs on this daeg now in the small ham in the brunnesweald as the last daeg that was good in all of my lif. it was the last daeg also when our men was free it was the last daeg that we was yonge lic cildren in the grene land before we was tacan to another place before what i was and what i was to do was gifen to me clere. long it was now since i had gan down to the treows under the mere but it was only now that their triewth cum to me in the light of the new time

it was a daeg of wundor and all folcs around us it seemed was triewe for these was the last good folcs in angland. if all folcs in all hams had been lic this there wolde haf been no frenc we wolde haf been full again but this is not the world it is not the world of men

in this small world though in this holt on that daeg all was good. the yonge wifmen we had seen gan off in to the holt gathran the grene and bringan it baec to the ham. yonge men wolde mac to go with them but they wolde scuf them away lic in plege and they wolde go gathran while the yonge men sat in the ham. then they wolde cum baec from the holt and bring with them all the leafs and blosms of the grene world and they wolde mac a great game of gifen them around

they wolde walc these yonge wifmen up and around the yonge men and loc at them all the time smercan and specan low lic they was locan ofer them deop. sum of these yonge men was smercan also and laughan but sum was almost locan afeart. then these girls they wolde gif the grene to efry yonge man and what they gifen wolde haf meanan that wolde be the ordeal of holt and ham upon them

to one man they wolde gif a nettle and this wolde mean he was a stunt and other men wolde laugh and laugh at this and he wolde loc ired. to another yonge man then they wolde gif the blosm of the blaec thorn and this wolde lead to much smercan and whistlan for this man was faford by the girl who had gifen it. another yonge man wolde be gifen the rowan for freondscip and then another the alor for his loose tunge. all yonge men in the ham was gifen sum grene thing to marc his place there while the ealdor men and wifmen locd on laughan

well we was standan locan on at this when one yonge wifman who was not of great beuty but seemed good and triewe she cum up to us and smercan she gaf to tofe a stocc of the blaec thorn what is also cnawan as sloe. sean this sum yonge men of the ham whistled and smercd though others locd sore. amongst my men there was micel smercan then and gamel hit tofe on the baec and saed it is time cilde for thu to becum a man now and tofe gan red lic the haw thorn in blotmonth

after this the yonge wifmen gan ofer to a waegn what was by the cross of wud and this they began to bury in grene leafs and in blosms. the yonge men gan off to the holt together and we gan with the gerefa and sat in the ham on bences where his wifman gaf us ealu and hunig cicels and we was eatan and drencan in the sunne and all the world then only for that small time was in stillness and beuty and efen in my heorte all was still

we spac to wulf the gerefa then and i telt him of what we had been and done and i telt him of the many frenc we had cwelled of our great strength and of the luf we had been gifen by all anglisc folcs. i did not tell him about cwellan the gerefa at creatas tun for there was no need to bring in small things on a great daeg. i gaf him also my sweord welands sweord to loc on and he locd on it with awe as all triewe men does and then he seen what cynd of man i was i still is efen here efen now without my sweord without naht

sum time later as we was still eatan and talcan the yonge men cum baec and with them they was draggan the litha pal. they had gan and cut down a tall treow an ac what was yonge yet strong and they had cut off all side scots and brought now the stocc in to the ham. micel callan and singan was there as folcs seen them and sum of the ealdor men gan to help then as they toc the pal to the place where the cross was where a hole had been macd in the eorth. the men then they tied lines to the pal near the corona and steered the pal in to the hole and stood it up and glad my heorte was when i seen how micel higher than the cross it stood. the lines was pegged out then so the pal did not fall and the yonge wifmen who had done macan the grene waegn cum ofer and begun tyan blosms and leafs to the pal also

oh i can sae these words and try to tell what it was lic there but naht can gif to thu what was in my heorte as i seen all of this cuman in to place. sum folcs who is dumb thincs the world is only what can be seen and smelt and hierde but men who cnawan the world cnawan there is a sceat a sceat of light that is betweon this world and others and that sum times and in sum places this sceat is thynne and can be seen through. on this daeg in this ham the sceat was thynne and scriffran in the light wind and through it i colde see all that the world triewely was beyond this small place of small men and deorc and strong and of great beuty and fear was what i saw

the pal reacced up to the heofon and grew grener as the yonge wifmen worccd on it and all stood locan on and a stillness cum down on this ham what had been so loud and we all loccd on at these yonge wifmen tyan the leafs and blosms to the pal and slow slow grew up a great treow and it reaccd to the heofon it called up it saed cum for we is in need in these grene daegs and through this pal then cum sum thing what i colde feel so strong that i colde almost see it climban up the pal up the stocc of this new treow. sum thing from erce sum strength it was climban climban up from the ground and it gan up the pal and from the corona it spread out in to the heofon abuf this small ham abuf us abuf me and i colde see all the hues of its cuman

oh it was the last daeg of the world

*he specs my nama the horned man he cums to me now in the*
*beorg of light the light is behind i sees only his scap he cums*
*near and now he specs again buccmaster he saes and dim*
*now i sees dim i sees his nebb grim it is and he saes the treow*
*buccmaster the treow waits for thu and when we is ready thu*
*will hang*

the eald grene game went on in that ham all of the daeg
after noon. the yonge men and wifmen stepped around
the pal singan and plegen then the ealdors did so while
the yonge rested. the waegn what was now grene with lif
was tacan around the ham with men and wifmen leapan
on and off and the wifs wolde throw blosms at folcs as
the waegn was drawn not by hors or by ox but by yonge
men laughan and mofan slow. there was drencan and
there was folcs plegen harp and pipe and singan the litha
songs. sum of these songs is songs of the circe thancan
the crist for the gift of sumor but most is ealdor songs of
the time before his cuman

by the time the deorc began cuman in all was blithe in
this ham. my men we had droncan micel and eaten also.
there was good swine mete and baerlic loafs there was
cicels and broth and micel good ealu and there was efen
ciseraeppels what had been cept for this daeg. after a
winter in the holt it was lic lifan again and we ate lic
wihts that daeg lic wihts of the holt after the snow

cum the efen the litha fyr was macd great and high in

242

a place on the ecg of the holt by the ham and my men we satt there with wulf and folcs from the ham. the gleoman was away specan rott and raedels to yonge folcs for the luf and the gold they wolde gif him and tofe also was gan. aelfgar saed he seen him gan to the holt with the yonge wifman who had gifen him the blosm and we was all laughan at this and talcan of him wieldan a sweord at last lic he had spoc of for so long. all was well and blithe and my heorte was still lic the heofon on that night

we spac all of us for micel of that night we spac full of ealu and mete as the gerefas wifman filled our cups and plates. we spac of the felds and what was growan in them we spac of this ham and others we spac of litha and luf and of what we was and wolde be. most of all we spac of angland and of the frenc

so buccmaster saes wulf the gerefa tell me triewe can we drif the frenc out

thu has seen my sweord i saes we can send them baec to the sea

ah we can not saes grimcell who is druncen

what is this saes gamel then why feoht why not stay in thy hus

i has no hus the frenc beorned it

as they beorned mine i saes so we will beorn them

i will beorn them saes grimcell specan slow beorn and hang and gutt them lic fisc i will do this all my lif but we will not mac them leaf now their grip is too tight on anglands throta we will cut their fuccan arms off then saes gamel and sum men from the ham roars to hiere this

we sees no frenc here saes wulf but the tales cum with this gleoman and with others and they gifs us micel sadness of heorte. but what can we do so small agan this

i thinc we moste wait for the crist saes another man from the ham he has thrown us down for our synn he will raise us up when we is triewe. i is drincan ealu at this point and nearly spits it all ofer this esol

feohtan saes gamel and he sounds strong feohtan is all there is now there is naht else. they cums to bring war to us we moste gif them war this is the way of things. i will not lie down and be fucced lic a wifman

yes i saes gamel is right all of the world is blud this is the way of things it is the way of the holt the way of the hafoc and the craw the way of all wihts and of men. gif blud or tac blud there is naht else

for sum time then there is naht saed. we all locs on in to the fyr locan at the sceaps in the flames hearan the spittan the breathan and eatan in the blaec what ringed us around the light

i fear for angland saes wulf then. this daeg i was locan on at our litha games and i was thincan that we may be the last of our folcs. i was thincan that it colde be a folc is lic a weddan. there is a cuman together what is triewe and deop there is sum time what is good and strong when all worcs well and all seems it will worc well for efer and then there is a fallan awaeg and an endan. things is fast and cene then they is slow and dull and then they is broc and no man or wifman can do naht for this is the way of things in this world. well it colde be it is the way of things for folcs to do this also and it colde be it is the time for anglisc folc to fall awaeg and if it is the will of erce then what can man do

thu specs of erce i saes. wulf then locs a lytel small

i specs with ealu in me he saes

no man i saes no thu is right to sae this thu is right to spec of erce for if mor men did so the frenc wolde not haf cum. i has hierde all these folcs saen the crist has sent these frenc hunds for not lufan him triewe but i thincs what if the bastard has been sent by others for lufan the crist too triewe

again there is a small stillness and then wulf specs again

thu is specan of the eald hus he saes

yes i saes yes man

well he saes there is not so many folcs lic thu in angland no mor. i locs about the fyr and i sees sum men of the ham locan at me sum lic in fear others in wundor others only locan with no cnawan what they is thincan

buccmasters eald gods saes grimcell lifs under a mere well when is they cuman up this is what i wolde cnaw

they is not cuman up as men i saes but in men

in men

in other men

in thu saes grimcell

in me in thu if thu wolde haf it but thu smercs and talcs druncen scit grimcell when thu sceolde be triewe to the gods of this land and this place and thy folc

the eald gods saes wulf i was telt a lytel of them when a cilde by my mothor. she wolde spec sum times of erce who was the ground and the holt and the heofon and she wolde spec also of frigg who loccd ofer wifmen at all times. my mothor cnawan all things what grow in the holt she colde spec to the wihts she was a wifman of the wicce craft. but she wolde gif it only to them who cum to her ascan for she cnawan that the preost and the thegn wolde not haf it spoc out

ah it is sceomu i saes sceomu upon angland that the eald ways is moccd. this man wulf i colde see that he was not dumb and to spec of the eald ways with an other was sweet for i had not hardly done so since my grand father was toc from me

men wolde laugh at my mothor saes wulf or mocc her in the ham but then they wolde cum to her in stillness at night to asc for her help. she wolde bind senep seeds and rue to their heafods to stop their pain or if they had hrifteung she wolde coc pic in milc and they wolde drinc it and all wolde be well. if a wyrm had bit them she wolde tac an egg and sum ealu and sum scit from a sceop and mac them drinc it though she wolde not tell them about the scit before they dranc. once i dranc sum of this and i was sicc for a wice

drincan scit well that is bad saes aelfgar laughan

yes but she was wise saes wulf and folcs wolde cum to her. she colde do other things also blaecer things but only at night and with no words saed. i seen her mac lytel poppets for folcs to harm their enemi she wolde put nails in them and the enemi wolde be in pain and none cnawan why. this was wrong i wolde always thinc for i had hierde of wifmen drencced or hanged for doan these things for the preosts wolde not haf it and the cyng wolde not neither

they is afeart i saes all afeart for the eald ways is stronger than their crist

men from the ham has been lystnan to this and saen naht but now one specs. i can not see his nebb well in the light of the fyr

this is blaec specan he saes we sceolde not spec lic this no mor

thu is a wyrm then i saes and no anglisc man

i is anglisc he saes as anglisc as thu but the eald ways is deorc and if the preost hears of this our ham will be deorc also

the preost has thy beallucs in his hands then i saes we feohts for angland we will spec as we wolde

but the eald ways the eald gods all of this is gan saes this man. it is all of the eald times the deorc times these is the times of the crist and we is his men. there is no need to spec lic this now

at this i stands from my benc by the fyr and all locs at me then and is stillness. the man who has spoc he locs lic he is ready for me if i cum at him but i does not cum at him i raises my hand and i points at the litha pal what is still standan by the cross and what can be seen dim and lit by the mofan light of the fyr lic the pal itself is mofan in the light

thu wolde sae the eald gods is gan i saes and thu wolde sae the eald ways is gan well loc at this pal loc at it higher than thy cross efen now. to thu it colde be this is only sum treow what is grene as the sumor is grene but this is the eald treow of the world what we anglisc folcs loccd up to before the crist cum

there is stillness then only the sound of the fyr and the mofan of fox and aelf in the holt

this pal that thu pleges around i saes it is the world treow what cepes the seofon worlds together by will of the eald gods. at one root of this treow is the world of the gods and at an other is the world of the dead and betweon is the worlds of men of the light aelfs and deorc aelfs of the ents and the dweorgs. the world treow the great aesc treow what ties all things it grows through all the worlds and its stics hangs ofer all the world of men

this pal i saes this pal what thu steps around this cums to thu from the eald gods. i has seen the eald gods they has spac with me they is ired for thy luf of this hwit crist for he is not a god of the ground of treow and leaf of mere and snow of sumor and all the grene lif in the land. he is a god of men only and he tells thu to loc up to the heofon not around at thy place in this land. he is an ingenga god from a land where there is no treows and no luf neither for any thing what is not man and for this great yfel the folcs of angland has been gifen the ire of the frenc. if thu wolde lif thu moste feoht and the eald gods will feoht with thu and if thu does not feoht thu will die for this is the way of things and the only way

i locs around me then and all men is stillness they is locan at me or at the pal or at the ground. i sits down again and tacs my cuppe and starts to drinc lic i has nefer saed naht but wulf then i seen he locs at me and he nods a lytel lic he is saen yes and then he stands and calls mete wifmen mete and it is lic sum thing is gan on the wind and the drincan begins lic all was aemty as a pond in the sumor heat


that night it was the last good night of the world. druncen i was a lytel only a lytel when i gan to sleep in a hus with my men and they was druncen too for the night had been long and the triewth of this good ham colde be felt all around. druncen i was a lytel but it was not the ealu what macd me see what i seen

i gan to sleep cwic but i woc sum time later and i was beornan all ofer. i satt up from the ground where i had been slepan and i seen that the straw on the ground was mofan with fleas and they had bit me all ofer. all around me other men was still slepan in the deorc fnaerettan lic swine

i colde not sleep again with this iccan it was lic fyr so i
gan up and out of the hus. the door macd a sound when
it mofd but there was no other sound but for the fnaerettan in the hus. out in the road i seen the mona was great
and hwit and sean it macd me fall to my cneows there in
the road and loc up at her and loc and loc in stillness.
when i was a yonge cilde i wolde do this to the mona i
wolde loc up at her lic a wif god i does not cnaw why
there was sum thing that brought me to her

the iccan toc me up again for i colde not stae still that
night and i colde hiere then the sound of the ea what ran
through the holt near the ham and i thought i wolde go
to it and bathe my self and cool the beornan that way. i
gan down the path past the hus of men and the hus of
swine and cicens and no sound but ules in the holt and
the small sounds of leafs and the runnan of the ea growan louder

the ea was hwit and still under the mona and i toc off
my tunece and brices and gan in and satt in the water
my scancs and arms in the water and it was good. the
beornan soon gan but when i cum out again it cum baec
so i gan in again to cool it and in this way i satt in the ea
for sum time locan up at the mona not sean how cold i
was until i colde not hardly feel my hands

well i felt at last the cold and i stood up in the ea and
then in the treows on the other strand of the ea i seen
sum thing mof

i stood there in the ea the water flowan ofer my feet

and i loccd and then i seen cum out of the treows a wulf. it was great and hwit and it was locan at me and this hwit wulf it had one eage only. on a rocc then in the ea this wulf stood locan at me and me stood in the ea half nacod locan at this wulf and naht mofd in all the night. long had i been in this brunnesweald and nefer had i seen efen one wulf though at one time we had hierde sum callan in far places. but this wulf was great and strong and locan at me for sure

and then as i stood there in the ea i seen behind this wulf a man in the treows. deorc it was in the treows on the far staed the monas light did not reac there but i seen the scap of a man with long cape and wide hat and he was stood behind the wulf and he called to him and though i did not hiere no words i hierde him call. the wulf then he locs at me and he mofs his heafod clere three times as if to say no as if to say do not

and as i stands then in the ea cold and growan colder this hwit wulf he leaps from the rocc and in to the treows and is gan and the capd man he teorns and i seen his nebb then dim but triewe and he too has one eage only and it seen me and beorned in to my deop sawol. and i cnawan then who i had seen and who had seen me and i was cold then colder than all the eas in angland colder than all the ys in the seofon worlds ah stan ford stan ford it was the last of all things

let me tell thu what i seen that daeg what was lic no other thing seen in the world. we woc in the ham sum of us with heafods what was broc apart. we ate and dranc and the gleoman telt us we sceolde go to stan ford for the castel was bean macd and soon it wolde be done and when castels was done there was no man colde tac them down. well this gleoman he seemed sore cene to get us out of the ham and to this place stan ford and it was odd as most times he cared not what we done

but i colde not thinc that mergen not after what had cum to me by the ea in the night for this was all in me and i was afeart and also thrylled. that he sceolde haf cum to me it was clere i had been ceosan and where was weland now when i was needan to spec with him. the wulf the wulf had spac to me and not any wulf but the wulf of the father of all

i colde not thinc that mergen if i colde haf thought well it colde haf been that things wolde not haf been as they was. micel things was goan on and my heafod was full and loud with what had cum to me. as we ate our foda by the mergen fyr tofe cum baec and we had not seen him since he gan to the holt in the efen with this yonge wifman and all the men sets up a roar when they sees him. he gan red and smerced a lytel as he toc loaf and ealu and all is saen to him where is the maeden cilde where did thu hide her and did thu gif it to her good tofe and how is thy litha pal cilde and run cwic now or she will haf thu wed and then it will be thu who is fuccd. tofe is locan at the ground and eatan and saen naht but he is lican it i can see

wulf cums to us then and i tells him we moste go for there is micel feohtan to be done and this daeg we is goan to tac the castel. he thancs us and he locs in to my eages then and he saes i hope our ham has gifen thu all thu needs. i is still thincan of the ea and the father of the gods it is lic i is not all here and i saes yes wulf we thancs thu for all that thu has gifen to us

the gods will go with thu he saes to me low

and with thu i saes

then louder he saes there is men from this ham wolde cum with thu and becum grene if thu wolde haf them. three men then cums to us and wulf saes this is godric siward and osbern these men is triewe and will feoht with thu. i locs at them then and they seems good men they is strong and triewe and carries scramasaxes and osbern who is a boy lic tofe he has also a good eald strong ax

thu is wel cum men i saes wel cum to the grene men we feohts for angland and agan the frenc and all who feohts with us moste be strong and triewe

we is strong and triewe saes this osbern and we will feoht all the frenc in angland and he seems to me lic tofe when he first cum yonge and cene. godric and siward they is ealdor they nods and locs at me and locan in to their eages they seems good men well then i saes well then we moste go. this ham is a good place and triewe and the gods will cepe thu. we thancs thu wulf for thy foda and ealu and for thy litha games and now we gan to tac the castel at stan ford and angland will be free again

at this men roars and wafs as we gan in to the holt. ten of us there was now with the gleoman and we walced and loccd lic a triewe fyrd with me at its heafod buccmaster of holland its ealdor and cyng my sweord on my belt and in my heorte the hwit wulf and the great ealdor of all men locan at me with his one eage beornan in to my sawol

stan ford was half a daeg through the holt we gan baec to earninga straet and gan south. my men my werod was specan light and strong and was in high sawol after our time in the litha ham. tofe was specan blithe to this osbern it was lic they was great freonds after only one mergen. gamel and grimcell and the gleoman was specan and smercan wluncus was singan to him self and to the treows and swingan his sithe and i spac a lytel with these two men siward and godric from the ham to see if they was right and they seemed to me to be triewe anglisc men

by middaeg we had cum to the tun. we gan from the straet in to the holt for many folcs was near now and who colde cnaw who was frenc and who anglisc who triewe and who a weasul. we gan to the ecg of the treows we ten men and from the grene we loccd out at the blaec

254

this was a thing lic i had nefer seen. this tun was greater than any place greater than the greatest ham in the fens and the hus and the barns and the circe here was greater also. so many hus was there in stan ford that i colde not tell and so many folcs also and so micel sound. smoc was in the heofon and folcs mofd specan and wagns and hors and ox was in the straets and there was sound in all parts the sound of specan and fyrs and the sound of wheels teornan of hors mofan the sound of the smith and the ceap

it was hard to lysten so micel sound was there. the gleoman then he telt us to go with him for he cnawan where to go in the holt to see the part of the tun what we moste see. the gleoman on this mergen he was cene it was not lic him moste times he stood baec i was wary but i toc my men for he did cnaw this place and we moste see what we colde do. the gleoman toc us then through the treows around the tun and micel time it toc for it seemed so great. mor hus we cum to and then to a circe what was not lic any circe i had efer seen. the circe in bacstune was of wud and eorth and thaecc and was small and deorc smellan of folcs and of straw and of the stencan candels of the preosts. here the circe was macd of wud and of stan and had a lytel torr and on the torr a cross of wud goan up to the heofon. it was lic the crist was in the ground it self and wolde nefer be mofd

we cept mofan past the ceap and past mor hus and it was not long before we seen the great wound what had been done to this tun. we cum through the treows round past a great hus what locd lic the hus of a thegn with a barn and a hall and then we seen it. it was lic sum wilde wiht had toc a great bite from this place and many folcs with it

what is this saes tofe in wundor what is this

it is hel saes osbern

it is the frenc saes gamel

mof slow now saes the gleoman there is many frenc here with hors and gar and sweord

what we seen was a great aemty place in the tun. we colde see that it had once been a place where folcs was lifan for we seen parts of hus and barns and halls but they had been tacan down and left flat for this was now to be sum thing what had nefer been seen in angland before and we colde see what this thing wolde be

we seen a great place of flat ground where the hus of the folcs had been and all around this was a high wall of wud and the top of this wud was scearp none colde climb it. ofer to the other side of the flat part of the tun there rose a great hyll of eorth with steps in it and up these steps climbed many folcs of the ham they was tacan things to the top of this hyll where there was was an other wall and in it was risan a great torr. locan on as the folcs worced was many frenc on hors with gars and sweords and it colde be seen they was macan these folcs worc though they was not wantan to

this is the deofuls worc saes grimcell and he specs for all

is these anglisc folcs macan this fuccan frenc castel i saes to the gleoman

they is anglisc he saes. thirtig hus was beorned by the frenc to mac the place where this castel wolde be. they has macd thralls of anglisc folcs from stan ford and macd them raise the walls and the hyll. they will mac a great torr of wud and will haf hus and halls where the anglisc hus was. in the torr they will cepe twentig of their cnihts on hors and within the walls they will haf the ceap of the tun and micel foda and hors and here they will lif and no anglisc efer will be able to mof them

thralls macs the castel to mac them selfs thralls saes gamel

and o i is ired we is all so ired so broc to see this. we has hierde of the frenc of what they done and sum of their yfel we has seen with our eages but this is a thing from an other world from a blaec place from hel itself. naht has there efer been in angland lic this naht efer in the world and standan there i feels we is lost all lost now for efer

we will tac them i saes we will tac them slit them cwell all these frenc fuccers we will beorn their fuccan torr it will beorn so high that the bastard him self will see the heofon alight with the fyr

none saes naht to this only locs on at the wound what is bledan as we locs

what will we do saes tofe

i locs on and i feels weac then standan there in the treows locan at this great synn upon our land. what will we do saes this cilde and he is right to asc but what can i sae. he locs at me ealdor of his werod ring gifer leader of these men and he saes what will we do well i is ascan the same. i is ascan my self i is ascan weland and the eald gods but i hieres naht but the sound of anglisc in thrall to frenc for efer. there is cnihts here cnihts on hors with sweords and what can we do wluncus with his sithe and two yonge boys and a man who can not walc an eald gleoman sum cottars what is we to do agan this

then the gleoman specs and in me i felt sum thing risan in my heafod i seen the hwit wulf it saed no it saed do not but i did not cnaw then what this meant i did not cnaw until it was far gan

i cnaw a hus saes the gleoman a hus what is aemty sum times it is used by the frenc for cepan things but there is no folcs there. if we go there we will be near to the castel we will see the cnihts and what is bean done there we colde thinc better of what to do

well lic an esol i saes yes then i saes lead us gleoman and the gleoman he tacs us around the holt away from the cnihts and he tacs us down a path and to an eald hus what is mor lic a barn the thaecc all fallan in sum straw and broc sithes and sicls on the ground

this is a good place he saes loc through the walls and thu can see the castel. well i locd a lytel but colde see naht but the gleoman then he is cene to go i sees o it stanc it stanc i sceolde haf seen

i is goan to see what is cuman he saes there is folcs i

cnaw in this ham i can spec to them they will tell me
what to do i will cum baec and tell thu how to tac these
frenc

then he is gan cwic cwiccer than he has efer gan and
we is left standan in this eald hus lic esols

i can not see the castel saes osbern locan through the
slits in the walls

this is wrong saes aelfgar it is wrong buccmaster

tac thy weapens i saes tac them out cum

we gan to the door of the hus then and it was good
that we did for if we had cept inside soon we wolde haf
been mete. we gan to the door and gan out slow and we
seen cuman to us from the castel three frenc cnihts on
hors with sweords and gars and two others on foot and
with them the fuccan gleoman walcan not lic a thrall but
lic a freond

the fuccan gleoman i saes that cunt i cnawan it i saed
so

he has sold us saes gamel

go to the holt saes grimcell run to the holt. who was he
bean the cyng here well it colde not be spoc of now for
we was runnan runnan. the cnihts seen us and they cum
on us they cum down cwic

sound of callan and sound of sweords and of callan
and wepan of hors and men runnan it was all cwic and i
colde not see. i had my sweord in my hand they was
cuman at me they had hierde of me of my greatness i was
ring gifer they wolde want to tac me. i mofd behind a hus

then out again to the treows then from them all of my men runnan then feohtan then runnan again. tofe before me i sees he is runnan from a cniht on foot he has his scramasax i cum from behind this cniht and with my sweord i strics him in the sculdor he calls and is down in blud i can not cwell him i has not time i moste cepe mofan to the treows all is mofan to the treows

the cnihts on hors is mofan cwic betweon and around us with sweords swingan and sum of them strics my men i sees blud but i is mofan all is mofan so cwic i can not see. i gan under a small hege in to a place where there is cycens and ofer another hege i teorns. baec on the ground i sees this cilde osbern he is under a frenc hors all in blud he is not mofan. i sees that grimcell and aelfgar has got to the treows and is callan for others i sees tofe runnan but teornan with his scramasax. i sees gamel he tries to run but his scanc it will not run he is slow there is cnihts cuman down on him

i teorns and i runs to my men i wolde haf toc mor of these frenc toc them all with welands sweord i colde haf done but we was sold and i moste get to my men. and then it was i was gifen a great gift. i teorned and gan cwic ofer the hege and i mofd behind a hus for the cnihts had seen me and one was cuman on his graeg hors so i run behind a hus and then another and in then behind the door of a small barn so none colde see me and there in that small place behind the door also was another man

he seen me cum in and he leapt and macd a noise and

it was the gleoman the fuccan gleoman hidan from what he had macd. i seen this and i seen cwic that the gods had gifen me a gift. he tries to go from me but we is both in this small place behind this door what can he do. i tacs my sweord and i can not mof it micel but i mofs it up hard from the ground in to his beallucs and pulls up hard and he calls loud and falls and the door mofs out and i seen cnihts then loc at me and one of them starts to cum. i tacs my sweord cwic and the gleoman lies on the ground screaman his beallucs out blud on his hands and i raises the sweord and swings it down hard on to his heafod and his nebb i nearly cutts off and a sound he macs not lic the sound of no man and writhes lic a cut wyrm fucc thu cunt fucc thu

and then i gan i run to the treows my men is callan to me good men they is if there is any good men now in the world but it colde be there is not. the last thing i sees in stan ford is wluncus mad wluncus who talcs to the treows and he has his sithe up lic death itself and he is leapan lic a mad man teornan round and round lic in a game from the other worlds and he is cuttan all who cums near him and he is macan a sound lic a hafoc in flight callan callan for blud blud blud

i gan to the treows and those of us what was in there we gan cwic deoper in to the holt. two frenc men followed us but we was good in the holt we cnawan it we used the treows to cum on them and we got them we got them down on the ground and when we got them we stabbed them we cut them we ciccd and fuccd them with so micel ire that there was no bodigs left only mete in strips the fuccers the fuccers the cunts

we cept mofan cept walcan for sum time until we was deop in the holt until we was sure no mor frenc wolde cum. then we satt down all of us by a great ac and saed naht for a long time

well these was my men i was ring gifer i moste cepe them safe and triewe. after sum time i stood slow and loccd around. osbern was gan the yonge cilde under a frenc hors tofe cept talcan of him wepan and greotan to him self. wluncus had not cum baec he of the game of death and gamel lame gamel that man who had tacan frenc style on sanlac who had feoht with harald cyng had seen the bastard him self gamel was gan. aelfgar his freond i seen locan at the ground lic he was aemty lic all of him now was used no small part was left. ten of us there had been in the mergen at the litha ham in the holt. ten of us smercan drencan ealu leafan to calls of anglisc folcs it had been the same daeg but it seemed a lif baec. ten of us and now there was six

*trust none*

fucc thu

*thu is ired thu specs lic an esol*

where was thu i called thu cums and thu is gan and when i is needan thu there is naht

*thu needed no other so strong so blithe*

i is strong we was blithe

262

> thy blitheness blinded thu esol thu was sold

i cnawan he was not triewe

> drincan laughan smercan lic a wifman

the first daeg of litha

> thu is no ealdor no cyng not lic the other

i was ceosan i

> always thu is weac

leaf me then go go

> thu was warned thu did not lysten

i colde not see it was not

> can thu do naht is thu a cilde. trust none trust no man

my men is triewe

> there is no triewe men now

> trust the gods trust the land do not trust men

thy sweord was strong

> do thy worc

i cnawan what i moste do when i was a cilde i cnawan it i leorned then what men is. lic woden i was hung upon the treow and beaten sent away teorned away lic woden i was gifen the triewth of what men is. at stan ford again i seen that triewth high and clere in a blue heofon

i cnawan what i moste do when my grandfather died. sum times thy wyrd is gifen to thu and thu moste walc with it efen if it may tac thu to the deorcest parts of all the worlds. gifen my wyrd i was the first time when i seen

my grandfather lyan long and hwit on his bier and when
i hierde my father tellan me what he wolde do to win
baec his name in the ham lic sum hund who has been
ciccd and wolde crawl to his mastor hwinan and hwinan

my dumb yfel father all wrong things cum from him.
my grandfather colde see in to the cracs in the world he
had eages that seen beyond what others see he seen into
the seofon worlds and when his bodig was still on the
bier i cnawan he had gan to that land

there is hylls to the south with great scips under them
and in efry scip a great cyng

to go to the crist to be sent to ingengas after all he had
gifen

in efry scip a cyng

i cnawan what i moste do and i felt it in me and strong
i was stronger than efer i haf been. it was the night of the
same daeg my grandfather died there was a half mona
and many clouds in the heofon. i gan up from the hus in
stillness for my father and my sistor aelfgifu was slepan.
i gan out then to the feld and i stood and i loccd all about
me. i was thincan of what my grandfather telt me about
the eald gods about erce and woden and i was thincan
they may cum then they may cum to tac him baec but
none cum

an ule called in the holt and i gan down on my cneows
in the feld. it was cold and the grass was wet and i gan to
my cneows and locd up at the mona mofan across the
heofon and i cnawan

i gan to the fenn i gan through the felds and holt and

in to the secg i gan in to the water up to my cneows. i was
felan about it was so deorc the mona was behind clouds
and i was wet my arms my scancs locan in the reods for
it. i hierde sounds in the water dabchiccs or otrs or nightgengas i colde not tell and i was afeart. then i found the
boat my grandfathers eald boat and i toc it to the ecg

it was a small boat and not hefig and soon i had it out
of the water and i dragged it up and out of the fenn
through the feld and the small holt and to the hus. then i
was afeart triewe for as i cum near i seen sum one standan still before the hus and loccan down at me. i thought
it was my grandfather and then my father and then a
deorc aelf i stopped and then i seen

it was aelfgifu standan locan at me cuman up through
the feld draggan the boat and she mofd towards me now
and the mona cum out and she in her hwit night scirt lic
the swan wif of weland she was scinan in the light

do not do this brothor she saes to me

there is hylls with scips in them i saes

she tacs my arm then and stills me she colde always
still me

brothor she saes this will bring a deorcness

it is right it is the eald way

thu is sic his goan has macd thu mad

i gan to her then and i toc her in my hands rough for i
was ired at this i toc her by the arms she fell the grass was
wet she fell to the ground and i with her she beneath me
abuf lic a man and his wif

on the ground we did not spec for a sceort time we

265

breathd i loccd down at her her eages was wide ah she was a beuty i held her

well i gan up and i lifted her and she stood and i loccd at her and for a time we saed naht only locan and then i spoc still

i is not sic sistor this is my wyrd

father will harm thu

he is no man

he is a man and thu is a cilde

this night i will be man

well what colde she do i was a man and she a wifman a maeden she colde not stand before me she colde not stop me. i toc the boat to the hus and i laid it by the door and in to the hus i gan. i toc my grandfathers sweord from the beam where it was still. i toc also a belt what was his i toc a scramasax and his treen what he ate foda from. i toc sum of the blosms and herbs what the wifmen had put on him. in the deorc of the hus his great hwit bodig was dim i felt lic it wolde rise and cum to me

i toc these things together from the hus to the boat and i laid them in it

brothor what will thu do saes aelfgifu who is standan there locan and frettan. will thu mac a hyll lic in the eald times thu can not brothor stop this is wrong

i can not mac a hyll i saes i has no freonds in this i is alone. we will put his bodig in the boat sistor and we will tac him to the fenn. we will fyr the boat and it will go away on the mere to the world of the dead at the root of the great treow of lif

266

well aelfgifu is locan at me lic she locs sum times at the swine what will be ate soon for mete. i cnawan it was my wyrd i cnawan what i was called to do and naht she colde sae wolde stop this in the heofon in the ground i colde feel it was tacan its path

sistor i saes i can not tac him alone

no

he is hefig thu moste

no i will not

i gan to her and i locd at her and toc her hands then and she loccd at me

for him i saes for grandfather

she macs a sound lic she is sic but still holdan her hands i tacs her in to the hus where he lies. my father is fnaetteran i hieres him loud. we gan slow to my grandfathers bodig and we is both afeart

tac his feet i saes help me and i gan then to his sculdors and i stands for a time locan and then i breathes deop. he is cold so cold i breathes again deop and i saes still i saes grandfather this is for the eald hus and i tacs him then by the sculdors and i worcs to tac him from the bier and on to the ground

oh he is hefig mor hefig than it seemed i can not hold him he begins to mof and i can not cepe him in my arms. aelfgifu sees what is cuman and she leaps baec and she cries loud and i tries to hold him but i can not. the bier and the blosms and the herbs and my grandfathers bodig cums down hard to the ground and it seems the sound they macs can be hierde in all the fenns in the scir it seems cwiccer than the hafoc that my father is upon us cuman out of the deorc in his hwit clothes and here here is the nightgenga not in the fenn not in the holt but in the hus. aelfgifu is wepan now wepan loud she locs up at him he strics her hard only one time across the nebb and she falls baec callan and wepan she falls in to the door and to the ground but it is me he has cum for. my father cums to me lic fenris wulf at the end of all things he cums down and he does not stop he is hittan me now in the nebb now in the guttas he saes naht he does not loc at me only beats and beats me in the guttas ofer ofer

this lifs with me now and will lif when all other things is gan. if he had spac called roared all this i colde haf ridden but he saed naht only came beatan and beatan lic there was naht to sae no mor lic he moste wear himself down on the stan before he colde efen spec. nefer had i seen this in him nefer had i cnawan it was within him and i his son his son

aelfgifu and i was on the ground wepan and callan and the bodig of my grandfather on the ground also twisted his scirt half off his eages open locan at the ground his tunge cuman from his mouth. my father he wears down and he stops he breathes micel and fast and then at last he locs at me and i seen his hwit eages in the deorc of his eald hus

out deoful he saes out out out

i cnawan it then i cnawan it always why had i forgot. when my yfel father cum at me i cnawan it when ecceard cum for my boys i cnawan it when my wifman my own fuccan wifman gan agan me i cnawan it always i cnawan it well now i cnawan it triewe and deop lic it was carfan in my flaesc. weland spac it all of the wilde world spac it when i wolde lysten

*trust none*

it is hard to tell now of what my father done of what i done it macs me feel small to loc baec it macs me feel sceomu. i wolde not tell thu of this but i wolde haf folcs cnaw of the yfel what has been done to our land and of the yfel what cums on them who worcs to right it. all my lif i has worced to right yfel i has worced to waecen men to mac them see and all my lif i has been beat in the gut- tas for it. trust none but the treows the meres the ground trust none but the dead

we sat the rest of the daeg in the holt we did not efen light a fyr we satt and loccd. i saed lytel all loccd at me to be ealdor to be ring gifer but they colde see i was thincan was thincan of what to do to sae. oft i gan in to the treows to thinc to sec my wyrd from the wihts and from weland and my men colde see this and loccd up at me for it

tofe for a long time was wepan for this osbern who was gan under the frenc hors. he did not sae micel only wept and sum times stopped and loccd around lic he colde see through all things.

tofe cilde saes grimcell do not weep do not weep

frenc gold saes aelfgar who is locan blaec and aemty frenc gold who will it not buy

i cnawan ulf for many years saes grimcell he was a good man but it bought him

it will not buy me saes tofe nefer

this gleoman saes siward he cum to our ham for years he always seemed good

there is no good men now i saes none

we is good men saes siward bound in blud

well i saes naht to this i did not cnaw this man well why wolde i trust him. the frenc has toc our anglisc gold and uses it to buy anglisc folcs

for sum time we satt there but as night cum i stood and i spoc to my men and i spoc strong

men i saes we has been sold none can be trusted now none. we has gifen our selfs too free to others. there is no triewth beyond this holt no triewth in men. triewth is in the ground in the treows i has lystned too micel to men. well i is ealdor of this werod and i will lysten no mor we will gan baec to the hus we macd so long ago in this wud and we will mac this place a castel of our own. no frenc will be safe from us no mor no man will be safe from us. if thu is strong cum if thu is weac stay

i teorned then and though the deorc was cuman i gan in to the holt and i cept walcan and after sum time i hierde behind me the steps of fife men

                                   *so this is thy castel*
strong as the treows

                          *and thu will lif here lic wifmen*
we will mac war

                                                *war*
thu will see

                                          *i sees naht*
no mor specan now

                                      *then what*
feohtan cwellan

                                *lic great hereweard*
lic the gods


hereweard hereweard oh still we hierde of him all this
year. hereweard has cwelled mor frenc hereweard has
beorned a tun hereweard has tacan a castel. hereweard
has one hundred men he has gan to an ealond in the
fenns there he macs a great torr and not efen the bastard
can tac him. the denes is cuman the denes cums in scips
they will cum to the ealond and with hereweard will tac
lundun and cwell the frenc and angland will be ours
again

     this is what was saed at this time by esols all ofer the
fenns and around. esols will belyf any thing what is telt
them this hereweard none had efen seen him. none had
fuccan seen him but he was a great cyng in their heafods.
they wolde see me they wolde see us they wolde see

                                   271

there was six of us now six in our place in the holt. this place it was my castel for the hus we had macd we now macd strong. we dug dicces around this place and we macd waepns and cept them in treows and under the ground. with lines we macd ladders up the treows and we locd out on to the land and colde see and hiere any folcs cuman. if any frenc cum here we wolde haf many ways to tac them and if anglisc cum we wolde see them cwic

i wolde let no man cum in to this place who we did not cnaw no mor gleomen wolde cum to us nor beorners nor no other men. i sent this siward out in to the holt to hiere what men saed of us and of the land and of angland. he wolde go out sum times for a daeg or mor and he wolde cum baec to tell us how things was and this way i wolde thinc of how we colde best do what now we moste do

siward had tales for us soon enough. it was only one wice or a lytel mor after stan ford that we hierde we had a new cwen in angland. the bastards wifman who was named matilda had cum ofer from the frenc lands and in lundun had been macd cwen of angland. it was saed that the bastard now felt safe in angland now felt this land was his and colde bring her here to see her new gems. well we wolde do to her what weland did to the cwen of nithad and he was thincan the same then and i colde feel it

it colde haf bene the cuman of the cwen that macd them rise but it was not long after this that siward cum to us with tales of men all ofer angland cuman together for war. in the northern parts of angland it was saed men was still free for the bastard had not gan so far and wolde not. in the south parts he had toc all things and macd his castels and sent out his cnihts to cwell and beorn but in the north the lands and the folcs was wilde still. nefer has i been to these north lands but then in the holt i wolde oft thinc of them and thinc that maybe these was places lic my grandfather had spac of where anglisc men and anglisc ground is still wilde and free

there was two eorls of the north lands they was called edwin and morcar they was the only anglisc eorls now all others had been cwelled and their lands toc by frenc hunds. many things was saed about these eorls it was saed that aetheling edgar who had been macd cyng after harold was cwelled though only a cilde it was saed he was in the north with these eorls and it was saed also that malcolm cyng of the scots was with them. efen the wealsc i hierde at this time efen the wilde wealsc whose cyngs was lic deofuls wilder than the fenns efen the wealsc now was specan to the northern eorls of standan agan the bastard for the scots and the wealsc colde see what this deoful was and that he wolde want them as he wanted us

that fuccan gleoman that fuccan lyan gleoman micel scit had he spac to us but in this it seemed he had telt sum small triewth for edwin and morcar now they spac of bringan anglisc folcs together in a fyrd. they was specan saed siward to the cyng of the denes who is called sweyn ascan him to cum in scips and feoht with them. in the north of angland there has been denes for many years the folcs there is half ingenga it is saed and this is why i wolde not trust them. well there is many folcs who is dene and half dene in the north and they saed to this sweyn cum and feoht with us agan the bastard and the corona of angland will be thine. this is where angland had cum to this poor fuccd land to asc one ingenga to cwell another ingenga to cepe it safe fuccd we was fuccd and beorned

well sum thing was cuman it colde be seen. by the sumor of that year siward cum to us with tidans efry daeg from the hams and the tuns and the straets around the brunnesweald. he wanted to bring folcs he had met on the paths who wolde spec to us and he saed wolde be part of my werod but i wolde not haf this no mor i saed we can not trust none no mor. but sum thing was cuman for sure for these eorls they had put out a call all ofer angland to grene men and triewe men be ready they had saed be ready to rise when thu hieres of what we will do

*and when will thu rise*

we has risen

*i sees nuthan*

when it is time

*thu is all words and lies*

it is cuman we is cuman

*we is waitan*

274

all things at this time seemed scearper deoper than before. weland he spac to me mor and he spac harder. the times they was cuman together the light in the wud was brighter the fyrs smelt scarper the mete we ate was stronger. sum thing was cuman now for sure it colde be felt in the heofon by all of my men

when it cum it cum in a scape i wolde not see. it was a daeg in sumor and siward had been out for sum time efry daeg now he wolde cum baec with tales from angland and the tales wolde be good he saed. he wolde tell us of grene men cuman together all ofer in holts and in fenns and on hylls there was gangs lic ours risan up they was cwellan frenc in their lands and they was waitan for the call from the northern eorls when we wolde all go to one place and mac a fyrd and tac down the bastard and mac angland ours again. well my men they was in thryll to hiere of this they was wantan frenc blud now but i was wiser always i was wiser lic i had been when the fugol cum and the haeric star lic i had always been

when it cum it cum in the scape of a preost. siward fuccan siward well he had seemed a triewe man but this daeg he cum in to the holt to our hus our castel in the holt and with him he brought another man though he cnawan i had saed no to this no others nefer. worse this man was a preost and this wolde be why siward cum in with his head low lic a hund for he cnawan my thoughts on these things. well he was seen cuman by grimcell who was locan out from the tall treow and so i called all my men to ready them selfs for war. who cnawan if this man was frenc or if siward lic the gleoman had sold us for gold

when siward cum in to the lea then he seen no men. grimcell was in the treow he had a bow we had macd from welig and straels and was ready and i was in the hus waitan with my sweord. tofe he was in a hole dug in the ground behind a lyttel treow with scramasax and line and aelfgar and godric was behind the stoccs of great acs with scramasaxes also

buccmaster calls siward as he cum in to the lea godric where is all of thu

we saes naht for my men cnawan what they moste do. many times we had done this and none wolde mof nor sae naht until i telt them. from the hus i colde see siward he was locan small and with him was this fuccan preost. the deoful was weran a blaec scirt lic a fuccan wifman and around his necc a cross of wud on a line. he was a thynne man not old no ire in his eages but still a preost

i cums out of the hus then and stands with my sweord in my hand and at this the preost his eages gan big and he locs afeart the wifman

siward i saes thu brings other men here when i has telt thu nefer to do this

buccmaster saes siward i cnawan thy orders but this is

sceolde i not haf opened my mouth i saes sceolde i haf sat here lic a cilde for thu to piss on me siward in my own place. i was walcan to him now with my sweord and him and this preost was goan baec as i cum

men i saes and at this my men cum out from their

276

places and stood by me. well i gan to siward and i strics him hard with the flat of my sweord on his sculder and then his heafod and he gan to the ground

buccmaster saes godric

yes godric i saes yes wolde thu lic sum also. he saes naht then and siward stands slow from the ground

buccmaster he saes i is sorry i cnawan what thu saed but this man is

a preost a fuccan preost

also a bringer of words for thu saes the preost

do not spec preost i saes

well saes the preost locan at siward and at me i wolde not be here but i has a burthen

tac thy burthen to others i saes and thy fuccan crist god also

thy man siward he saes not lystnan not hearan me cum to me on the straet for he had been sent by others to hiere what i has to sae and he ascd me to cum and tell his men for he feart they wolde not belyf the words if they cum from him alone

what words is these saes grimcell who has cum down from the treow but holds the bow still in his hand

words of callan saes the preost

good words saes siward loccan at me lic a beat hund good words for all anglisc

may i spec saes the preost locan at me and in his eages no sign of whether he is yfel or good or where he is from o i is ired

spec then i saes spec

277

i is cum from northanhymbre saes the preost. i and other men has been sent out by eorl morcar and his brothor edwin who is eorl of mierce what is not under cyngscip of the bastard. two years we has all had of great sorness and war and i need not tell thu men of what we has had at the hands of the frenc. well it will now end for a fyrd has been called by edwin and morcar and all men who feohts for angland is called on to go north to eorfic and there stand agan all frenc in this land

oh a fyrd a fyrd saes tofe an anglisc fyrd. he is in thryll lic sum maeden

eorfic i saes cold

the preost locs at me

eorfic he saes yes men is gathran there now in great numbers

and what then i saes

edwin and morcar will cum to eorfic he saes and so also will malcolm cyng of the scots. the wealsc will send their wilde men and aetheling edgar our triewe anglisc cyng will stand with them

and then

then the bastard will hiere of this and will go north

and then

then he will be strac down by anglisc style

thu will stric down the bastard

an anglisc fyrd will stric him down

anglisc men has not a sweord among them thu has seen what this bastard will do when he is ired buccmaster saes siward what is this

mens words i saes not cildes

but a fyrd saes aelfgar a fyrd buccmaster

a fyrd with no sweords no cyngs but edgar the cilde and sum scuccas from the scots and wealsc lands. where is our cyngs where is our great men

we can tac the bastard saes tofe cwell him

this is scit i saes scit spoc by men who has naht else to sae. these northern eorls they is half dene they is ingenga who wolde trust them

the preost then he locs at me stiff

i can see thu and thy men is not what i was telt he saes

we is we is saes siward

we is anglisc men feohtan for angland i saes and this is our land here in this place. those who wolde go north may go north but if the bastard gan with thu thy men will die or flee for there is naht to be won that way

well saes the preost i has spac my words

and thu is right to saes siward right to buccmaster this is what we has cum for this is it now this is the time it is time to stand

why not stand saes tofe why not buccmaster stand agan the bastard

we will nefer stand saes grimcell we only runs

well it has been a long time since grimcell spac to me in this way. for sum time he had seemed blithe with us and he spac naht and yet always i cnawan he was locan for other things. sum times around the fyr he wolde spec of hereweard and in his eages there wolde be sum thing what was not here sum thing what wanted to be with others. i has been locan at him long

i tacs my sweord now and i gan to him with all men locan at us and he tacs his bow with its strael and he lifts it and he points it at me

no man saes this to me i saes

he saes naht

put it down grimcell i saes do it now

he saes naht

then what wolde thu do man i cries cwell me. well try then grimcell try and cwell me for i has the gods with me i has great weland of the beorgs with me i has his sweord i can not be cwelled grimcell i can not

grimcell then he smercs wid and this i did not thinc to see. he smercs wid and he puts down his bow

thu can not be cwelled he saes loud and he is laughan. o men did thu hiere these great tidans o preost thu is well cum for thu has found here the first man since the crist who can not be cwelled

scut thy fuccan mouth cottar i saes i has welands sweord

ah thy sweord of wundor he saes and thy bodig what can nefer die o buccmaster tell us why is it that with all this thu sits in a hut in the holt with fife men while angland beorns all ofer

scut thy fuccan mouth i saes or i will do to thu what i done to the fuccan gleoman and the gerefa and the frenc thegn does thu cnaw who thu specs to a man whose madness is full now lic the mona saes grimcell and he does not smerc. specan to treows muttran to the wind talcan of eald gods wafan sum fuccan eald sweord lic a cilde. o this is my werod i is thy cyng o buccmaster thu is naht naht and nefer has been

i gan at him i had to there was naht else to do. i gan at him with my sweord and he toc his bow and he tried to haf me but i was too near and i fell on him with my sweord and i cut him but i colde not cwell him for other men had me and was tacan me off it was fuccan aelfgar and siward the cunts

do not do this aelfgar saes to me and to grimcell

six anglisc men together saes siward and he is callan loud six only and they tears at eacc other lic hunds they does the worc of the frenc

thu does not spec to me this way i saes thu fuccan does not nefer nefer. o the fuccers the esols the scuccas o this will not be the last it will not

tofe cums and he helps grimcell to stand and he is bledan i sees on the arm where my sweord has stracc and he locs at me lic he is on fyr but i will not stand for this and i mofs hard away from these fuccan thralls who holds me

i is buccmaster of holland i saes does thu hiere this i is buccmaster of holland i is a socman a man of the wapentac i has three oxgangs and this is my werod. this is my werod and this is my sweord and those who wolde leaf with this fuccan preost go now go north go to sec thy eorls and beorn lic the landwaster did in northern fyr none saes naht only locs at me. the preost all this time has gan baec into the stocc of a treow lic he was part of it but his eages is scearp and always is locan ofer me

go i saes fuccan go all who wolde be weosuls lic that dead gleoman go and if again thu cums to me the next time the gods will not cepe thu. on fyr then i was on fyr and i teorns and gan baec to the hus in the holt and fucc them all fucc them fucc them fucc them


                              *trust none buccmaster i has telt thu*
there is none i trust none
                              *all is agan thu i has telt thu*
all is agan me
                              *great hereweard rises while thu is sincan*
fucc hereweard he is a ghast only
                              *he gathers a fyrd while thu does naht*
this is scit
                              *this sweord i gaf thu and what will thu do*
tell me
                              *all thy cynn locs on in sceomu*
tell me tell me what moste i do
                              *thu moste go*
go where
                                        *go baec*
baec
                                        *baec*

on the mergen what came after there was four men by
the fyr when i had thought there wolde be none. grimcell
was gan and i was blithe to see this but i saed naht only
sat and ate sum baerlic loaf. tofe and aelfgar and godric
and siward saed no words as i cum only ate and dranc
slow and loccd at me. tofe though was a yonge man and
colde not for long cepe his thoughts to himself

what will we do buccmaster he saes

do i saes

it is odd that grimcell is gan he saes he was the first

he is a hund we will spec of him no mor

for sum time naht is saed but the words is in tofes
eages before they is in his mouth and i is sittan waitan for
them

the fyrd he starts to sae at last

go if thu wolde i saes go now none will stop thu but as
long as thu is with me there will be no mor specan of this
fyrd or of eorfic or the eorls of the north

then what saes siward and he saes it bold. buccmaster
when thu and thy men cum to our ham on the first daeg
of litha we cum to thu cene to feoht with the frenc cene
to feoht for angland. we cum to thu with waepens and
with strength and with full heortes but what has we seen.
we has lost men to the frenc in stan ford and then we has
sat here macan walls diggan dicces

waitan saes godric but for what

waitan for what saes aelfgar this is what we wolde
cnaw. grimcell he spoc with us when thu was gan he bid
us cum to the fyrd and we was thincan hard

we wolde go saes siward but we does not cnaw if we colde trust the northern eorls. they saes the men in the north can be weosuls and we cnawan naht about where to go or what will be when we gan there

it colde be thu is right buccmaster that this fyrd will be weac saes godric. but if we staes with thu what will thu gif us feohtan men for thu moste gif us sum thing

it is not time for talcan now saes siward it is time to feoht

well it seems they is all agan me now they has bene talcan without me here it seems they wolde be cyngs all. well i had nefer thought to stae here we was gathran our strength that is all gathran our strength waitan for our time

men i saes now lysten to me. in all things this werod has been triewe always and we has cwelled many frenc folcs since we cum together. we has lost men in stan ford when we was sold by a gleoman for gold but i cwelled him triewe and we is still here. now lysten to me of what we is. we is grene men we is men of the holt of the fenns we cums from a grene place we cums from the ground none can see us if we does not asc them. we cum up in the night and in the grene light and we cuts out the deorcness that has cum to our land and we gan baec again in to holt and fenn before the frenc efen cnawan what we is

this is what we is i saes it is what we do. we hears all ofer of others lic us all ofer angland in efry ham in efry tun in efry wud and feld there is men who will rise with the sunne and cut the throta of the frenc in stillness and then becum the treows again. we is not fyrdsmen we does not feoht on hors on hylls in lines with cyngs and huscarls. we is men of the hidden places of our own places and our worc is to stand for the lands we cnawan and cum from to cepe our own folc free. and when there is enough of us angland will not be ham for no ingenga and none will stand to be here for none can lif if the treows the ground the hylls them selfs is waepened agan all comers

i loccd around the fyr then at these men who is locan at me now still and it seems they is cene to hiere these words from me and blithe that i is leadan them for a hund wolde always be led. tofe and aelfgar and siward and godric that is all now they is not many men but they is mine

men i saes we is not many but we is strong. we has stayed in this holt now for enough time we has macd us a place that we can cum to when we is needan to cepe safe if again we is needan to run. grimcell that hund who is gan thu has hierde him moccan thy gods and thy land well he may mocc but the treows the holt the ground itself here has macd us strong

again i stops talcan and locs only at my men and they is still still loccan on

men i saes this daeg we is goan

goan saes tofe where. he locs blithe and the others also

seems to waecen when i saes these words as i cnawan they wolde lic hunds is men walcan at the right words

we is goan to the fenns i saes baec to the fenns from where i is cum for it is there that we will stand it is there we is needed. this i has been gifen this i has been telt the holt is not our place we must cum to water and there we will see what is gifen to us and what we moste do. tac thy waepens tac foda tac all things that we will need

well i cnawan no mor i cnawan lytel of what i colde do or where we sceolde walc. all i cnawan was that my men was weac and agan me and wolde not stay and so we moste go. i cnawan this fuccan preost had macd them thinc there was other ways to feoht and they was thincan all the time of the north and the eorls and i moste gif them other things other ways

but it was not only this that macd me go for i colde feel sum thing in the heofon that wolde tac me baec to the fenns. in my sleep in these times i had been dreaman of the fenns of the meres and pools of my eald hus of the gods of my cynn and my folc and the great deorc holt of the brunnesweald in these daegs seemed to be a place of ingengas and deorcness. there was eald wicce craft in this holt and aelfs and scuccas it was not my land

i was a man of the water not the wud the fenns was callan me. i had always seen things felt things no other colde and again now we moste go to the water lands for there was no other place triewe in this world *and there is light now light under the mere. and so flat in the daegs beginnan and deorc all ofer until so lytel so lytel but so strong a fyr can be seen a fyr deop under the water a fyr in the treows hard and lytel lic a candel fyr but growan lic a treow to the light*

we gan through the holt for four daegs to get to the blaec fenns always cepan to the treows cepan off the paths and the roads. sum times we hierde others in small hams or on roads sum times we seen them but nefer near not now none colde be trusted. it was three daegs walcan before the brunnesweald gan baec and the land becum small farms and hus and hams felds and paths. we gan through stillness and in another daeg the eorth teorned blaec the meres began the secg was seen and in the heofon was the eald feel of my lif and of my folc

tofe seemed to cum alyf as we cum near to the fenns. lic me he was a man of these parts and sum times i wolde loc at him and see the cilde becuman man. it had been sum time since he had been to his ham and i also and we had becum other whilst we was in other places for man tacs on the ways of the place he is in and the holt had cum in to us without us cnawan

it is good to be here saes tofe i has missed the fenns

it is thy place cilde lic it is mine

it is not lic no other it is not lic the wuds or these hylls that is in the wealsc lands or these great tuns lic stan ford. it is the triewest place in angland

287

it is

in the holt all is deorc and it is aelfs and wihts what is
ealdors there. in the tuns all is so great and blaec and
there is so micel sound that no man can be free or triewe
but in the fenns

in the fenns

there was not no need to sae mor

it was lic i was tacan it was lic weland or sum other
mofd me as weland had mofd my sweord when i had
cwelled the esol gerefa. i did not thinc where we wolde
go when we got to the fenns but only walcdd without
stoppan without thincan and it was midday in late sumor
when i cum to where i did not cnaw i was goan

what is this place saes aelfgar

it is my ham i saes

i had cum to the ham that i had left two winters before.
i had gan with ecceard who was dead now in his graef in
the holt and with grimcell the esol cottar who had now
gan north to be cwelled in frenc fyr and he wolde see he
wolde see who was wise. i had stood here in the deop
winter locan at all the hus smocan locan at the folcs
cwelled and dyan on the ground after the ingengas had
cum through. now in sumor cuman to haerfest i stood
again locan and things was not the same

the frenc was here then saes aelfgar

the frenc was here i saes and i was not. all was beorned
all was cwelled

why

we wolde not gif geld to them

none saes naht now only locs at what has cum to the ham. two winters only it has been but already it is lic there was no ham here. ofer the blaec deaths of the hus of the folcs grass is growan and secg is crepan in from the fenns. the paths is goan also undor grass and leafs. there is no bodigs of the folcs now it colde be sum has cum baec to put them in graefs or it colde be that wihts has ate them but undor the high grene i colde not efen see bones. stillness there was nefer in this place always the specan of wifmen and cottars and geburs i wolde not cum to this place so micel talcan scit was there but now all that colde be hierde was fugols and the wind

cum i saes to my men and i tacs them up the path where i cnawan i moste go

this path is not so high and grene it is lic folcs has been this way since the beornan though i can not see why. up we gan up the path my heorte hefig but i gan lic i was macd to go and it was not long

thy hus saes aelfgar to me. he is not a dumb man

my hus i saes

this is a hard thing saes siward a hard thing for thu

well my hus also is gan undor the high grene grass. in my eald felds there is baerlic growan and flax with micel grass in it all fallan down now no folcs to haerfest it. where my great hus was is blaec aesc and sum grass and there is lytel welig and alor treows cuman up near the eald barn. the holt is cuman baec the treows and the grass and the secg is cuman baec to tac what was theirs now their waitan is ofer

the frenc beorned thy hus saes tofe did thu feoht them

they wolde not feoht me cilde i saes i cum up to this place with welands sweord in my hand and i called on them to stand and feoht lic men but they gan on their hors and they ran when they seen me

we stood locan there for sum time it was lic i colde not mof

buccmaster saes aelfgar tell us why did thu bring us here

well as i had walced here not cnawan where i was goan now i spoc without cnawan what words wolde cum but words did cum and it was not me who spoc

this is my ham i saes this is my land my ground. in this place i was born as my father and grandfather was. when the ingengas cum i was macd to leaf here i was macd to go gathran to get men to mac a werod to leorn of the world beyond. all this we has done and now we cums baec to the fenns stronger and ready

ready saes godric for what

we is grene men i saes our place is in the sceados by the ecgs. when the enemi is seen we cums at him from the deorc and we tacs him before he can sae any words. there is mor of us now we is all ofer and when there is enough then no frenc man sceal lif in angland. those who gan north to fight in fyrds with mad wealsc men they will be cut down but we will lif lic the treows lic the secg lic the grass after the beornan lic the grass saes tofe lic the secg

the esol grimcell i saes he wolde mocc me but he cnawan i has seen things that other men can not see he cnawan i is ceoson and this is why he is afeart. thu men is triewe to me for thu has been tested and thu has stayed. sum has gan north to fight with the eorls and sum has gan loccan for this fuccan hereweard who walcs in these parts callan anglisc men to cum to him but who is nefer seen. but thu men is triewe thu is triewe to me and now we will go huntan

what will we hunt saes aelfgar

and i saes we will hunt a man

*then thu is ready*

i is ready

*ready for the hunt*

who is the prey

*he is near*

always thu talcs in raedels

*wolde thu haf me holde thy hand cilde*

i wolde haf thu tell me what i moste do

*loc to thy self loc to the land do not loc to me*

thu called me

*go to them buccmaster go to them*

that night we stayed on my land. we lit a fyr by the holt where i had slept the night i had cum baec to find all gan

291

and we ate and dranc. i gan and toc sum aels from the
fenn and we ate foda and we dranc and we spoc and i telt
my men what we wolde do

when i had ate and as my men was still drencan in the
deorcness by the fyr i gan walcan. i gan walcan until i
found the graef of my wifman odelyn. grassed it was now
but i colde see it high lic the beorgs of the eald cyngs

odelyn i saes odelyn it is me. i has tacan wergild from
many ingengas for thu

i hierde naht only my men specan around the fyr

it is not enough i saes there will be mor for thu there
will always be mor

i stands and i locs at all that i was

i gan baec to the fyr then and i dranc the last of the
ealu we had on the straet and when i had dranc i gan
down in my cape around the fyr and i slept lic i had not
nefer slept in the deorcness of the eald holt that is called
the brunnesweald


*i becum it i becum it i was a man no mor. was i a wyrm a*
*hara a broc i was sum thing that was not a man but was not*
*lic any wiht i cnaw. i gan down a deop hol in to the ground*
*deop and blaec and i colde feel the eorth in my haer on my*
*nebb cold and wet. down i gan until i cum in to a great light*
*place in the eorth and all around me i seen dweorgs worcan*
*to dig gold from the rocc worcan with hamors and with*
*hands. i flowan through this and i cum up abuf the eorth*

again i was in the heofon i was a fugol with a carfan bec and i flowan then flowan across water what nefer seemed to haf an end

i cum then to an ealond where there was great blaec treows higher than all things and ealdor than the rocc in the eorth and to the ground i gan and becum again a man. abuf me the blaec treows gan up to the heofon i colde not see the place where they ended deorc it was deorc with the sound of the water mofan on the blaec strand. and i stood and i called to the heofon called in to the treows in words i do not cnaw and then i seen her

she cum from the treows slow and small lic a graeg sceado. naht in her eages naht in her nebb she wore cloths but not lic no wifman in the world of men and her eages they loccd at me and i was scoccd when i seen them i wanted to run. they was her eages but dead and yet they loccd at me lic i was no man lic i was a ghast lic all things was cnawan about me efen deop in to my sawol

my brothor she saes

aelfgifu

thu sceolde not haf cum

thu is thynne thu is in fear

there is no fear here brothor

aelfgifu cum baec with me to the fyr we has ealu i has men we is cyngs of angland now

all cyngs is dust

do not go

why does thu cum after what thu done

*aelfgifu*
*what thu done and will do*
*cum with me*
*angland is dead brothor do not raise the dead*
*aelfgifu*
*do not raise the dead*
*i wolde be with thu*
*thu will*


for micel time the next mergen i colde not spec colde not eat for in the night this deorc dream had cum to me and i cnawan it was gifen to me. why had this cum i did not cnaw it macd me cold lic ys i ascd weland but weland wolde not spec nefer wolde he spec when he was ascd only when he ceose

this mergen i had thought to begin walcan for we moste go huntan and my men was ready. the night of the dream when i had spoc to my men it had again been lic the words was not mine. we is goan huntan i had saed to them and then i had telt them mor. to mac the frenc afeart i saed we moste stric at them in their strongest part lic we wolde cut the heafod of a snaec or spere the heorte of a bera or a great wyrm. cwellan frenc scuccas on the roads was a good thing but always there wolde be mor. to be great men to do great things we moste stric at a great man so all the world wolde see

my men was in sum gladness when they hierde this

and was ascan me what will we do who will we tac. well i
wolde not sae mor at that time for in triethwe the words
was dry so all i saed was we will hunt a man a great man
we will mac the bastard ingenga duc himself teorn his
eages to us in fear. saen this then i colde not sae mor and
i did not cnaw why i had saed any thing or what wolde
cum from it. but by this time i had gifen my self to the
gods to weland to my wyrd i was walcan paths laid down
for me and when the words cum i moste spec them

but i seen on this mergen that the dream of aelfgifu
ascd sum thing of me and that i moste gif a good answer.
it seemed to me that i moste go to the eald hus again and
it seemed then that this was why i had cum baec though
i had walced here cnawan naht. i had spoc to odelyn at
her graef and now to aelfgifu in the deorc world and now
i most go in my lytel boat to the eald deop treows. though
it is not seen by men there is a way to this world and sum
times it can be seen as the sunne can be seen through
cloud and then the eages for a lytel time is blind again

this colde be why i did not go alone this time this colde
be why i toc tofe. i wolde nefer haf thought before to tac
any other to the eald hus or to the treows but on this
mergen with aelfgifu thynne and graeg still in my heorte
and with my worc hefig on me i did so. to myself i saed
that this cilde neded to see of what i spac for the eald
gods was moccd by so many folcs now that their men
moste gif their tales to the yonge so that the hus wolde
not be forgot in the cuman deorc times when ingenga

cyngs and biscops wolde together mac angland their poppet

so i telt tofe to cum with me from the fyr and he cum gladly for he was blithe about what we wolde do. i had gan locan in the fenn and i had found my eald boat there still tied with line though full of water and weods and i had clened it and it was not holed. i telt tofe to cum with me to my boat and i macd him tac the ars and row in to the fenn what on this mergen was loud with fugols and wyrmfleages as if no war had efer cum to this land. tofe saed lytel at the start but after sum time of rowan he spac

buccmaster he saes where is we goan

thu will see

is it far

far enough

well he saed naht mor then only rowed as i telt him to with his yonge mans strength until we had got to the place i wolde cum to. as i cum through the yeolo secg to the mere of the eald treows i felt a great thing i felt lic i sceolde be here that this was my place that i was wel cum baec that they had been waitan

> thu has cum

now i seen why

> it is past time

but i is here

> thu brings the cilde

i will tell him of the eald hus

> he is not of this place

296

i needs a son

*thu needs strength*

stronger i is now stronger than efer

*strong men is needed for the hunt*

the hunt

*spec to them*

i will

*spec and hiere thy wyrd*


tofe cilde i saes we is here stop rowan. tofe does so and
locs at me as the lytel boat sits roccan in the still mere
   what is this place buccmaster he saes to me
   it is the eald hus cilde i saes
   the eald hus
   the hus of the eald gods cilde the place of the treows i
has telt thu of this place before. tofe then his eages growan big as he locs at me
   eald gods he saes lic he is afeart
   loc in to the water cilde i saes loc down. tofe does so
and as i did when a cilde he seen the treows
   do not be afeart cilde i saes i has telt thu of this. and i
telt him then as we sat in the boat all that my grandfather had telt me when a cilde. i spoc of woden of thunor
of ing of balder and frigg of what the preosts done and of
the cuman baec we awaited the cuman baec what wolde
cum when angland was triewe and in need
   when i has stopped talcan tofe locs at me and then

again ofer the boat in to the water where the great blaec stoccs colde be seen deop under the mere

this is a fearful place he saes

no i saes not fearful all men here feels as they sceolde feel when in the hall of a great ealdor. they is here they is still here they is locan at us tofe and they is waitan for us to be waecened. hope for angland now is not in fyrds in eorfic or ingenga cyngs it is under this mere cilde in these treows

tofe saes naht only cepes locan down

what will we do here buccmaster he saes

i has cum to asc them the way

the way

i moste haf stillness cilde i saes stillness now. i colde not stand and spec to the gods with the cilde there so instead i moste be still. in the boat then roccan slow on the mere in the mergen sunne i closed my eages and i spoc to them that only i colde hiere

we gan huntan i saes huntan for angland

i has cum to asc thu

who sceall be hunted

who sceall be hunted

and as i satt then in the boat roccan on the water all the sounds of the mere they cum baec to me as one. the wind the fugols the wyrmfleages the mofan of the secg and the water on it all of them cum together for me and i hierde them then i hierde the gods spec through the world itself i hierde the words they gaf to me in the

specan of the wilde and the words was clere as ys in a
winter well

    *the crist*

    *the crist*

    *the crist*


*blaec water blaec and deop and naht mofan. night time the
mona full the secg still the ule callan the fenns is still this
night there is no sound in no place but the ule far from here
far in another world*

    *the mere is deop and wid and from this strand can be seen
an ealond blaec in the night hwit undor the mona. the ealond
is long and on it a great hus of stan lic a castel but not a
castel for there is a cross on it this is a hus of the crist an
abbodrice. around this abbodrice a wall and around this wall
a mere and no way out*

    *the mona has risen it is high and hwit only now to loc at it
seems it is sum other thing also for the mona is becuman
sum thing else. it is becuman a heafodpanne it is red now red
lic blud ofer the abbodrice and now the mere the stan of the
hus of the crist the secg all is red and still no sound in all the
world only the fenn growan deorc under the heofon the
waters growan red and men all ofer angland mofan to this
place to stand for the last time as men of their cynn*

well what to do with this what to do. when the gods specs a man moste lysten but they specs as in the raedels of a gleoman or the song of a fugol. my men is by the fyr in the aesc of my hus waitan for me to lead them in the huntan of a great ingenga waitan for the eages of the bastard duc to teorn on us in the fenns and see our great strength at last but raedels is all i has to follow

so micel to thinc of and my mind deorc all deorc all deop lic the mere of the gods. cuman baec on the boat to the secg by my hus with tofe rowan and the lytel boat mofan under me i was thincan of the last time i left this place when i was a yonge man when i was sent away i was thincan of how deorc things was then also and how deorc my mind

well i tried to tac my grandfathers bodig i tried to put him in the boat to send him in fyr to the gods well i seen now i is a man that this was a dumb thing to do but i colde not let my esol father gif my grandfathers bodig to the preosts. but to the preosts he went for i colde do naht and my father my dumb father he beat me beat me so hard i colde not thinc my own father nefer wolde i thinc this of him efen of him

in the mergen after in the dawn my father cum to me with a sacc and in this sacc was sum loafs sum ealu a scramasax sum clothes and shoes a fyr stan and sum other things. well in the night he had left me on the ground bledan and breathan and he had toc my grandfathers bodig and put it baec on the bier and put the blosms baec on it so that all was the same and he had not saed one word to me

now he cums to me in the light of the daeg and he gifs me this sacc

son he saes these is thy things today thu will be goan from this hus. thu has broc all things here now and thu is wel cum no mor

father

thu is a man now son thy lif is thine thu is my son no mor. thu has brought sceomu on me lic thy grandfather before thu and i has telt thu son i has telt thu there will be no mor of this no mor in this hus. on my death this hus and land will be thine for thu is the only son of mine what lifs. but after this daeg i will not loc upon thu again in this world

well my father was dumb an esol a scucca for all that he done but i was a cilde and he was my father and on this daeg my heorte was broc. aelfgifu she ascd my father so many times not to do this not to send me away but he wolde not hiere her and put her in fear so that she saed no mor. on the land then we stood and i gripped her and she me and there was tears efen from me for i was a cilde and not yet strong as i wolde becum

brothor she saes

aelfgifu

i wolde cum with thu but

i will go alone i is man now mor man than him

he may cum to sum other thincan he may thinc again

thu colde cum baec in sum lytel time when our grandfather is in his graef it colde be that our father will wel cum
thu

i will not wel cum him

brothor

i will not and when i sees him again he will be on his
bier with blosms on him and i will send him on a fuccan
boat in to the mere and i will fyr that boat with blitheness and the gods will see how angland has been sold

aelfgifu she saes naht only mofs her head with tears
cuman from her eages

aelfgifu my sistor i will cum baec for thu

brothor

i go now i go in to the fenns i go to lif in other parts
and when thu sees me again sistor i will be ealdor of this
land

well i colde say no mor i colde stay no mor i wolde
weep i was still a cilde and though i had becum a man
this daeg to leaf aelfgifu was a hard thing my sistor my
dear sistor my luf and

i gan then i teorned and i i walced the path that toc me
in to the holt. i toc the sacc from my father and all other
things i left behind not cnawan if i wolde efer see them
again. all was blaec in my mind and in my heorte but in
the heofon was sum thing that wolde cum for me in time
and bring me to what i wolde be

tofe and i cum up to the secg and gan from the boat in to the water. i hid the lytel boat what was so eald now i hid it in the secg for i did not cnaw if i wolde be baec here and we gan baec to the fyr on my land to find my men

well we colde see before we got to them that they was not alone. we had left aelfgar and siward and godric only by the fyr but we colde see now that there was two other folcs with them and they not frenc they was specan lic all was well lic they was freonds and when i gan near i seen them and they seen me

it was one man and one wifman and to see both of them it was lic a strael in me

buccmaster saes the man and he stands as i walcs to the fyr

thu

buccmaster what was saed will not be saed again

i will cwell thu esol go from this place now

it is my place also

why is thu here grimcell

why is thu

we has cum baec to my lands we has worc to do in the fenns

we has cum here also for we had no other place to go and we wolde see what had becum of our ham. we did not cnaw thu wolde be here

now i locs at the wifman who is with him and i cnawan her i had cnawan her when i seen her from far off

buccmaster of holland she saes to me she does not

smerc only locs at me lic she is ascan sum thing. it is annis the gebur of my dead wifman i had thought her gan in the fyr

annis i saes why is thu with this man

i will tell thu this saes grimcell and i will tell thu what has becum of the fyrd of the north and the eorls if thu will hiere it

all i will hiere from thu is scit i saes

cum now saes aelfgar who stands now also. we has all spoc hard things for these is hard times but we is all anglisc folcs agan the bastard can we not sitt and spec

i locs hard then at grimcell and at annis. then i saes spec then spec for we wolde cnaw the tidans but if there is any words of ire or any scit spoc about the eald hus or buccmaster and his cynn there will be blud

by the fyr then we sits and we eats loafs and tofe who seems blithe to see grimcell again saes to him so tell us tell grimcell what has been. has thu been with the fyrd of the north has thu been feohtan

grimcell then he bites from a loaf and he eats slow and then he specs

i gan from the brunnesweald he saes not locan at me and i gan to earninga straet and i gan north. on the straet i found other men who also was gan to eorfic for we had all hierde about the eorls and the fyrd and we was thin-can we wolde be in a great war agan the frenc and we wolde haf our blud for the blud of our cynn and cyng at sanlac and angland wolde be anglisc again well we walced for two daegs on this straet but we did not get to eorfic for soon we seen men cuman south and they was in fear and ire. when we spac to them they saed they had cum from eorfic and that the fyrd of the north was gan for the men had run there had been no feohtan

what cum saes godric

a fyrd cum together saes grimcell in eorfic with edwin and morcar and cyng malcolm of the scots and sum wealsc folcs and many anglisc. the bastard hierde of this and he gan north also he toc his cnihts up the straet and he cum to eorfic and efen before they seen him cum malcolm and the wealsc they gan baec for they was full of great words when alone but when they seen a fyrd of the frenc with the flag of the bastard at its head they scat their brices and they fled lic wifmen

fuccan ingengas i saes i telt thu do not trust them

and what of the anglisc fyrd saes tofe

the anglisc fled also saes grimcell and i sees he does not loc at me as he specs. none wolde feoht the frenc cnihts on hors in style with sweords. so the bastard he gan in to eorfic and the tun gan on its cneows to him and the northern eorls runs for the holt and all is worse efen than before the risan. now the frenc they has macd castels in eorfic and in grantabrycg and huntenadun and efen in lincylene in this scir and these castels they is macd by anglisc thralls and is full of frenc cnihts so that if efer again there is a risan in these places there will be anglisc blud before efen it has begun naht is saed for sum time after this tale but my heorte is full. i locs at my men and i can see they is thincan yes buccmaster was right. yes we was agan him and we did not lysten but he was right there was no hope with this fyrd for he has seen the triewth when other men is esols.

after sum time i spac to annis

and thu annis i saes what does thu do here with this man

i cum baec down earninga streate saes grimcell to me and i did not cnaw what to do or where to go. i wolde not go baec to the brunneswealde but where else colde i go. i did not cnaw so i walced to the fenns for it colde be there was folcs there i cnawan it colde be i might lif there again in sum way. and then on the straet i cum across annis who i cnawan well as the gebur of thy wifman odelyn

do not spec her name cottar

and i also was lost saes annis. she specs slow lic she is not afeart. nefer had i trusted this gebur. she was a scort wifman scort and eald her haer graeg her nebb lined and her eages blaec. when she was my wifs gebur i had thought she was agan me always she wolde stand by odelyn and when i needed to beat my wif or to tell her what she most do in the hus annis wolde stand there still saen naht locan most times at the ground but i colde feel she was agan me

i was lost she saes and had been since i left this ham. i had been in sum other hams with folcs i had cnawan but always i was mofan i had no place to go to be. on the

straet i seen grimcell and we thought to cum baec here to
see what had becum of this place

and thu was hiere

what does thu mean

thu was here gebur when the frenc cum to my hus

annis she does not loc at me now only locs in to the fyr
and for sum time is still and then she specs

yes she saes i was here

i sees aelfgar and tofe locan at me but i does not loc at
them

then thu will tell me i saes tell me now of it

annis saes naht

annis i saes i wolde cnaw what cum to my wif

well at this annis she loccd at me and her eages was
lytel and it was lic she was locan in me for sum thing.
why wolde i asc her why wolde she tell me why wolde i
belyf her belyf any folcs

buccmaster she saes and she specs soft to me lic i is a
cilde buccmaster we did not cnaw where thu had gan

i gan to get aels i saes i telt odelyn i gan to get aels for
foda

she locs at me again then and then she specs. well she
saes it seemed lic a good daeg i will always see it in my
heorte. the heofon was wid and clene that daeg

it was i saes it was

well it was only a daeg she saes lic any other daeg and
we was doan things in the hus. odelyn began weafan on
her loom she was macan a rug and i gan down to the

barn to fecc milc from the cu so i was not in the hus when
she stops then

i milcd the cu she saes and i cum out of the door of the
barn and from there i seen two men cum to the hus on
two hors. i colde see from there that these was not men
from the ham or any men i had efer seen and they did
not loc lic they brought us good things

annis stops specan again and locs at the fyr

i did not go to the hus buccmaster she saes. i gan baec
in the barn so i colde not be seen and i loccd ofer

tell me i saes tell me wifman

what to tell she saes slow. they gan in thy hus buccmaster and i hierde wepan then callan from odelyn and
still i loccd when i sceolde haf gan to help or to get help
but i did not cnaw what i wolde do. there was wepan and
callan from odelyn and i colde not stand to hiere it but
then it stopped and then there was stillness i colde hiere
fugols callan in the holt

and then

after sum time i seen the fyr gan up in the thaecc of
thy hus buccmaster and it teorned the heofon blaec and
that mofd me that woc me and i gan from the barn in to
the holt and i ran to the ham

at this i saed naht what colde i sae

i got to the ham saes annis still locan at the fyr i got to
the ham thincan to call men to cum for odelyn but there
was mor of these folcs in the ham and mor beornan and
then i cnawan what had cum and what colde i do what
colde i do

grimcell then he puts his hand on her sculdor though he saes naht

thu ran then i saes. annis locs at me her eages deorc

i ran she saes lic thu ran. lic all who wolde lif run from the frenc lic the hara from the hund. i ran to the holt i ran to folcs i cnawan and here we is now here we is under the treows of angland

and all hunds i saes

and all lifan saes grimcell

and we will feoht saes tofe we will cwell these hunds lic we has cwelled many in this place


that night we slept in the small holt by my hus me and my men that is tofe aelfgar siward and godric. grimcell i wolde not let him stay with us not to sleep he was not triewe and he did not want to stay he wanted to go in to the ham to see his eald place and if there was any mor folcs there. of course there wolde not be i telt him all was gan but he wolde go and i was glad for he was an esol who colde not see my triewth

but annis staed and she slept with us around the fyr by my eald beorned hus not far from the grassed graef of my wifman and it was this that macd my ire rise lic that fyr had done. this gebur had let my odelyn die when she colde haf cept her alyf. if she had not been in the barn with the fuccan cus it colde be the ingengas wolde haf fuccd and cwelled her and not my wifman or she colde haf gan to the ham and raised sum men to cum well i

309

does not cnaw but she was lifan while odelyn was gan and this was not right. she was here again walcan about and talcan wifman scit and locan at me lic sum wyrm and my odelyn in her graef

what is a man to do in these times what was a man to do with all this scit. now i seen why harald cyng had been fucced by ingengas anglisc folcs they was not triewe not straight always they was plegen games. none was right none was triewe and i was feelan lic i wolde run from this from these men this wifman all these ingengas from all these lytel folc what wolde not hiere me run into the fenn and lif there on aels and all the world colde go to fuccan hel

i slept thincan these things and i did not dream no mor of my dead sistor and of this i was blithe. when i woc in the mergen all the others was waecened. it was cuman to the end of sumor and in the heofon colde be felt the first sign of the cold that was to cum. the fyr was up and i colde hiere muttran as i woc and i stood and gan ofer to see what this muttran was for i feart they was talcan of me

well they did not efen loc up so cene was they to hiere what this fatt gebur annis had to sae. she was sat by the fyr and tofe aelfgar and godric was satt round her locan at the ground. only siward was not sittan there he was at the ecg of the fyr drincan from a cuppe locan ofer at them and not locan blithe

annis was talcan to aelfgar as i cum up to them. on the

ground around her was small twigges of berc and on eacc was carfan scapes and when i seen them i cnawan what she was doan and i did not efer cnaw when she was in my hus that she colde do this

no annis is saen to aelfgar this thing can not be done thu sees this rune here it is called ea it is the rune of death of the graef it saes that if thu tacs that path it will be the end

then what saes aelfgar

then we moste throw again saes annis and we will see what it is that thu is called to do. and she gathers up the twigs to throw again on the ground

what is this i saes runes what is a gebur doan with runes

annis locs up at me there is naht in her eages. i was gifen the runes by my mothor she saes it has always been with my folcs

these is the runes of the eald gods i saes of the eald hus these things is from before the crist

and the crist is agan them saes siward who is not with them but sittan awaeg. the crist is agan them the preost and the circe is agan them i has telt them these is deorc things

well thu is talcan scit then i saes these is eald triewe things but they is not things for geburs

well i is no gebur now saes annis locan up at me then in sum ire i is no gebur of thine buccmaster of holland i is a free wif now and i will throw my runes where i will.

i was gifen this by my cynn and i does not need to asc thu
if i may do my worc no mor. then to aelfgar she saes we
will stop this now we needs the stillness of the land for it

i locs at her then and i is wundran what she is for i has
nefer triewely cnawan this gebur. what was she doan in
my hus was she throwan runes for my wifman was they
ascan the eald gods about me was she tellan her to go
agan me what was they doan while i was gan

well i colde not thinc for then there was sounds in the
treows and the esol grimcell cum in to where our fyr was.
he was bade wel cum by others but not by me and again i
seen this werod was broc it was weac and i moste stand
again to get my men baec for i moste do the gods will

grimcell he cums and sits straight down at the fyr and
tofe gifs him a baerlic loaf and water and he begins to eat
and then he specs

so what is to be done here he saes

done i saes

what will thu men do he saes specan to all not only me

what this werod does is no thing of thine cottar thu
has left us

grimcell he does not efen loc at me only cepes specan

the fyrd in eorfic was a weac thing he saes but still men
is risan all ofer the land. so many grene men is there now
that the bastard cyng him self is afeart and he has
brought a new law agan us

a law saes tofe what law

it is a geld saes grimcell for all those who cwells frenc

in angland. so many frenc is bean cwelled by grene men that the cyng secs to stop this by use of gold. thu may cwell any anglisc thu lics and our cyng does not gif one scit but if thu cwells a frenc man thu moste gif gold. this fine it is called the murdrum

murdrum saes aelfgar this is good it means we is cwellan many

the cyng is afeart saes grimcell all saes so the bastard is afeart of the anglisc risan agan him and they is risan now in all places. here in the fenns great hereweard is risan with a fyrd and the bastard talcs of cuman at him imself so great is he now

hereweard hereweard fuccan hereweard again

ah i saes here we is again great hereweard this ghast who we all hears of but is nefer seen

oh he is seen saes annis i has met those who has seen him

many sees him now saes grimcell for he gathers a fyrd in elge and macs a castel agan the frenc and efry daeg his men gan out and cwells frenc so that they is afeart all ofer the blaec fenns

ah i saes smercan another fuccan fyrd grimcell let us hope it is as great as the last one thu wolde tac my men to that fyrd that ran when they seen the bastard cuman ten miles away. i was hopan to ire grimcell hopan to stand agan him before my men but he wolde not rise

tell us of hereweard tofe saes to annis and i sees he is a cilde still hereweard saes annis is a thegn of elge he is a great tall man and all who sees him is mofd by him. his cenep is long and yeolo and he is strong as a cyng in war

he has led fyrds in other lands saes grimcell he has led many men

yes i saes and he is one mile high and macd of gold and breathes fyr also thu is all esols to lysten to this

he builds a castel saes annis not fuccan lystnan at the abbodrice of the crist in elge

*at the abbodrice of the crist*

he macs it a place for anglisc men to cum and eat and spec together and gather to feoht the bastard saes grim-cell. he has a great hall where all eats together and in the castel all daeg they trains to feoht and macs waepens and sum gan out efry daeg to bring down any frenc they finds

*the abbodrice of the crist*

none can cum to him until he calls them saes annis for none cnawan the fenns around elge lic him and if the frenc cums they will be drencced in the fenns

he sets fyrs saes grimcell fyrs all ofer

fyrs saes tofe what fyrs

fyrs from his great mouth of course i saes

fyrs in the fenns saes annis he puts ele on the secg if there is frenc there and he lights it and the fyr gan down efen to the blaec eorth and it beorns for daegs and nights and the frenc is afeart and many is drencced

he will beorn the bastard saes grimcell and he is callan for anglisc men to cum to him in elge and mac a great fyrd and he is not lic the northern men or the ingenga scots who is weac and afeart he is a triewe anglisc man and he will feoht

tofe i sees is locan lic a cilde who has seen a ghast or a god

i is goan to him saes grimcell

what i saes. i had telt my self i wolde not spec to grimcell no mor but i colde not help this

i is goan to hereweard saes grimcell. since i cum baec to the fenns i has hierde micel about him and i wolde be with him he is a triewe ealdor and leads a triewe werod

well of course grimcell does not loc at me but i cnawan what he is saen and he is not now the only one who saes this

i will go also saes godric for it is time now to feoht. he does not loc at me neither the cunt

and i saes siward. now all of them is agan me and this is what weland had saed this is what i had always cnawan and in sum ways this macs things good for now i cnawan i owes them no triewth. only aelfgar and tofe saes naht i seen them locan at me but i cnawan what they is thincan and i cnawan also what i moste do

well this is good i saes for this is what i had cum to tell thu all this mergen. i is goan to tac thu to hereweard

*to the castel of the crist*

thu saes grimcell and i is blithe to see i has fryhted him into specan with me

i leads this werod cottar i saes and i has telt thu all we

315

is goan huntan well now we gan we will go to elge

huntan what saes annis

this is worc for my werod i saes not for wifmen nor geburs. now men we is goan to elge for i wolde spec to hereweard angland needs great ealdors now who leads great werods and he will see what i has to bring him

he will saes godric who is already standan

well i saes then cum men tac thy things for we is goan to elge

*thu gan to him*

thu will see what i will do

*thu gan to gif thy weac small self to great hereweard*

thu will see what i will do weland smith and no mor will thu spec lic this

*is this so*

this is so

*well there is sum thing new in thu this daeg cilde*

i is no cilde

*then what is thu*

i is buccmaster of holland thu will see what i will do

i did not cnaw where the path wolde lead that daeg but i cnawan it was the right path. i felt that daeg sum new thing had cum in to me and weland he seen it too. as we ciccd ofer the fyr on my eald land by the graef of my cwen odelyn by the hus of my grandfather and all his cynn as we macd ready to leaf i seen in my heafod again the fugol what had cum to me that daeg two sumors ago and i was thincan again of the words i saed then. sum thing is cuman i had saed sum thing is cuman i had felt it then and i felt it now. in the eald holt of the brunne-sweald i had lost the way for i is a man of the water not the wood but here in the blaec fenns here where i was grown from here now again i was cum in to my self

and so we gan for elge all of us aelfgar siward godric tofe and grimcell and this annis also. they had thought to leaf me but they wolde not leaf me now and together we all walced down the fenn ways

well i cnawan the gods wolde gif me a gift this daeg and i will tell thu now what it was and how it ended. lif is gan from angland now and from all this deorc world so why not spec why not tell there is naht left in this dead land for any good man to lose


*there is mist all ofer the blaec fenns this night and from behind the mona sum thing rises. before the mona stands the ealond with the cross the ealond with the circe reaccan to the heofon and from behind the mona sum thing rises sum gathran of wihts and men and thu cilde thu they cums now for thu* we walced that mergen on the paths towards elge though we nefer seen it for it was still sum daegs awaeg. there was a mist on the land and high was my heorte to be baec in the place i had cum from and wolde always be of. the paths here was not the paths of the holt with great deorc treows all around these was fenn paths. sum times they gan through meados and past eald small hams but micel time they gan through the fenns with secg on both sides and this gladdened my heorte. the fugols that sang here was the fugols i cnawan and the heofon was the heofon of my cildehood and for a small time i felt that my heorte had cum baec to where it sceolde always be. the mist cum round the secg cold as we walced saen lytel and sounds colde be hierde that was lic the sounds of my eald lands when i was still a man

but we had not walced for long before we hierde other sounds and these was the blaec sounds of men. we was cum from a small fenn to a place where the path we was on met a straet what wolde taec us to elge. the mist was still on the land as we cum to the straet out of the wet secg of the fenn and we hierde as we cum the sound of hors cuman up from the west

well we all gan baec in to the secg as we hierde this for we was cepan awaeg from all men. there was many frenc in these parts and they cnawan of the grene men and was ired. the sound cept cuman in the mist and then out of the hwitness of it cum three scapes and in these three scapes was the end of it all for me it was three men on hors and two of them was frenc cnihts lic we had seen at stan ford. their heafods was scafd they wore clothes of style and had sweords at their belts. but the man in the middel of them he was no cniht. this man wor clothes of deorc brun and ofer them a cape of blaec and on this cape was wofen lines of gold and a thing of beuty it was if beuty is to be found in the things of men. this man he had a nebb set lic style as all frenc do and a lytel blaec cenep but his heafod was not scafan lic the cnihts it was scafan lic a munc and around his throta on a line of gold he wore a great cross of wud

a preost i saes a frenc fuccan preost

he is no preost saes annis he is a biscop

*the crist*

well it had cum it was my time and nefer has i done a thing so triewe and so fast. the gods had spac to me and this had been sent and this now this was my wyrd this wolde bring the eald gods baec to angland and again we wolde rise again from our land again we wolde cum in to our selfs and be men in angland for efer

i calls tac him and i runs from the secg to the frenc men. i tacs my sweord from my belt and i strics one of the cnihts hard on the scanc and cuts him deop and he is afeart for he did not see us and he grips his hors and his scanc and begins to fall and the other cniht and the biscop they tacs their bridels and tries to stop their hors and they begins callan in their fuccan ingenga tunge and goan for their sweords well my men is not ready i had not spoc to them of this it had all had started from naht but when they seen me go they moste go also. tofe cum first callan and grippan his scramasax and when he seen him aelfgar cum too and siward and godric and when he seen them grimcell he cum also and here again now was my werod feohtan in our fenns agan the frenc lic we always sceolde haf been

well the cniht i had struc with my sweord was off his hors now and on the ground and my men done him fast lic we had done many frenc scuccas. now the other cniht he was cuman round on his hors strican at us with his sweord and the biscop the fuccan biscop of crist he had in his hand a great clubb and he too was on his hors standan and callan and strican at the heafods of my men and efen i cnawan that the crist tells his scepe nefer to cwell no man so what was this

well my men gan for the other cniht first and they tacs him off his hors with hardly no cutts on them and to the ground he gan and is cwelled fast tofe goan in to his throta with a scramasax now lic he is cuttan a snaec a man he has becum. and then we is left only with this biscop. we is all ofer the straet so he can not go past on his hors without cuman to us and on efry side of the straet there is fenn

men i saes men do not cwell the biscop

why not calls aelfgar this is a great gift from the bastard

320

a great gift i saes so we will do mor than cwell him

and then the biscop specs. it is not oft that any frenc men specs to anglisc in their own tunge but this biscop he cnawan what we spoc

then thu is hereweards men he saes and this is thy wel cum to me. thu will be wel cum to hel before this daeg is done by the will of thy cyng geeyome

he is not our cyng i saes he is a fuccan frenc ingenga scucca and we is anglisc men and thu now is ours

if thu wants me he saes still on his hors grippan his clubb then thu moste tac me anglisc man

well he is harder than the cnihts this one and mor than one of us tacs a beatan from his fuccan clubb befor we can tac it from him and throw it in the secg. but we is six and he is one and though he tries to cicc his hors for it to tac him awaeg we gets him down from it and we gets him to the ground and tofe and aelfgar sitts on him while the othors tacs the sweords of the cnihts and gathrs their hors and ciccs their bodigs in to the deorc waters where the bodigs of all frenc sceolde be

*thu has done well*

this is my time

*done well for thy land and thy cynn*

risan again we is risan again

*and now*

now the gods will feed

ah to loc down and see this great frenc biscop lyan on an anglisc straet with two grene men sittan on him oh it macd me laugh out and this macd the others laugh out also and on the nebb of this biscop colde be seen an ire so great it macd him red lic the sunne on a winter mergen

who has line men i saes. grimcell it seems carries sum and so i tells him to tie the hands of the biscop and get him to his feet and grimcell does this with aelfgar and tofe. i is blithe to see grimcell worcan with us in this for though he is a scucca he is an anglisc one

so we has this biscop tied with line his blaec and gold cape all eorthd now and his nebb set hard locan at us with eages of fyr but saen naht. as before i cnawan what to do in this place and i spoc to my men lic the cyng i was now lic the ealdor i had becum lic the ceosan man of the eald gods buccmaster buccmaster ham at last

tac him baec to my land men i saes it is not far. we will tac the hors also we moste be slow with them on the fenn paths but they can be tacan that way. tofe and i will lead the hors aelfgar and siward thu will tac the frenc sweords and lead the biscop and if there is any scit from him thu may cutt him a lytel for i cnawan thu is wantan to

well they colde see what i was now and none saed naht only cum with me baec again to my eald lands. annis who had been in the secg all this time she cum also and lic the biscop she nefer saed naht only loccd on and what was in her eages i did not cnaw

*baec to the eald hus*

the eald hus the triewe hus

322

                                        *thu tacs the preost*

he is a biscop he is mine

                                *and what will thu do there*
no mor words now weland smith no mor words


so my men tacs him baec to my land and in doan this
they is my men again triewe. i has them tie the two hors
to a treow near where my aeppels grew and we lit a small
fyr by the eald fyr where my hus had been. the biscop we
macd to sitt on the ground still tied with the line and he
satt and he loccd slow at us and saed nuthan

   it was noon time and my men was weary. eat men i
saes and drinc and soon thu will cnaw what will be

   well my men locs at me lic they is wundran what is
cuman but they does what i ascs. i puts tofe and aelfgar
to loc ofer the biscop as they is my moste trusted men if
any men can efer be trusted on this eorth and then i calls
ofer annis to me. i does not lic to do this i does not lic
efen to haf her with us and i can see she is only here to
loc ofer the other men and to see what will happen to the
esol biscop. well soon i wolde gif her a sight but first i
moste cnaw what i needs

   buccmaster saes annis befor i can spec lic a fuccan
fugol she is in talcan buccmaster what will thu and thy
men do with this biscop

   this thu will see i saes thu will see this night. but i
wolde haf thu tell me how thu cnawan he is a biscop and
what mor thu cnaws for thu has been in these fenns for

sum time now while i has been gan

she locs up at me for she is scort this wifman scort and
fatt. there is nefer naht in her fuccan eages

he is turold biscop she saes and he is a freond of the
frenc cyng

he is not a cyng

well he is frenc and this is a frenc biscop and he has
been gifen the abbodrice of petersburh as his. this was
not one month ago and all of the fenns is specan of it for
when hereweard hierde that the abbodrice was to go to a
frenc biscop he gan in and he threw out all the muncs
and toc all the gold and all things from the abbodrice to
say to the frenc that this place can nefer be theirs

so he is the crists man in these parts

he is the cyngs man at petersburh and he is a strong
man it is saed mor of a cniht than a preost thu has seen
him with his clubb. it is saed the bastard sent him here
for there is many grene men in these parts and also
hereweard in elge and so a feohtan man is needed

so this is turold

this is turold biscop buccmaster and now thu has him
and efen hereweard who so many specs of has not done a
thing lic this

efen great fuccan hereweard no no he has not i saes
and i gan ofer to my men around the fyr and to the biscop who sits by them stillness his arms behind him tied
with line

men i saes we has here not sum lytel preost but great
turold biscop of petersburh freond of the bastard and

enemi of hereweard. i locs at the biscop who locs at me and saes naht

i is telt thu and hereweard has been feohtan lic cildren i saes to him but it seems efen great hereweard who so many lufs has not tacan thu lic i has done

then thu is not hereweards men saes the biscop

i is no other mans i saes. i is buccmaster of holland a man of these parts i is a socman with three oxgangs this is my anglisc werod and thu is our frenc mete. men does thu hiere we has done greater than hereweard i has done greater now see what we has in this gift

this is good saes tofe and he smercs with his mouth full of loaf but the other men they locs only at me and at the biscop

what will thu do with him saes grimcell

thu will see grimcell i saes thu will see this night. but now thu most cepe him for i has things i moste do

i left my men by the fyr and i gan ofer my eald meados and down to the fenn. it was late in to the daeg now and sumor was endan. ofer the yealo secg i colde see lines of fugols high in the heofon goan south lic they does when efry sumor ends. it is saed that these fugols fleages all year all ofer the seas and all the lands of man and does not go down to land until they cums baec to the fenns in spring. i locs up then at these fugols small and blaec in the heofon. they does not cnaw of the bastard or the biscop or of what men suffers in this land they does not cnaw naht but what is gifen to them by the winds

weland smith i saes where is thu

                                                        *i is here*
thu cums at my call
                                    *thu has done a great thing*
a great thing
                                            *now thu is strong*
strong lic the heofon
                                            *strong lic the land*
stronger than hereweard
                                    *what will thu do my freond*
i will show thu smith i will show all


standan locan out ofer the secg i hieres a sound then and
i sees a hraga rise from the water and feoht to rise up to
the heofon lic it is feohtan to lif. we all is feohtan to lif i
saes to this hraga all wihts men and others all is feohtan
to lif in this deorc world. and now i moste stric

    i teorns then and i mofs baec through the fenn on a
path that only i cnawan and i gan baec to the small holt
near where the men was cepan the biscop. here i colde loc
through the treows and see them sittan eatan and drincan and talcan and i colde see the biscop sittan also his
hands still tied with line saen naht. i is stillness lic the
hara lic the fox none can see me on my land on the land
what i cnawan best of all folcs in angland

    and here it is lic i had cnawan it wolde be they is talcan
of me for i is not there

    fatt annis scort fatt fuccan lytel wifman annis she is
talcan of me and the others is lystnan. all is lystnan as

they eats and drincs and none is saen no it is not triewe and none is walcan awaeg cuman to find me. efen the fuccan frenc biscop can hiere all that is saed about buccmaster of holland

where is he gan tofe is saen

to the fenn saes grimcell

what does he do there

who cnawan what he efer does

and what will he do with this biscop does thu thinc saes godric

all locs ofer then to turold who locs baec not smercan not specan

tell us then of what he done after his father sent him out saes godric

oh the fuccers she is talcan of my cynn

well none cnawan what becum of him saes annis. it was spac about in the ham micel for folcs thought the buccmasters was always odd folcs and so this cept them specan for months. well i was a yonge wifman then and not lifan with them so i did not see it but he was gan for sum years and none cnawan where. sum saed he went to the holts and lifd with out laws and others that he was a beorner of col. i was telt by a gleoman that he gan ofer the seas for sum time

buccmaster gan ofer the seas saes grimcell and he laughs

well it was a tale saes annis and i can not sae if there is triewth in it

and then saes godric

and then saes annis he cum baec

and

he cum for his father who had sent him out. his father had saed he wolde nefer see him again but buccmaster he wolde cum baec. he wolde haf his place and his land and his sistor

and what becum

none cnawan for none was there but the three of them buccmaster and his father and his sistor there was no others. it was a daeg of ys in geola when he cum baec. we seen the smoc risan to the heofons from the ham

smoc saes tofe for efen he efen he is lystnan to the scit from this fuccan fatt wifmans mouth

they was beorned in the barn saes annis the lyan esol. the barn was beorned and in it was his sistor and his father. men did not find them until sum time later and none cnawan what cum to them. i spoc to sum men in the ham saed buccmaster was seen later that daeg in his boat on the fen druncen lic a hors on aeppels at haerfest specan to the wind lic he was gan in the heafod

i has spac to men also saes grimcell who found him after for he wandrd in the holts near his fathers land and when men cum to him he wolde sae out laws had cum from the holt and cwelled his folcs and beorned the barn.

well this colde be triewe saes tofe why wolde thu thinc it not. he is a good cilde a triewe cilde aways he has been triewe and now he is bold for he is growan

why sceolde we lysten to thy tales of him saes tofe now

to annis. buccmaster sum times is odd but thu is saen he cwelled his own cynn that he is mad and yfel but we cnawan naht of thu annis wif. he is not here to spec his triewth and this only is why thu specs we does not cnaw why thu might sae these things or who thu is or why thu wolde spec agan him

many in the ham belyfd these tales saes grimcell and now that i cnaw buccmaster i is thincan them triewe also

thu may saes tofe for thu and buccmaster is both strong men and has been feohtan but these is words only and we has had naht to tell us if there is any triewth in them

annis them she sits still for a time and then she locs at tofe and specs slow so i can hardly hiere.

cilde she saes i did not want to thinc of buccmaster of holland efer again. nefer to spec of him nefer to see him and i does not want to be here in this place neither but thu sceolde cnaw who leads thu. ah of course he wolde lead thu for always he moste lead always he moste haf men loccan up at him lic sum ealdor when in triewth he is cilde only. i tell thu this man is of the cynd what moste be tied down always lic a hund moste be tied by the law by the eages of other men. all ties is gan now broc by the frenc and with no bridel on him a man lic this can do any thing for all the world is his enemi all the world tell me what thu thincs of this fuccan scit tell me

*i thincs lic thu*

the fatt hore moste die

*all is agan thu*

all sceolde die all of them

*my sweord was gifen to thu*

all has been agan me since i was a cilde what colde i do

*what colde thu do*

my father was agan me my own father my wifman my
sons

*all agan thu*

aelfgifu she who i lufd when a cilde my sistor

*thy sistor*

she gan agan me when i cum baec

*all of them all of them*

i did not mean to tac her that way

*thu had thy right*

she was my sistor

*she lufd thu*

it was my right

*any man wolde do the same*

it was my land

*thy land*

all is broc

*what will thu do*

i will rise smith i will rise

*loc up buccmaster of holland*

up

*gan to the secg loc up to the heofon*

the secg the heofon why

*do it now*


well i gan out of the holt then to the ecg of the fenn
where the yeolo secg met the land and the efen was
cuman in across the low waters. fugols was callan and
climban up and cuman down again and the sunne was
startan to fall down to eorth and with it cum its yeolo
light across the flat lands of my folcs

*now see how the word is cept*
and i seen them i seen them cuman then and always will
this stay with me until i is in the ground under a beorg or
in a great beornan scip lic all anglisc ealdors sceolde be.
ofer the fenn from the place where the hus of the eald
gods lay ofer the secg ofer the heofon i seen the eald
hunters. i colde not tell all of the riders who was mofan
with them there was so many and they mofd in a way
that colde not be loccd at for micel time by men. all was
deop blaec and there was no sound to be hierde

at the head of the hunt was eald woden who i had seen
at the deorc ea that night his cenep long and hwit his one
eage locan at me specan to the blaec hunds what ran
before him in the heofon their eages great and scinan and
with the hunds was the great hwit wulf i had seen by the
ea the wulf what had loccd at me. great woden rode a
great blaec hors but many of the hunters was on goats

with eages of fyr and was blowan horns though no sound was macd by them. sum loccd lic eald cyngs with helms and sweords but others was ealdor than cyngs ealdor efen than angland they did not loc lic men they was lic eald wihts lic the treows them selfs blaec and carfan into scaps not of this world. they had cum up from the treows cum up from the mere cum up into the heofon they had cum baec for angland lic my grand father had telt me. they had cum for me cum for me and i cnawan now that it was time and i cnawan what i moste do

i gan down to my cneows then in the secg and i felt them go ofer me and i felt great weland locan ofer as he gaf them sige and i cnawan again who i was what i was what i had cum here for

i is buccmaster of holland and the eald gods has ridden for me


i colde feel the efen cuman in stronger now and the deorcness cuman down on the land. ofer in the treows where my men sat i colde see a fyr beginnan to rise. i stood up then and i gan ofer again to the graef of my wifman odelyn and i stood locan down at the grene beorg for sum time and i saed naht for naht was there now to sae

then i gan from the graef i gan baec in to the holt and i found where i had left what i was locan for. i found where i had put in a scealo graef the things i had toc from the fyrs aesc two years befor and i had cnawan one daeg i wolde cum for when i needed. things what my grand father had gifan to me before he gan eald things what my father had nefer cnawan about. these was things of the eald times my grand father had saed these is the things of feohtan men of eald angland and when the feohtan cums again when thu moste cepe thy land and thy freodom agan ingengas and cyngs thu moste tac welands sweord and tac these things and then cilde thu moste stand agan all

> *thy cyngs was weac*

harald cyng edgar cyng all of the ealdors

> *angland was weac*

angland moste haf new cyngs

> *great men*

all in bright helm and with great sweord

> *all in gold and the luf of the eald ways*

strong and blithe in the dyan light

> *stand cyng*
> *stand*


stronger was i then stronger than efer again in anglands dyan light. great in what i was gifan great in what i had toc. i gripped welands sweord in my hand as i walced through the holt in to the light

when i cum to the fyr all my men loccd at me in wundor. i stood before them in the eald war helm of my grand father all macd ofer with boars with seolfor and gold in the eald carfans of the eald cyngs. i has welands great

333

sweord in my hand and my grene cape on my baec an eald sigil on my sculdor all of me scinan scinan brighter than the crist brighter than the bastard cyng and all his deorc cynn

what is this saes godric standan from the fyr

buccmaster saes grimcell and he stands also and gan baec locan waery at me but i has no time for these men now i has time only for one

i walcs slow to the biscop who is sittan his hands tied behind him i walcs to him all in helm and with sweord in the light of the fyr with wodens hunters at my baec gifan me sige

this is thy death biscop i saes

the biscop locs up at me. my men is standan now all around the fyr locan on but none specs

thu has cum from the sea to cwell what we is and here thu sitts afeart on anglisc ground thy frenc hands tied

the scucca saes naht

there is ways to see this world i saes. there is the way of the boc and the way of the wilde there is the god of the boc and the gods of the mere there is the way of the crist and the eald ways of this land. i is cum from the mere i specs for the wilde for the eald gods under the blaec waters in the drencced treows. i is the lands law ofer mens i is eorth not heofon leaf of treow not leaf of boc

still he saes naht

i is raedwald i is raedwulf i is beowulf i is harald cyng last of the anglisc i sceal be

334

buccmaster saes aelfgar but i will not spec with him

turold biscop then he locs at me slow and locs at the holt and at my men and at all he fears and he specs

then this is why we cum he saes. this is why the fathor of rome in his triewth has gifen his flag to thy cyng geeyome for in the deorc holts of angland eald satan is lifan still

there is no satan here i saes

in the deorc holts of angland the yfel engels our god cast from his heofon pleges games for dumb esols saes this fatt frenc cunt. here in the treows and in the meos and the water and in the deop ground is the eald yfel one and his fyrd and here is anglisc men callan the yfel one their god. for thy god threw satan from his heofon and he macd his ham in the wilde world in the water and the holt. he is in the call of the crow the rind of the treow the sound of the fox. he is deop in thy eald duns he hangs lic the bat from thy ac treow. in all that thu calls thy gods in the grass and in the wind in all things wilde and grene is the deorcness of the yfel one

what scit thu talcs thu frenc scucca i saes but he does not stop

now i sees in triewth he saes as i nefer has seen before that thy synn has been so deop angland. and for this thy triewe god he has sent thu a cyng for whom satan is an enemi true yes on the hylls of war and in the dreams of a cyng

*he is a weosul*

thu is a fuccan weosul i saes and these is weosuls
words. behind this helm lies thy death biscop behind
this masc lies the eald things thu wolde scit on but what
now rises high lic a fyr agan thu. i is grim i is woden of
the high duns i walcs the chalc roads mascd by the mona
i has hung upon the treow i is cwelled and again cum alyf

   thu is lost he saes that is all thu is lost in the deop
grene deorcness. what wolde thu haf of me half mad man
of the grene holt wolde thu haf me cepe thy sawol for it is
too late for thu to be ascan

*tell him*

   any sawol of mine will go to my folcs in anglisc ground
i saes not to the sands with thy ingenga crist. in the high
eald beorgs sceal i lie with my cynn

   and the lord will stric down the heathen saes the
biscop

   he locs up at me from where he is cnelan

   i has seen hereweard he saes

   why wolde thu sae this to me

   i has seen him he is not so mad as thu

   fucc thu

   thu fears him does thu not small man with thy eald
masc

*why does thu let him spec thus*

   his men follow him thy men is laughan at thu

   i will not let thu spec thus biscop thu will scut thy
mouth

   as thu saes


336

we is anglisc men here and triewe and greater than any
he saes naht

                                                    *he moccs thu*

does thu mocc me
i does thy will great masccd man
thu will call me thy cyng
i will not
thu will call me thy ealdor
i will not

                                        *spec for angland*
lysten to me biscop does thu thinc this is sum game i
will slit thy fuccan throta lic a cycen
      if it be his will
do not spec lic this here do not gif me thy scit biscop
                        *spec for angland spec for angland*
there is naht to spec for now naht lysten biscop lysten
men i has cum from the eald gods i has been sent here we
has been gifen a gift and now this biscop will gif a great
wergild for the synns of his cynn and his circe for his
synns agan the land and all anglisc folc
      what wergild saes tofe. efen my cilde now he specs lic
he does not cnaw me none is triewe none
      i saes we will carf the blud earn on him
      blud earn saes tofe
      o thu is fuccan mad thu is craccd and broc calls grim-
cell who has been standan loccan on. thu is writhan lic a
wounded wiht buccmaster what is this scit thu and thy
sweord and thy eald masc and thy eald fuccan gods there

is naht left for thu naht thu moste see this. men why is thu here with this mad man we moste go cum with me cum now

i has telt thu cunt this is not thy feoht

this is no mans feoht buccmaster none will follow thu in this thing

does thu want my fuccan sweord again grimcell this time i will not let thu lif

what is the blud earn saes tofe

there is no blud earn saes grimcell it is a cildes tale of the eald times what buccmaster thincs he lifs in still

it is triewe i saes it was done and will be done again here. the blud earn is the death gifen by the eald cyngs to ingenga enemis

the blud earn is denisc saes grimcell it is an ingenga thing not anglisc thu is broc and mad buccmaster let us go

the blud earn is the death of the eald gods i saes. thu lays down thy enemi on his nebb ties him with line weights him with stans. then thu tacs thy scramasax and thu slits his baec and thu cutts all the ban in it and thu pulls up the ban and pulls his lungs out of his baec and then he has fethras lic a great hafoc lic a great earn with a carfan beac and he will fly to the gods and woden and his hus sceal feed

o saes tofe o this is a fearful thing fearful

it is not a thing of these times saes grimcell

it is not a thing of the crist saes siward

338

fucc the crist i saes fucc the crist can thu men not see that the crist and the cyngs has led thu into deorcness has tacan thu from thy land from the eald ways

we sceolde go with grimcell saes aelfgar

thu will not go i saes this biscop moste die it is the will of the gods

there is no gods saes grimcell but in thy deorc heorte man

my men will stand

we is not thy men no mor saes godric we is goan with grimcell we is goan to hereweard. enough of this bucc-master now enough

well here it was here now was the weacness and the smallness of angland. these man is standan locan at me their cyng their great ealdor the man who had macd their werod all in helm and with sweord the man who had led them to sige and in the eald times all wolde haf gan with a man lic this and done his will but now all was weac lic wifmen. i locs around me at these men what had been mine at this land what had been angland. all was standan by the fyr locan at me annis was standan locan at me also and she saed naht lic the fuccan biscop still on his cneows locan on saen naht but with sum lytel fuccan smerc on his ingenga nebb

*all is gan*

i locs then at the cilde tofe who had cum to us with his swine wantan to feoht thincan us great. tofe who i had tacan to the hus of the eald gods who i had telt of the greatness of them who i had macd in to a man by my own strength. he is locan at the fyr he is not locan at me

    tofe cilde i saes will thu help in this thing

    tofe does not loc up but cepes locan down at the fyr what now is beornan low. he is still for sum time and when he specs it is low also

    i thinc he saes that i will go to hereweard

*hereweard*

    well there is naht else to do then but tac my sweord and use it as great weland had telt me to cwell them what has torn down all that we is in angland. this time grim-cell is not fast enough he is not locan not thincan i wolde tac him on and no other cums betweon him and welands sweord. it gan cwic into him with a sound lic the cuttan of mete undor his sculdor and he calls out and locs at the blaed what has gan right through and cum out his baec and he wolde sae sum thing but his muth is all blud. i locs in his eages what is not agan me now not agan me no mor and i pulls out the blaed hard and he calls then lic a cilde and falls hard on to the fyr and for a sceorte moment he writhes lic an ael on the glaif and then he mofs no mor

    well then there is all callan and runnan and roaran and annis mofs lic she wolde go to him but i tacs welands great sweord what is all ofer with his blud and i saes thu

*hore*

    thu also is the enemi of this land and of all men and of my wif what thu cwelled and *the eald gods*

i mofs to go to her but she is fast and though she is scorte and fatt she is gan

*in to the treows*

before i can get by the men who is cepan her from me and callan to me buccmaster buccmaster this moste stop and gettan out their scramasaxes and annis is gan then gan in to the treows and

*the gods is callan*

i is callan and then from the treows on the path what we had cum down with the hors and the biscop we hieres a great sound what is not the sound of one wifman but is the sound of many hors and then the biscop is worcan to stand and he is callan callan in his fuccan frenc ingenga tunge and then we seen in the treows cuman ofer to us men on hors in style with

*sweords*

the frenc the frenc calls aelfgar and he tacs his scramasax

hoi hoi calls turold biscop or sum succ ingenga words hoi hoi

*they ran they will die*

thu men i calls thu fuccan esol scuccas thu has cwelled angland thu has cwelled the eald gods. but my men does not lysten for they is standan now by the cwelled bodig of grimcell and they is grippan scramasaxes and axes and bows. tofe aelfgar gamel and siward they is standan and now cuman through the treows on all sides is

frenc cnihts on hors and they cums first for the biscop
and cuts his line and puts him on a hors what they has
brought for him and he calls to them and then he calls to
us in the holt lic he is sum mad wiht and he cepes callan
thu will cum in to the light thu will cum in to the light

*cum in to the light*

and did they thinc i wolde stand did they thinc i wolde
stand and die with them these esols these cwellers of
angland these wifmen who has not been triewe to me

*their cyng by right*

did they thinc this why wolde tofe loc at me lic i sceolde
not run run through the holt in to the yeolo secg by the
path that only i cnawan before the frenc colde see me
before they colde tac me why did he call

*buccmaster buccmaster*

why wolde he thinc i wolde be with him now in his death
in the death of my small

*weac werod*

well he was a cilde a cilde only and i an ealdor of this land
and angland beornan now and these ingengas these men
of style well they was triewe men strong men and we was
weac and eald and the biscop is callan callan thu will cum
in to the light and my men is callan also lic catts lic cildren and there is sounds of style and i is mofan mofan
down the path

*baec to the eald hus*

to the eald ways i will not stay with this i will not gif my
self to this i is

342

                                    *buccmaster of holland*
what colde i do what sceolde i do naht naht none stood
with me
                           *they wolde not lysten wolde not see*
i will gif them naht none is triewe
                                 *wolde not lysten wolde not cum*
brothor she saes no brothor
                              *what man can stand ofer me*
brothor leaf me
                                             *trust none*
all saes no all is agan me
                              *beorn the hus beorn the land*
beorn them all
                                      *cepe it cepe it*
out deoful
                                 *all of the world is blud*
thu is my brothor no
                                        *buccmaster*
deop in the ground deop
                      *they calls they calls lic cildren they calls*
where is he he has gan
                              *i will not cum i will not cum*
the hafoc has tacan the crow
                           *none is triewe none is triewe*
spec to the land cilde spec to the land
                           *she wolde not do what she sceolde*
beorn then beorn
                              *a hwit wulf a boar a fox*


                              343

beorn sistor beorn father

*this sweord i has gifen thu*

beorn my weac werod beorn

*out deoful out*

it is deorc it is late

*none cums when called*

out

*late late*

none lystens none sees

*deoful*

deoful

*deoful*

beorn angland

*beorn*

# A partial glossary

ABBODRICE – monastery

AC – oak

ALOR – alder

BLOTMONTH – November (lit. 'blood month',
   when livestock were killed for winter)

BLUD EARN – (lit. 'blood eagle.') Mythical Viking
   sacrifice in which the victim's lungs were cut from
   his body and pulled up through his back to resemble
   the wings of an eagle. Historians still argue about
   whether it was ever used outside the sagas

CARUCATE – measurement of land; 8 oxgangs
   make up a carucate

CEAP – market

CENEP – moustache

CICEL – cake

CISERAEPPEL – dried fig

COTTAR – free tenant farmer owing obligation to a
   thegn. At least one step below a sokeman on the
   social ladder

CROCC – cauldron

DANELAUGH – Danelaw; area of northern and
   eastern England under Danish settlement and law
   from the 9th to 11th century

EA – river

EARN – eagle

ECED – vinegar

ELE – oil

ENT – giant

EORCA – demon or evil spirit

EOSTURMONTH – April (Easter month)

ESOL – ass

FLOTA – fleet

FNAERETTAN – snoring

FORHEAWAN – cut down

FUGOL – bird

FYRD – conscript army

GAR – lance

GEBUR – landless peasant farmer who owed labour
    services to a thegn or sokeman

GELD – taxes

GEOLA – December (Yule)

GEREFA – local official, later known as a reeve,
    representing the king or thegn at village level

GLAIF – three-pronged fishing tool used in the fens

GLEOMAN – travelling storyteller, poet and news-
    bringer

GREOTAN – crying

HAERIC STAR – 'hairy star', comet

HARA – hare

HAFOC – hawk

HEAFODPANNE – skull (lit. 'headpan')

HRAGA – heron

HRETHMONTH – February

348

HRIFTEUNG – stomach ache

HUSCARL – royal bodyguard and elite fighting force

INGENGA – foreigner

LEA – meadow, open field

LEAC – onion

LESCH – reeds

LITHA – May and June

MELU – flour

MICEL – much

NEBB – face

NIGHTGENGA – demon of the night (lit. 'night-traveller')

NITHING – outcast, villain

OXGANG – measurement of land, equivalent to around 20 acres, said to be the amount a single ox could plough in a season

PETERSILIE – parsley

SCEOMU – shame

SCOPMAN – similar to Gleoman, travelling news-bringer, storyteller. Also shortened to 'scop'

SCRAMASAX – dagger

SCUCCA – demon

SENEP – mustard

SIGE – victory

SIGIL – brooch

SLEGE – slaughter

SOCMAN – free tenant farmer. sokemen were found only in the eastern counties of the Danelaw. They owed alleigance to the king rather than the thegn, owned their land, and seem to have been a high class of independent landed farmer

SOLMONTH – January

STOCC – trunk

STRAEL – arrow

STUNT – stupid or stubborn person

SWAMM – mushroom

SWEALWE – swallow

THEGN – lord, squire

THRALL – slave

THRIMILCI – April (when cows were milked three times)

TREEN – woodenware

WAPENTAC – wapentake, the Danelaw's equivalent of a shire court, the basis of local justice in England

WEALSC – the Old English word for both foreigner and slave was applied to the pre-English ('Bryttisc') population. It became the modern word 'Welsh'

WELIG – willow

WEODMONTH – July (month of weeds)

WERGILD – blood price. A monetary measure of a life, the wergild was a price put on someone's head. If you killed them, you had to pay it. A king cost a lot more than a cottar

WEROD – war band

WIHT – living being, creature, animal

WITAN – gathering of the highest men in the land – earls, powerful thegns and bishops. Before the Normans introduced automatic hereditary monarchy, English kings were elected by the Witan

WITHIG – wreath

WYRD – fate, destiny

WYRMFLEOGE – dragonfly

WYRT – herb

# A note on language

What we now call 'Old English' was the language of the English people until the invasion of 1066, when it rapidly began to mutate with the arrival of Norman French, the language of the new ruling class. This novel is not written in Old English – that would be unreadable to anyone except scholars. It is written instead in what might be called a shadow tongue – a pseudo-language intended to convey the feeling of the old language by combining some of its vocabulary and syntax with the English we speak today.

The language of this novel evolved as I wrote it over a period of three years, often seeming to do so beyond my control. Eventually, in an attempt to prevent things getting entirely out of hand, I tried to hem it in with some rules.

The first and most important rule was that I wanted to use only words which originated in Old English. The vast majority of the vocabulary of this novel consists of words that, in one form or another, existed in English 1000 years ago. The exceptions are cases where words did not exist for what I wanted to say, or where those that did were so obscure today, or hard to pronounce or read, that they would have detracted excessively from the flow of the tale.

The second rule was that I did not use letters which

did not exist in Old English. The OE alphabet was more limited than ours. There was, for example, no letter 'k' – it is replaced by 'c', which is always pronounced like the modern 'k', never like the modern 's'. There was no 'v' either; 'f' takes its place in words like 'seofon' (seven). 'J' and 'q' were similarly absent.

The matter of spelling was more complicated. I wanted to render as many OE pronunciations as I could on the page, rather than translating them into their modern equivalents. So the OE words daeg (day), for example, or deorc (dark) – though pronounced in much the same way as they are in modern English – are offered up with their OE spellings intact. This is a rule that I found I had to break more often than I wanted to – if I had stuck to it with every word, the novel would have been ten times harder to read. I had to use my judgement as to when to use OE spellings and when to modernise them, and if so by how much.

Choosing OE, or pseudo-OE, forms for the novel's vocabulary means that the reader has to initially wrestle with OE pronunciation. This can be tricky to compute at first, but once grasped it becomes, I hope, second nature. So 'sc', for example, is pronounced 'sh' – as in biscop. 'Cg' makes a 'dg' sound in words like bricg (bridge). 'G' can be pronounced both as a hard letter, as in mergen (morning) or as a soft equivalent of 'y' when it appears in words like daeg. 'Hw' sounds like 'w' in words like hwit (white).

354

Finally, it's worth stressing the catholicism of my approach to the language, old and new. To achieve the sound and look I wanted on the page I have combined Old English words with modern vocabulary, mutated and hammered the shape of OE words and word endings to suit my purpose, and been wanton in combining the Wessex dialect with that of Mercia, Anglia and Northumberland – and dropping in a smattering of Old Norse when it seemed to work. The syntax used is mine, its structure often driven by the limitations placed on me by the available vocabulary.

There was one final rule I set myself, and it was this: all of the previous rules could be overridden, if necessary, by a meta-rule, which functioned as a kind of literary thegn: do what the novel needs you to do. This, in the end, was a matter of instinct, which means that I have no-one to blame for the results but myself.

Why bother with all this? Why make life harder for myself and for the reader? There are two answers to this question. The first is that I simply don't get on with historical novels written in contemporary language. The way we speak is specific to our time and place. Our assumptions, our politics, our worldview, our attitudes – all are implicit in our words, and what we do with them. To put 21st-century sentences into the mouths of eleventh century characters would be the equivalent of giving them iPads and cappuccinos: just wrong.

Which leads on to the second reason for playing with language in this way. The early English did not see the world as we do, and their language reflects this. They spoke their truth, as we speak ours. I wanted to be able to convey, not only in my descriptions of events and places but through the words of the characters, the sheer alienness of Old England.

The early English created the nation we now live in. They are, in a very real sense, the ancestors of all of us living in England today, wherever our actual ancestors come from. Despite this link, though, their world was distant from ours; not only in time but in values, understanding, mythopoesis. Language seemed the best way to convey this.

This novel is written in a tongue which no one has ever spoken, but which is intended to project a ghost image of the speech patterns of a long-dead land: a place at once alien and familiar. Another world, the foundation of our own.

# A note on history

The Norman invasion and occupation of England was probably the most catastrophic single event in this nation's history. It brought slaughter, famine, scorched-earth warfare, slavery and widespread land confiscation to the English population, along with a new ruling class who had, in many cases, little but contempt for their new subjects. It wasn't until 1399, over three centuries after Duke Guillaume of Normandy launched his successful invasion, that England again had a king who spoke English as his first language.

The cataclysm of 1066 sparked nearly a decade of risings, rebellions and guerrilla warfare across the country, as populations in north and south struggled unsuccessfully to repel the invaders. This resistance finds contemporary parallels in the struggles of the Viet Cong against the US army or the French against the Nazis, yet today the English are remarkably ignorant of this period of our history. This is all the more regrettable as the effects of Guillaume's invasion are still with us. In 21st-century England, 70% of the land is still owned by less than 1% of the population; the second most unequal rate of land ownership on the planet, after Brazil. It is questionable whether this would be the case had the Normans not concentrated all of it in the hands of the king and his cronies nearly 1000 years ago.

Other Norman legacies remain with us too, or have only recently been purged from our society. Automatic hereditary monarchy, the 'ownership' of a wife by her husband, the inheritance of land and titles by the first-born son, the legal ownership of all land by the monarch: all are Norman introductions. Historians today tend to sniff at the old radical idea of the 'Norman Yoke'. History, like any academic discipline, has its fashions. In my view the Yoke was very real, and echoes of it can still be found today.

Though any resemblance between most of this book's characters and any person living or (more likely) dead is coincidental, the narrative is hung carefully on the known facts about the history of the period and the religion and mythology of the Old English. The green men are not a fiction, and Buccmaster's tale is built around the known timeline of post-1066 resistance to the Norman occupation. Events like the northern rebellion of 1068, the risings of Eadric and Hereward and the construction of the castles were all realities. The various instances of atrocities committed against the English by the Normans are either taken from or are in keeping with contemporary reports.

There are, however, three deliberate historical anomalies in the text (I leave it to readers to spot the accidental ones).

The first is Buccmaster's name: it is not an Old English name. But it came to me and refused to yield to anything more historically correct, and so, it stays.

The second anomaly is the allusion to the word wake (wacan or waecnan, meaning awake, or to become awake) in reference to Hereward, leader of the Ely resistance, who is popularly referred to today as Hereward the Wake. While Hereward was certainly real, as is the tale of his remarkable last-ditch stand against the Norman king, there is no evidence that this nickname was. 'Hereward the Wake' does not appear in any contemporary records; the name appears to have surfaced late in the 12th century, when the Wake family of Lincolnshire began claiming ancestry from Hereward, and it was later popularised by Charles Kingsley's patriotic Victorian novel *Hereward The Wake*. Novelists can do that sort of thing.

The third and final anomaly is the timing of the kidnap of Bishop Turold. Unlike the other speaking characters in this novel, Turold was a genuine historical figure, and his kidnap and eventual ransom is said to have occurred (it was claimed for Hereward and his men) in 1070. I have taken the liberty of bringing it forward two years, along with his accession to the bishopric of Peterborough. Since historians seem to agree that the kidnap tale is of dubious veracity in any case, I consider this to be merely a continuation of the original storyteller's artistic licence.

I swam through a deop mere of books and articles in piecing this tale together, as well as as spending time tramping and mapping the fens, and exploring their landscape. Key among the written sources were Peter Rex's *The English Resistance*, and his companion volume *Hereward: the last Englishman*. For the myths and religious beliefs of the pre-Christian English, I looked to the two Brians, Branston and Bates, whose *The Lost Gods of England* and *The Way of Wyrd* were invaluable. In developing the language of the novel, I referred extensively to Stephen Pollington's *Wordcraft*, J. R. Clark Hall's *A Concise Anglo-Saxon Dictionary* and Douglas Harper's *Online Etymology Dictionary* (etymonline.com).

A full source list follows for those who want to explore further. Any errors which remain in this book are mine alone.

# Sources

## PRIMARY

*Anglo-Saxon Chronicle*
*Beowulf*
*Chronicle of Battle Abbey*
*Domesday Book*
*Gesta Herewardi*
*Liber Eliensis*
Bede, *Ecclesiastical History of the English People*
Geoffrey of Monmouth, *History of the Kings of Britain*
Hugh Candidus, *Peterborough Chronicle*
Orderic Vitalis, *Ecclesiastical History*
Simeon of Durham, *History of the Kings*
William of Malmesbury, *Deeds of the Kings of the English*

## SECONDARY: BOOKS

Astbury, A. K., *The Black Fens*. London, 1958.
Atherton, M., *Old English*. London, 2006.
Barlow, F., *The English Church 1000–1066*. London, 1963.
Bates, B., *The Way of Wyrd*. London, 2004.
Branston, B., *The Lost Gods of England*. London, 1957.
Cantor, L. (ed), *The English Medieval Landscape*.
　　London, 1982.
Clanchy, C., *From Memory to Written Record: England
　　1066–1307*. London, 1993.

Clark Hall, J. R., *A Concise Anglo-Saxon Dictionary*.
Cambridge 1960.

Darby H. C., *The Medieval Fenland*. Cambridge, 1940.

English Companions, The, *Members Handbook*. Leek, 1998.

Faith, R., *The English Peasantry and the Growth of Lordship*.
Leicester, 1999.

Frazer and Tyrell (eds), *Social Identity in Early Medieval
Britain*. London, 2000.

Griffiths, B., *Aspects of Anglo-Saxon Magic*. Swaffham, 1986.

Hare, R., *Without Conscience*. New York, 1993.

Hadley, D. M., *The Northern Danelaw: its social structure,
c.800–1100 AD*. Leicester, 2000.

Hill, D., *Atlas of Anglo-Saxon England*. Toronto, 1981.

Hill, P., *The Anglo-Saxons: the verdict of history*. Stroud, 2006.

Hooke, D., *The Landscape of Anglo-Saxon England*.
Leicester, 1998.

Lees, C. and Overing, G., *A Place To Believe In: locating
medieval landscapes*. Philadelphia, 2006.

Leyser, H., *Medieval Women: a social history of women in
England 450–1500*. London, 2005.

Millar, R., *The Green Man*. Seaford, 1997.

Myers, J. N. L., *The English Settlements*. Oxford 1986.

Owen-Crocker, G., *Dress in Anglo-Saxon England*.
Manchester, 1986.

Owen-Crocker, G., *Rites and Religions of the Anglo-Saxons*.
Newton Abbot and Totowa, 1981.

Pelteret, D., *Slavery in Early Medieval England*.
New York, 1995.

Pollington, S., *Anglo-Saxon FAQs*. Swaffham, 2008.

Pollington, S., *Leechcraft: early English charms, plantlore and healing*. Swaffham, 2008.

Pollington, S., *Wordcraft*. Swaffham, 2006.

Rathbone, J., *The Last English King*. London, 1998.

Rex, P., *Hereward: the last Englishman*. Stroud, 2007.

Rex, P., *The English Resistance*. Stroud, 2004.

Reynolds, A., *Later Anglo-Saxon England*. Stroud, 2002.

Samson, R., *Social Approaches to Viking Studies*. London, 1991.

Shadrake, D. and S., *Barbarian Warriors*. London, 1997.

Stenton, F,. *Anglo-Saxon England*. Oxford, 1971.

Stenton, F,. *The Free Peasantry of the Northern Danelaw*. Oxford, 1969.

Thomas, H.M., *The English and the Normans: ethnic hostility, assimilation and identity 1066 – c.1220*. Oxford. 2005.

Ward, J., *Women in England in the Middle Ages*. London, 2006.

Wilson, D.M., *Anglo-Saxon Art from the Seventh Century to the Norman Conquest*. London, 1984.

Williams, A., *The English and the Norman Conquest*. London, 2000.

Wood, M., *Domesday: a search for the roots of England*. London, 1987.

Wood, M., *In Search of England*. London, 2000.

## SECONDARY: ARTICLES AND PAPERS

Abels, R., 'Interpretations: bookland and fyrd service in late-Saxon England', Morillo, S. (ed), *The Battle of Hastings: sources and interpretations*. New York, 1996.

Briggs, A., 'Saxons, Normans and Victorians'. Hastings and Bexhill Historical Association Lecture, 1966.

English Companions, The, *Widowinde*. Ongoing.

Frank, R., 'Viking atrocity and Skaldic verse: The Rite of the Blood-Eagle', *English Historical Review* XCIX, 1984.

Hill, C., 'The Norman Yoke', *Puritanism and Revolution*. London, 1958.

Horsman, R., 'Origins of racial Anglo-Saxonism in Great Britain before 1850', *Journal of the History of Ideas* 37, 1976.

Reynolds, S., 'Eadric Silvaticus and the English Resistance', *Bulletin of the Institute of Historical Research* 54, 1981.

Vann, R.T., 'The free Anglo-Saxons: a historical myth', *Journal of the History of Ideas* 19, 1958.

Wormald, P., 'Engla Lond: the making of an alleigance', *Journal of Historical Sociology* 7, 1994.

Young, M., 'History as myth: Kingsley's Hereward The Wake', in *Studies in the Novel*, Vol. 17, 1985.

## OUTSIDE THE LIBRARY

Battle Abbey and battlefield, West Sussex
Bayeux Tapestry, Bayeux, France
Ely Cathedral, Cambridgeshire
Greensted Anglo-Saxon church, Essex
The Staffordshire Hoard
Waltham Abbey, Essex
West Stow Anglo-Saxon village, Suffolk
Wicken Fen National Nature Reserve, Cambridgeshire

# Subscribers

Dear Reader,

The book you are holding came about in a rather different way to most others. It was funded directly by readers through a new website: **Unbound**.

Unbound is the creation of three writers. We started the company because we believed there had to be a better deal for both writers and readers. On the Unbound website, authors share the ideas for the books they want to write directly with readers. If enough of you support the book by pledging for it in advance, we produce a beautifully bound special subscribers' edition and distribute a regular edition and e-book wherever books are sold, in shops and online.

This new way of publishing is actually a very old idea (Samuel Johnson funded his dictionary this way). We're just using the internet to build each writer a network of patrons. Here, at the back of this book, you'll find the names of all the people who made it happen.

Publishing in this way means readers are no longer just passive consumers of the books they buy, and authors are free to write the books they really want. They get a much fairer return too – half the profits their books generate, rather than a tiny percentage of the cover price.

If you're not yet a subscriber, we hope that you'll want to join our publishing revolution and have your name listed in one of our books in the future. To get you started, here is a £5 discount on your first pledge. Just visit unbound.com, make your pledge and type BUCCMASTER5 in the promo code box when you check out.

Thank you for your support,

Dan, Justin and John
Founders, Unbound

David Abram

Cathie Ackroyd

Jack Adams

Lorcan Adrain

Akshay Ahuja

Kutlu Akalin

Edoardo Albert

Robin Anderson

Eric Angel

Adrian Arbib

David Armstrong McKay

Rose Arnold

Rajan Arulganesan

James Atkins

Simon Austin

Rachael Avery

Karen Badlan

Ashley Balachandran

Laurence Baldwin

Nathan Banks

Laura Barber

Roger Barnes

Michelle Barnett

Gill Barron

Francis Barton

Geertje Baugh

Darren Beale

Helen Beetham

Graham Benjamin

Niall Benvie

Rhys Bethell

Emma Louise Prue
Billingham

Charlie Bing

Jacob Birch

Ian Blackaby

Owen Blacker

Sharon Blackie

Jeff Blackshear

Steve Blacksmith

Matthew Blake

Tim Blanchard

Chris Blythe
Nicalas Boardman
Nicola Boella
Chris Bone
Marina Bonomi
Jon Bounds
David Boyle
Phil Brachi
Ian Bradbury
Tim Bradford
Richard W H Bray
Andy Brewin
Christopher Brewster
Lucy Brill
Mark Brown
Ralph Brown
Richard Brown
Gareth Buchaillard-
    Davies
Monika Bulsiewicz
Elrond Burrell
Jake Campbell
Richard Campbell
Susan Canney
Xander Cansell
Tony Carnell
Jackie Carpenter
Jonathan Carr
Breyten Cats
Colette Cavanagh

Melanie Challenger
Nicky Chambers
Alan Chapman
Jean Chater
Navdeep Chater
Navpreet Chhina
Al Chisholm
Rebecca Clark
Ian Clarkson
Cary Collett
Richard Collins
Fiona Conn
Oliver Cooper
Paul Cooper
Andrew Copson
Adam Court
Gary Cowd
Gordon Cowtan
Colin Crewdson
Jim Cummings
James Curran
Robin Curtis
Kevin Danks
Deborah Danowski
Miriam Darlington
Stuart Davidson
Peredur Davies
Simon Day
Jennie Dennett
Christian de Sousa

Ben De Vere
Antonio Dias
Anthony Dinsdale
Keith Dodds
Therese Doherty
Lawrence T Doyle
Warren Draper
Charlotte Du Cann
Fintan Dudleston
Sam Dyson
Robert Ellis
John English
James Fairbairn
Sarah Farley
Tane Feary
Charles Fernyhough
Jemima Fincken
Alys Fowler
John Fox
Alex Fradera
Isobel Frankish
Dan Franklin
Simon Frazier
Kevin Frith
Richard Frost
Robert Frost
Simeon Gallu
Chris Gannon
Carolyn Garcia
Bob Geary

Helen Gee

Ray Georgeson

Julie Giles

James Gillespie

George Girod

Matthew Glover

Ben Goldsmith

Zac Goldsmith

Jonny Gordon-Farleigh

Chris Gostick

Suzanne Gotro

Dan Grace

David Graham

Jeppe Graugaard

Chris Green

Alex Griffiths

Jay Griffiths

Mike Griffiths

Fiona Guest

David Guy

Thomas Haas

Stephen Hall

Andy Hamilton

Rosie Hamilton

Susan Hannis

Matthew Harffy

John Harkcom

Jane Harris

Karey Harrison

Edmund Harriss

Helen Harrop

Louise Hart

Caitlin Harvey

Corina Hatfield

Christopher Hawkins

George Hawthorne

James Heartfield

Collin Heinz

Caspar Henderson

Olivia Henry

Stephen Henry

Justin Hill

Dougald Hine

Harry Hine

Tom Hirons

Tom Hodgkinson

Richard Holland

Anke Holst

Tony Holyoak

Robin Home

Rob Hopkins

Eric Horstman

Matthew Howells

Rosemary Howes

Jason Hubert

Nick Hunt

Marmaduke Dando
    Hutchings

Ceri Hutton

David Jennings

Alex Johnson

David Johnston-Smith

Julie Jones

Neale Jones

Keith Kahn-Harris

Wendy Keenan

Matthew Keer

Andrew Kelly

James Kelly

James Kemp

Chris Keppie

Linda Kingsnorth

Navjyoat Kingsnorth

Neil Kingsnorth

Peter Kingsnorth

Zsuzsi Kingsnorth

Cal Kinnear

Iain Kitching

Laura Knappenberger

Xavier Kruger

Séamus Laffan

Shaun Lambert

Antonia Layard

Alison Layland

Jimmy Leach

Chris Lees

Huw Lemmey

Rich Lennon

James Lester

John Letts

Owen Lewery
Hywel Lewis
James Lewis
Mark Lilley
Sylvia Linsteadt
David Lister
Paul Lock
Sidney Lock
Kim Locke
Patrick Logan
Kari Long
Laurence Lord
Catherine Lupton
Rebecca M.
Keith McBurney
Colleen McCulloch
Justin McCullough
Gavin McGregor
Alastair MacIntosh
Sophie McKeand
Bridget McKenzie
Angus McLellan
B. Cameron McMinimy
Lucy Mangan
Susannah Marriott
Drew Marsh
James Mason
Greg Masztal
Stephen Matthews
Will Merrow-Smith

Dr Mike Mertens
Deborah Metters
Mina and Rohan
John Mitchinson
George Monbiot
Daro Montag
Matt Morden
Benjamin Morris
Kate Morrison
Lindsay Morrison
Matthew Murrell
Meesha Nehru
Gregory Norminton
Dennis North
Mick North
Phil Oakes
Freda O'Byrne
Allen O'Leary
Deborah Orr
Ava Osbiston
Mat Osmond
Daniela Othieno
Gill Parrott & Nick
    Parfitt
Rupert Parson
Sarah Patmore
Chris Pendleton
Jon Penney
Ian Pettman
Faye Pirie

Duane Poliquin
Dave Pollard
Justin Pollard
Michael Poulter
Arthur Prior
Eddie Procter
Rosy Prue
Huan Quayle
Kate Rawles
Rebecca Rennie
Tracey Riley
Sabine Roach
Francis James Roberts
George Roberts
Nick Robins
Meg Roper
Rose and Crown PH
    Oxford
William Ross
Sean Rovaldi
Claire Rowe
Chris Rowley
Stefene Russell
Sally Ryder
Mark Rylance Waters
Andrew Sadler
Katrin Salyers
Christoph Sander
Bri Saussy
Jonathan Schofield

Adam Scott
Tom Scott
Matthew Sellwood
Emma Seymour
Ayres Simeon
Mark Simpkins
Mark Sleboda
Bradon Smith
David Smith
Jos Smith
Mike Smith
Molly Smith
Laura Sorvala
Jeremy Sowden
AllieK Stewart
Nick Stewart
Joan Stonham
Douglas Strang
Peter Stroud
Mark Sundaram
Linda Swartwout
Mark Sydenham
Graham Symmonds
Clare Symonds
Ashli Szczerbaniwicz
Pete Tayler
James Piers Taylor
Phil Teer
Jim Thomas
Kristine Thompson

Gordon Thorne
Adam Thorogood
Steve Thorp
Beth Tilston
Emma Tinker
Alistair Todd
Martin Togher
Kristine Tompkins
Steve Tooze
Emma Townshend
Rob Tucker
David Turner
Elizabeth Van Pelt
Mark Vent
Lucy Vickery
Ashley Vido
James Vincent
Roger Wade
Ben Walker
Della Walker
George Walker
Gordon Walker
Helen Walker
John Walker
Scott Walters
Rich, Lexi & Rosa Ward
Hugh Warwick
Dave Watson
Jonathan Watts
Peter Webber

Gregory Webster
Stokely Webster
Tim Webster
Francoise Wemelsfelder
Steve Wheeler
Stephen White
Eliot Whittington
Matt Wicking
Rob Widdowson
Andy Wightman
Matt Wilde
David B. Wildgoose
Keith Wildman
Samantha Wilkinson
Heathcote Williams
Dixe Wills
Chris Wilson
Richard Wilson
Richard Wiltshire
Laura Wirtz
Eva Wojcik
Chris Wood
Steve Woodward
Alex Wright
Andrew Wright
Gareth Young
Neville Young
Paul John Young
Susan Zasikowski
Liag Zeppetello

# A note about the typefaces

The period of history in which *The Wake* is set pre-dates typographic printing in Europe by almost 400 years. The typeface we have chosen to set this book is Jenson, one of the earliest and finest roman printing types. The Jenson typeface used here is a historical revival drawn for Adobe by Robert Slimbach in 1996.

The printer and designer Nicholas Jenson (1420–1480) had been a pupil of Gutenberg. Jenson is credited as the inventor of roman type. Based on the inscriptions of Ancient Rome, it is the letterform all Western books and screen fonts use, the basic currency of literacy and learning. Previously, books had been set in the difficult-to-read gothic 'blackletter' style.

Jenson's belief in simplicity and elegance of design and his business acumen created a new industry in Venice. By the mid-1470s, the city was producing a fifth of the world's books, and Jenson not only ran 12 presses, he also set up two successful book trading companies, selling books to high net worth individuals all over Europe.

Jenson was much admired (and imitated) by William Morris (1834–1896), the founder of the arts and crafts movement, who commented: 'Jenson carried the development of the roman type as far as it can go'.

The titling uses a modern version of a blackletter font called Aeiou, designed by Pia Frauss in 2007. It is based on actual handwriting from around the same time Nicolas Jenson was developing his roman types.